Miss Petrie was far from dull.

Edward Barraclough was not quite sure why. She dressed quietly enough, with no attempt to attract. If he had not seen those honey-gold curls that had tumbled about her shoulders at their first meeting he would never have known they existed. Miss Petrie wore her hair in a firmly disciplined knot, or even under a cap. She was not particularly tall, and her figure, from what he had seen of it, was slight. Apart from her forget-me-not-blue eyes, he would not have said there was anything interesting or attractive about her.

But Miss Petrie wasn't dull. She was quick-witted and amusing. And there was something about that small figure… Her carriage was graceful, her manner unassuming, but Miss Petrie was neither humble nor respectful, not underneath.

Edward Barraclough was intrigued. Perhaps he should spend more of the time he was forced to spend at Wychford in getting to know his nieces' governess!

* * *

A Very Unusual Governess
Harlequin® Historical #790—February 2006

Available from Harlequin® Historical and
SYLVIA ANDREW

**DON'T MISS THESE OTHER
NOVELS AVAILABLE NOW:**

Please address questions and book requests to:
Harlequin Reader Service
U.S.: 3010 Walden Ave., P.O. Box 1325, Buffalo, NY 14269
Canadian: P.O. Box 609, Fort Erie, Ont. L2A 5X3

A Very Unusual
Governess

Sylvia
Andrew

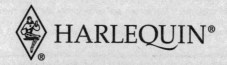

TORONTO • NEW YORK • LONDON
AMSTERDAM • PARIS • SYDNEY • HAMBURG
STOCKHOLM • ATHENS • TOKYO • MILAN • MADRID
PRAGUE • WARSAW • BUDAPEST • AUCKLAND

ISBN 0-373-29390-9

A VERY UNUSUAL GOVERNESS

www.eHarlequin.com

Printed in U.S.A.

A Very Unusual
GOVERNESS

Chapter One

Tall, with black hair, broad shoulders and a powerful stride, Edward Barraclough was an impressive sight as he walked through Green Park on his way back to North Audley Street. Though he was plainly dressed, his dark green superfine coat, silver-mounted cane, buckskins, and boots were all of a quality which indicated to the discerning that he was a man of wealth and distinction. The discerning might also have wondered what such an obvious member of the *ton* was doing in London, for this was the time of year when Society deserted the town for the pleasures of their country estates and the capital was very thin of company.

So, when Viscount Trenton saw Mr Barraclough emerge from the Park and prepare to cross Piccadilly, he hailed him with surprise and pleasure.

'Ned! What the devil are you doing in town?'

'The same as you, I imagine,' said Mr Barraclough. 'Business.'

'I didn't think the Foreign Office did any work till next month.'

'They don't. This was family business—bankers over here from Vienna.'

'Ah! What a bore, old chap!'

Mr Barraclough gave his companion an amused glance. 'Not at all! I enjoy talking to bankers.'

In Viscount Trenton's experience, interviews with bankers, or any men of business, were usually to be avoided at all costs, but he knew that Ned Barraclough did not suffer from the same reluctance. With good reason. The Barracloughs were enormously wealthy, with large estates in the West Indies and interests in banking and trade all over the world. And though you would never have guessed it, Edward Barraclough had a strange liking for work. Not only did he keep a personal eye on his own family fortunes, he also spent hours giving the Foreign Office the benefit of his considerable experience in the Americas. But, though it might seem odd, it did not prevent him from being a popular member of London society, and welcome wherever he chose to go. Jack Trenton liked him.

As they went up Clarges Street towards Grosvenor Square, he gave Ned a sly look and asked, 'Is Louise in town, too?'

'I wouldn't expect her to be anywhere else,' Mr Barraclough replied. 'She hates the country. Though she informs me that she wouldn't object to a trip to Brighton.'

'Are you going to take her there?'

'I might.'

'You want to keep a careful eye on that particular bird of paradise, Ned,' said Jack. 'If you hope to keep her, that is. Louise Kerrall is a damned handsome creature. You're a lucky dog to have such a prize. There's quite a few fellows in London who would soon take her over if you gave them half a chance.'

Mr Barraclough's teeth gleamed in a mocking smile.

'Are you one of 'em, Jack? I don't advise you to try. I've no intention of letting Louise go at the moment.'

'Oh, Lord, Ned! I didn't mean—! Y'needn't worry about me. I couldn't afford her! And I'm sure she's devoted to you—'

'Devoted?' Mr Barraclough's smile took on a cynical twist. 'Louise's devotion is in direct proportion to the value of the last trinket I happen to have given her. Particularly if it is diamonds. She's very fond of diamonds. But you needn't worry, Jack. It's not *devotion* I look for when I'm with Louise. Nothing so abstract.'

With a picture in his mind of Louise Kerrall's dark hair and languorous brown eyes, her creamy skin, red lips and generous curves, Jack said appreciatively, 'I dare say not!'

'So if you're not planning to take my mistress away from me, Jack, we'll forget her. Tell me instead why *you* are in town.'

Lord Trenton's expression grew gloomy. 'That's business of a sort, too. I've been seeing the lawyers.'

'Your father disinheriting you at long last?'

'No, no! Just the opposite. I've finally given in and made an offer for Cynthia Paston.'

'Have you, begad? Which one is that? The one with the teeth or the one with the nose?'

'The one with the teeth and a dowry of thirty thousand pounds.'

'And she accepted you?'

'Oh, yes. I may not be much myself, but the title is quite a draw, y'know. The Pastons like the idea of having a future Countess in the family.'

Mr Barraclough looked at the expression on Lord Trenton's face and burst out laughing. 'You're obviously the happiest of men! My congratulations!'

'It's all very well for you to laugh, Ned! Y'don't know how lucky you are! No one's putting any pressure on *you* to marry. No one's reminding you day after day that you're the only son and there's the damned title to consider. I'm not like you, with two brothers both older than me!'

'Only one now, Jack. My eldest brother was killed earlier this year. So was his wife. I thought you knew.'

'I'd forgotten. Sorry, Ned!'

'It's all right. Antigua is a long way away. Why should you remember?'

'All the same I ought to have. Carriage accident, wasn't it...? Is your other brother still out there in the West Indies?'

'Not at the moment. He and Julia are on their way here—they should arrive any day now.'

'Staying long?'

'Till next year's Season. They have my two nieces with them, daughters of the brother who was killed. Lisette, the elder one, is to be brought out next Spring. She's a lovely girl, I don't doubt she'll be a success. But I'm not looking forward to their arrival.'

'Oh?'

'I'm fond enough of my brother. And Lisette and Pip are delightful. But Julia, Henry's wife... Believe me, Jack, she's the best argument I've come across for a man to remain single!'

'I say, old chap, that's not very tactful!'

'Why? What's wrong?'

'It's downright unkind when you know I've just put my head in the noose!'

'If you feel that badly about it, why did you?'

'I've told you! *Noblesse oblige* and all that! Don't look at me so—you've no idea what it's like to have the family at your back all the time, rattling on about duty, preserving the line and all the rest. In the end I just gave in. It's enough to drive a man to drink.'

'Come and have one, then,' said Mr Barraclough sympathetically. 'The lawyers will wait.'

Lord Trenton met a few other cronies at White's, and after a while seemed to be drowning his sorrows so effectively that Mr Barraclough felt able to leave him. He resumed his walk back to his house in North Audley Street. The afternoon breeze was agreeably cool, and as he walked along he considered how very fortunate he was. At thirty, he was still free, rich and comparatively young. He had a mistress who was everything a man could want, beautiful, passionate and very willing—and, unlike a wife, she had no other claims on him. He was free to come and go as he pleased, and, when he tired of her, she would find someone else without any effort on his part.

Yes, his life was particularly well arranged. Unlike poor Trenton he was under no pressure to settle down. He could, and would, remain unencumbered for as long as he wished.

The only shadow on the horizon was the impending arrival of his sister-in-law. He frowned. It was an unfortunate truth that he and Julia cordially disliked one another. When to her chagrin he had inherited his uncle's fortune, she made no secret of the fact that she thought he should have stayed in the West Indies instead of choosing to travel the world as he had. His later decision to live in England was another source of displeasure. But he suspected that what really made her angry was the fact that, unlike his poor brother Henry, he took not the slightest notice of her.

This was as well, he thought as he crossed Berkeley Square and turned into Mount Street, for there really was no pleasing her. Far from neglecting his family responsibilities, he had allowed them to keep him out of England for a large part of last winter's hunting, and most of the London season this spring. What had started as a simple visit to Antigua had developed into a series of crises. Overnight his elder brother's two daughters had been made orphans, minors in the care of his brother Henry and himself. Making sure of their safety had been a major consideration, and he believed he had done more than his duty in that respect. It was now up to Henry and Julia to look after them.

Edward himself planned to make up for the last year's sacrifices as soon as he could leave London. He might spend a few days in Brighton with Louise, but afterwards he had various invitations from his friends to spend the later months of the year with them on their country estates. If and when that palled, he would return to London to enjoy town life again. A very attractive prospect, and one that he deserved, whatever Julia said!

Heartened by this thought, he leapt up the steps to his house, nodded cheerfully to his footman as he handed over his hat and cane, went into the hall, and started towards the stairs. But before he got to the first step he was stopped by his butler.

'Sir! Mr Barraclough!' Harbin looked as disturbed as Edward had ever seen him.

'What is it?'

'You have visitors, sir.' Harbin held out a salver on which was a card.

Edward read it. 'Lady Penkridge…? What does she want?'

'I don't know, sir. She has two young people with her.'

Edward frowned. 'I'd better see her, I suppose. Where are they?'

'In the library, sir.' Harbin went to the library door, opened it and announced Edward. Then he withdrew.

'Edward!' He was attacked by a small whirlwind. 'We've been waiting ages for you! Where've you been?'

Edward laughed, took the little girl into his arms and swung her round. 'I wasn't expecting you so soon, Pip! You should have warned me.' He put the child down and surveyed the room. Raising his eyebrow, he smiled at the other young person he saw, and went over to give her a hug. 'Lisette, I'll swear you're prettier than ever.' Then he turned and looked at the other occupants of the library. One was dressed in black, and stood ramrod straight. She had what looked like a permanent expression of disapproval on her face, with pursed lips and a nose like a hatchet. She was soberly dressed in rusty black, and what looked like the quills of a porcupine sticking out of an ugly bonnet. Not Lady Penkridge. He turned with relief to the other female, who was obviously waiting to speak to him. 'Lady Penkridge? I don't believe we've met?'

'No, indeed, Mr Barraclough. But I am very well acquainted with your brother and his wife.'

'Henry?'

'Yes. And dearest Julia. I have been a friend of hers for many years.'

'Indeed? Then I am pleased to make your acquaintance, Lady Penkridge. But…but I don't quite understand. Are my brother and his wife not here?'

'Julia is still in Antigua. And so is your brother.'

Edward looked at her in astonishment. Clearly enjoying the drama of the moment, Lady Penkridge nodded solemnly and added, 'They were unable to travel, Mr Barraclough. Julia broke her leg the day before we were all due to sail and Mr Henry Barraclough has stayed behind to look after her.'

'But…' Shocked, Edward demanded details of the accident. Lady Penkridge told him the tale, with frequent interruptions from his younger niece, who seemed to find the gory details of the accident more interesting than sad. But the conclusion was the same. It would be some time before Julia Barraclough could walk, and even longer before she could attempt the voyage to England.

At the end, somewhat bewildered, Edward said, 'But I still don't understand! Why, in that case, are my nieces here in London?'

'Edward! Don't say you don't want us here! We thought you'd be glad to see us!' This came from the small girl who had greeted him so rapturously a moment before.

Smiling reassuringly at her, Edward said, 'I am, midget, I am! I'm just a little puzzled, that's all. What are you going to do in England without your aunt?'

'It's all settled! We're to have Miss Froom as a governess. And you are to come with us to Wychford to look after us all.'

Edward's smile abruptly disappeared. *'What?'*

Lady Penkridge frowned at Pip. 'Philippa, I wish you would remember not to speak until you are spoken to! You must allow me to give your uncle the facts.'

'That would be helpful,' said Edward grimly. 'At the moment I don't believe what I've just heard!'

'First, may I present Miss Froom to you, Mr Barraclough?'

Edward loved his nieces, and the last thing he wanted was to upset them. But he had no intention of giving up his plans for the autumn in order to look after them, especially not in such an out of the way place as Wychford! So as he nodded to the dragon-like figure standing next to Lady Penkridge he said, 'Perhaps Miss Froom would take the girls into the saloon while you explain, ma'am? I'm sure Harbin could bring them some refreshments.'

Pip would have protested, but a look from her uncle silenced her, and she and Lisette followed Miss Froom meekly enough out of the room.

Edward waited until they had gone, then said, 'There's obviously some misunderstanding. I can't have heard properly. Would you oblige me by sitting down and telling me everything, Lady Penkridge? Slowly.'

His visitor settled herself, then began, 'You can imagine, Mr Barraclough, the confusion caused by Julia's accident—so unexpected and so immediately before the packet boat left Antigua. The Barracloughs were deeply worried. It was really impossible to change all their plans completely. So, since I was coming back to England on the same packet, I volunteered to bring the girls with me. It was a great relief to them, as you can imagine. Julia cannot possibly look after her nieces until she can walk. So, it was agreed that I should bring the girls and hand them over to you to look after until their aunt is able to travel.'

Edward considered this for a moment. Then he said carefully, 'You mean that *I* am to be responsible for my nieces? I alone? Without any help from my brother or his wife?'

'You will have Miss Froom.'

'Miss Froom!' There was a short silence during which Edward struggled to find some way of expressing his feelings which would be acceptable to the ears of a gently bred female. He failed.

Lady Penkridge went on in an encouraging tone, 'Julia is in good health. It shouldn't take long for her leg to heal. Perhaps only six or seven weeks.'

'Six or seven weeks! *Only* six or seven!' Edward's feelings got the better of him. 'This is a bachelor's establishment, Lady Penkridge. How the *devil* do you suppose I can keep Lisette and Pip here for six days, let alone six or seven weeks? I refuse! I damned well refuse!'

Lady Penkridge replied coldly, 'Your sister-in-law had the gravest doubts about your willingness to help her, Mr Barraclough, though she did not allow this to deter her. But I confess that your lack of sympathy surprises me. It is of course out of the question that Lisette and Philippa should remain here. I have taken a suite of rooms at the Poultney on Julia's behalf, and your nieces will stay there in Miss Froom's charge until you can arrange to transfer them to the house in the country where they were due to stay. The place is called Wychford, I believe.'

'Yes, yes, I know it. We had settled on a six months' tenure there some time ago. But it is in the heart of the countryside, over twenty miles out of London. I have other engagements, invitations I have accepted, commitments that would make it impossible for me to spend the autumn at Wychford. You must make other arrangements, Lady Penkridge.'

'I, sir? I'm afraid you are under a misapprehension. I brought the girls to England as a favour to your sister-in-law. But I now have to think of my own concerns. You will have to cancel these commitments of yours. I leave London in two days' time for the north.'

Edward gazed at her blankly. 'You can't!' he said.

'I can and will. I agreed to bring the girls to England, but my task ends there. As Julia said to me, they will now be entirely your responsibility.'

'My responsibility! Oh, yes, I can imagine Julia said that! This is all her confounded doing!'

'Mr Barraclough! Are you completely devoid of feeling? Your sister-in-law is at this moment lying on a bed of pain—'

'That is *nothing* compared with what she has done to me! And what was Henry doing all this time? Why hasn't he come up with a better solution? Dammit, *he's* the girls' guardian!'

'Your brother was naturally more concerned about his wife. And, as I understand it, you are also your nieces' guardian.'

'However, there is a substantial difference between us—Henry is married, and I am a bachelor!'

'That is why Miss Froom is here, Mr Barraclough. By a fortunate coincidence Julia had written to her some time ago to engage her services—'

'Fortunate! There is nothing fortunate about any part of this catastrophe!' muttered Edward.

Lady Penkridge ignored him. She went on, 'And I fetched her yesterday to join us. I am sure you may safely leave the girls in her hands. She comes with the highest possible recommendations. All that will be required of you is to take charge of the household at Wychford.'

'But I live in London, dammit!' Edward almost shouted the words. 'And I already have plans for the autumn! Why the devil did Henry agree to this cork-brained idea? Just wait till he gets here. If he wasn't my own brother, I swear I'd call him out!'

Lady Penkridge rose. 'I am sorry that your reception of my news has been so unfavourable, Mr Barraclough,' she said frigidly. 'Particularly as you express yourself in such immoderate terms. But there is nothing I can do about it. I leave London in two days. You have that time to make your arrangements. And now, if you don't mind, I shall collect the girls and return to the Poultney Hotel. Good afternoon.'

She gathered up her things and waited stiffly for him to send for Harbin to show her out. With a considerable effort Edward pulled himself together. It would do the girls no good at all if he antagonised this woman. Lisette was to come out in the spring, and for all he knew Lady Penkridge might have considerable influence among the London *ton*. He took a breath and gave her a charming smile.

'You are right, ma'am. It was quite wrong of me. It's just that…' He took another breath. 'It's just that I was a little upset at the notion that I would have to abandon all my friends, break the promises I have made, leave London and bury myself in the country for eight or nine weeks at least, with only my two nieces and their governess for company. And all within forty-eight hours. Absurd as it might seem to you, I was just a little shocked.'

He drew another breath and forced himself to smile again. 'But you have been very kind. I am sure Julia would wish me to show you our gratitude. May I call on you at the Poultney this evening? I should like to offer you and my nieces dinner there, if I may.'

Edward's charm was potent when he chose to exercise it, and Lady Penkridge was no more immune than many another lady in the past. Her manner was perceptibly warmer as she said, 'Thank you. Yes, the…the girls would enjoy that. And so should I. At what time?'

That evening Edward exerted himself to erase the unfavourable impression he had made on Lady Penkridge with such success that she began to wonder whether Julia had after all been mistaken in him. They parted on the best of terms, and after an exhausting two days of rearrangements, meetings, notes of apology and excuses, Edward saw Lady Penkridge safely launched on her journey north, then set out for Wychford accompanied by his nieces and Miss Froom.

As they left London behind them, he saw that something of his own gloom seemed to have affected the rest of the party. Lisette was gazing sadly out of the window, Miss Froom was sitting with a gimlet eye on Pip, and Pip herself was quite remarkably subdued. Edward roused himself. It was not his nieces' fault that he had been forced into exile. The poor girls had had a terrible time in the last year, first with the upheaval caused by the accident and the loss of their parents, and then the business with Lisette and Arandez. And now this…

'I dare say you would like to hear a little about Wychford,' he began.

'Has Aunt Julia bought it?' asked Pip.

'Don't be silly, Philippa,' said Miss Froom. 'Your aunt will have leased it through an agent. It would be unnecessary to buy it when you are to stay there for such a short time.'

Edward regarded Miss Froom. This wasn't the first time she had put the child down, quite unnecessarily. He would have to keep an eye on her. Pip's lively interest in everything she came across was one of her main attractions, and he didn't want it suppressed. He smiled warmly at his little niece as he said, 'I'm afraid you're both wrong. There's more to it than that.'

Pip's face brightened. 'A story, a story! Tell us, Edward!'

'Well, when we first heard about Wychford it belonged to Thomas Carstairs. Thomas owned some plantations in the West Indies, and he and his wife became friends with your grandfather. Some years later—just about the time you were born, Pip—Mrs Carstairs came out to see us again after her husband had died. She promised your father then that we could all stay with her at Wychford when you and Lisette were old enough to come to England.'

'Like a good fairy at a christening!'

Edward smiled. 'Something like. Though she looked rather more like a witch than a good fairy.'

'Will she be there now?'

'No. She died not long ago—'

'And left the house to us!'

'Not quite.'

'Philippa, how many times do I have to tell you not to interrupt? And get back down on to the seat, if you please!'

Edward felt a spurt of irritation. Pip was standing on the seat, leaning half against him and half against the cushions at the side of the carriage. It wasn't safe, and Miss Froom had been perfectly right to object, but he had been pleased to see Pip once again her lively self. He ignored the governess and went on, 'That would have been quite wrong. Mrs Carstairs had no children, but she had other family. She left the house to her niece.'

'A niece? Like us?'

'Mrs Carstairs was about eighty, so a niece would be much older, wouldn't you say? Probably even older than I am!'

'Have you met her?'

'No, I've only dealt with her agent, a Mr Walters. But you must let me finish my story. I visited Mrs Carstairs several times at Wychford, and when I was last there, and told her you were all coming to England this year, she remembered her promise to your father.'

'But she's dead!'

'That's true, but she stipulated in her will that Wychford was to be available to the Barracloughs for six months after your arrival.'

'That's a very strange condition, Edward,' said Lisette.

'Mrs Carstairs was a very strange lady. But I liked her.' He fell silent, remembering the last time he had seen the old woman.

She had been wrapped in shawls and huddled in her chair, obviously ill. But her gipsy-black eyes had been fiercely alive. She had looked at him hard, and then she appeared to make up her mind. She said, 'You'll do! The house likes you and so will she.'

Puzzled, he had asked, 'Who is ''she'', ma'am?'

Whereupon she had given one of her cackles and said, 'Never you mind! But she will. Eventually! Make sure you come back here! But there! I know you will.'

Edward had been tempted to dismiss her words as the wanderings of an old lady whose life was almost spent. But they had stuck in his mind, and now here he was, about to return to Wychford, just as she had said...

Chapter Two

Some thirty miles away, Mrs Carstairs and her house were also the subject of discussion between Rupert, fourth Earl of Warnham, and his daughter, the Lady Octavia Petrie. The day was cool, and Lord Warnham, who was in his seventies and felt the cold, pulled his shawl closer round his shoulders and gave his daughter a worried frown. In his gentle way he said, 'I wish your Aunt Carstairs had not left you Wychford, Octavia. It was most inconsiderate of her. I knew it would be a burden!'

'But, Papa, I assure you, I don't find it any sort of burden.'

'How can that be? You tell me that you must go to see it next week. All that way through the countryside to see a house that can be of no conceivable use to you! Of course it is a burden. She should not have done it. If she had consulted me in the matter I would have advised against it. She cannot have thought of the worry it would be to you to possess a house like that.'

'Papa, it is no worry at all! I am very *happy* to be the owner of Wychford.'

'But you cannot possibly keep it. You have no notion of what it means to look after a large house!'

'I look after this one, Papa.'

'That is quite a different matter, my dear. This is your home, and you have me to protect you.'

Octavia Petrie permitted herself a wry grin. It might be her home, but it was her father who needed protection. Even the most trivial of problems worried him. Much as she loved her elderly parent, she found shielding him from unnecessary distress far more demanding than looking after a house, however large it might be. She set about reassuring him.

'Wychford won't cause me any trouble, Papa! You know it won't. The Barracloughs are to rent it for six months, as Aunt Carstairs wished. The agreement is signed and sealed, and so far I have had nothing at all to do. Mr Walters has dealt with it all.'

'Walters is a good fellow. An excellent man of business! But he has done no more than he should. It would not be at all the thing for a lady to be concerned in property agreements and such matters. But I still cannot like it. Your Aunt Carstairs should have left her house to someone else. You would do much better to stay at home with me next Tuesday and let Walters get rid of it for you.'

Octavia smiled. Her father must be unique among parents. No other man would find it distressing that the youngest of his eight children, twenty-two and still single, had been left a large estate, including a house, by her godmother. But Lord Warnham's intense dislike of any threat to his unvarying routine quite blinded him to the advantages of such a handsome inheritance. Octavia hardened her heart and said firmly,

'I am not so very young, Papa. I shall be three and

twenty next spring. And I really shan't find it a burden to make a simple visit to Wychford. I merely wish to see the house before the Barracloughs arrive. It will take less than a day.'

'A day! You must not be so foolhardy! It is all of ten miles.'

'Fifteen. But it is still quite light in the evenings and the roads are good—'

'You would subject yourself to travelling *thirty miles* in one day! I will not hear of it! Even with a closed carriage—'

'Oh, I would take the gig. I'd like to drive myself. Will Gifford would accompany me, of course.'

This suggestion so outraged the Earl that it took several minutes of Octavia's most skilful coaxing before he could be brought to resign himself to her absence. Eventually he said wistfully, 'I suppose you will have to go, but I shall miss you.'

'I hardly think so, Papa. Have you forgotten that Cousin Marjorie arrives tomorrow? You like her, don't you?'

'She is a very pleasant person, certainly, and plays whist and cribbage better than you do. You know you can be a little impatient, my dear. Yes, I like Marjorie.' He sighed and added, 'I can see you are quite set on this escapade, Octavia, so I shall say no more on the subject. But I do wish that Mrs Carstairs had not left you her house. I cannot understand why she did!'

'Nor can I, Papa. Though…she did say when she was last here that Wychford would like me.'

The shawl dropped off her father's shoulders as he sat up and stared. 'Wychford would *like* you? A house *liking* someone? What a very strange thing to say! But then, I was often puzzled by the things she said. She did not resemble your dear mama at all.'

'No, indeed! Harry and I were afraid of her when we were children. We used to call her the Witch of Wychford. But I got to know her better when she was here last spring, not long before she died. She…she seemed to understand…'

Octavia fell silent. It was true that there had been something witch-like about her mother's half-sister. Though nothing had been said, she, of all the family, had seemed to divine Octavia's growing restlessness, her boredom with life at Ashcombe. Octavia had found Mrs Carstairs's gypsy-black eyes resting on her more than once and had wondered what the old lady had been thinking. But it had certainly never occurred to her that her godmother would leave her Wychford.

'Understand? What is there to understand?'

'Nothing, Papa. Nothing at all.'

'A very odd person. Why should she leave you her house?' He was obviously still struggling to understand. 'What do you need a house for? Surely you're happy enough here?'

Octavia longed to say, 'I'm bored, Papa! I sometimes think I shall go mad with boredom!' But she was a kind-hearted girl and genuinely fond of her father, so she merely said, 'Of course. And I have no intention of living at Wychford, Papa. In any case I couldn't. The Barracloughs take possession in just a few weeks' time.'

'Who are these Barracloughs? Do I know them?'

'Old Mr Barraclough was a friend of Uncle Carstairs. They knew each other in Antigua. They are now both dead, of course, but the present Barracloughs have some daughters, who are to be presented next year.'

'That seems a very odd sort of arrangement. But the Barracloughs sound respectable enough.'

'They are extremely respectable, Papa. Mr Walters has had the highest reports of their standing in Antigua, and Mr Barraclough is at present in London working as a temporary adviser to the Foreign Office. I am very unlikely to meet them. Certainly not this time, for they won't be there.'

'Well, I suppose you must go. I shall do as well as I can with Marjorie.'

Octavia laughed at his tone of resignation. 'You'll do very well indeed, Papa!'

'You must see to it that she has the tapestry bedroom. She likes that.'

'Indeed, she does. She has used it every time she has paid us a visit for the past twenty years!' Octavia shook her head at her father in affectionate exasperation. 'Really, Papa! What do you think of me? The room has been ready for two days now. It only needs fresh flowers, and I shall put those in it tomorrow before she arrives.'

'And a warming pan for the bed, Octavia! Remind the housekeeper to make sure the bed is properly aired!'

'I shall do nothing of the sort! I have no wish to offend Mrs Dewey. If I know her, there's a hot brick in the bed already, and it will be renewed tomorrow. You may be easy.'

As soon as her father settled down for his afternoon nap, Octavia changed and made her escape to the stables. She collected her mare and Will Gifford, her groom, and set off over the fields. A good gallop might rid her of the feelings of impatience, boredom, weariness even, which were taking an ever-firmer hold of her spirits. Much as she loved her father, she sometimes felt an irresistible desire to get away. The fact that she had made her own trap, had chosen of her own free will to stay at Ashcombe, was little consolation now. How could she leave him? But she was looking forward to the following week when she would see Wychford for the first time. She began to feel more cheerful. Cousin Marjorie's visit was something to look forward to, too. She might belong to an older generation, but she was still young in spirit, and a very sympathetic listener.

Octavia's Cousin Marjorie, the Dowager Lady Dorney, was a widow, and lived some distance away in the Dower House of a great estate now owned by her son. She and Lord Warnham had always been good friends and since Lord Dorney's death a year or two before she had been a frequent visitor to Ashcombe. She spent a great deal of time gossiping about the family with him, or playing backgammon, whist, or the many other games he enjoyed. Lord Warnham liked her company and her visits had always been a success. Octavia had no qualms about leaving her father in her care.

When Lady Dorney arrived the next day, Lord Warnham was still having his afternoon nap, so, after greeting her warmly, Octavia took her off to her own little parlour. For a while they exchanged news of the two families, then Lady Dorney said,

'You're not looking as you should, Octavia. What's wrong? Is it this house your mother's sister has left you? Wychford?'

'Not you too!'

Lady Dorney raised an eyebrow at the exasperation in Octavia's voice, and Octavia went on, 'Papa wishes it had never been left to me. He thinks it too great a responsibility. Don't tell me you feel the same!'

Lady Dorney laughed. 'I am not as unworldly as your father, I'm afraid. No, I am glad for you. But if it isn't that, why are you looking so unlike yourself? You're obviously under some sort of strain.'

'I had hoped I wasn't showing it!'

'Perhaps not to others. But I know you too well. What exactly is wrong?'

Octavia hesitated. Then she said, 'You're right, it is the house. When I first heard about it, it seemed like a way of escape. But I soon realised that I couldn't possibly take it.'

'I'm not at all surprised at your wish to escape! The life you lead at Ashcombe is no life for a pretty young girl. You should have married years ago. I've never understood why.'

'That's soon explained. I never met anyone I wanted to marry!'

'You've never been in love?'

'Not really.'

'Never?'

Octavia gave a small smile. 'When I was younger I thought I was. With a very handsome young soldier, called Tom Payne—tall, blond, blue-eyed, and full of fun. He came down here on leave with my brother in the summer of 1812, and he and Stephen got up to such scrapes that I don't think I stopped laughing for the whole of that fortnight. I've never forgotten it.'

'That's hardly my idea of a great romance! Did he make love to you?'

'Of course not. I was only fourteen! I don't think it entered his head. But if he had lived...I might have met him again...'

'He was killed?'

Octavia nodded. 'At Waterloo. Both of them. He and Stephen together.' She paused then went on, 'I got over it, of course. Our acquaintance had been too short for real heartbreak. By the time I went to London for my come-out I was quite my old self. But…I never had an offer there that I wished to accept.'

'Oh, come now! That is absurd! You can't have been short of choice! You're not only a very pretty girl, you are rich and related to half the best families in England. You must have attracted any number of eligible young men!'

'Perhaps so. But not one of them attracted *me*!'

'You were surely not still pining for Tom Payne?'

'Oh, no! It wasn't that exactly, but…but he was always my ideal—blond, blue-eyed, and *fun*. And no one quite measured up to him. Compared with Tom they were so dull! I couldn't face spending the rest of my life with any one of them. And then London was noisy, and dirty…and full of scandal…'

'Then your mama died and you left town.'

'Quite without regret.'

'And you decided to stay at Ashcombe, to put off even considering marriage until your father could manage without you. I said at the time it was a mistake, if you remember.'

'But there wasn't anyone else! Harry couldn't stay— he was already in the Army—and the rest of the family were married and established elsewhere. Papa would have had to move in order to live with any of them, and you know how he hates change. He even refused to move to Warnham Castle when Grandpapa died.'

'So your brother Arthur took over the family seat. I must say, the Castle is more Arthur's style! How is he?'

'Much the same as ever. Pompous, opinionated and prosy! Sarah is expecting another child, and Arthur is full of hope that she will give him a son at last.'

'How many daughters has he?'

'Four.'

'And no son. His poor wife. She won't get much sympathy from Arthur if she fails him again. I can quite see why your father wouldn't wish to live in the Castle with Arthur! But I still don't see why you had to sacrifice yourself?'

'I assure you, ma'am, it was no sacrifice—at the time! But now…I feel trapped!' She gave a little laugh. 'Sometimes I feel quite desperate!'

'You need to get away for a while. Could you not visit one of your sisters?'

'What? To be a nursemaid to their children rather than to my f—' She stopped short. 'Rather than manage Ashcombe for my father? Here at least I only answer to him! But…with your help I shall have a brief holiday—all of eleven or twelve hours.' She got up and walked about the room. After a while she turned and said with an impatient gesture, 'Oh, pay no attention to me, ma'am! I wasn't forced into my life here—I chose it. Marriage would not be the way out. From what I have seen of my sisters' husbands, I would merely exchange one form of boredom for another.'

'You still haven't met the right man,' said Lady Dorney with a smile. 'He'll turn up, you'll see!'

'That is romantic nonsense! At fourteen I might have believed in fairy tales, but at twenty-two I've given them up. No, when I no longer have Papa to look after, I shall turn into a crotchety old maid living at Wychford with a pug and a downtrodden companion, and children will think me a witch, as I did Aunt Carstairs!'

'She had the air of one, certainly. She had a way of looking at people…I only met her once, but I felt she knew what I was thinking before I did myself! What is this Wychford like?'

'I've never seen it. My aunt never invited any of us there, she was something of a recluse. I shall see it for the first time next Tuesday. I'm so relieved you'll be here to look after Papa. I know how tedious it can be…'

Lady Dorney looked at Octavia in astonishment. 'My dear girl, you are quite wrong! I shall look forward to it!' She laughed at the expression on Octavia's face. 'You needn't look at me like that, Octavia. I am quite serious. I love looking after people, especially someone as sweet-natured and gentle as your Papa.'

'Really?'

Lady Dorney took Octavia's hand. 'Since Dorney died there's been such a…a hole in my life that I sometimes hardly know what to do with myself. Coming here might seem dull to you, but to me it's most enjoyable! Indeed, I'd be happy to keep your father company for longer than a day if you wished! Now, tell me how you intend to travel. How far did you say it was to Wychford? And what do you know about these Barracloughs? Might there be a charming young, blond, blue-eyed Mr Barraclough who will "amuse" you?'

Octavia laughed. 'If only there were, ma'am! But, according to Mr Walters, the Barracloughs are a sober, upright and highly respectable family. And since there are only two daughters, there are absolutely no prospects there for me, I'm afraid. In any case, I shan't meet any of them—the Barracloughs won't be there. They're not due at Wychford for another week at least.'

Meanwhile, some three miles from Wychford, the 'sober, upright and highly respectable' Mr Barraclough, grim-faced, got out of his carriage, which was leaning drunkenly to one side, examined the broken wheel-pin and swore fluently and comprehensively. Three heads popped out of the window, one interested, one nervous and the third dressed in a black bonnet, its feathers quivering with outrage.

'Mr Barraclough! Sir! You forget yourself,' said the black bonnet severely. 'Lisette! Philippa! Sit back this minute and put your hands over your ears.'

'You'd do better to tell them to get out as quickly as they damn well can, Miss Froom,' said Edward brutally. 'I cannot promise that the whole lot won't topple over any moment. Out with the lot of you!'

'But there's too much mud on the road!'

'Better muddy shoes than bruised bottoms! Out with you! You first, Pip!' Ignoring Miss Froom's gasp of outrage at his language, he lifted the youngest of the three occupants out and swung her over to the dry verge of the road. 'Now you, Lisette. Don't hang back, you'll be perfectly safe with me.' Lisette was lifted and deposited next to her sister. 'Miss Froom?'

'Thank you, Mr Barraclough, I'll get out by myself,' Miss Froom said with dignity.

'As you choose, ma'am,' said Edward with ironic amusement. But when Miss Froom landed in the pool of mud and would have slipped he caught her by the waist and bundled her to the side to join the others, where she stood, ramrod straight, bristling with indignation.

He left her there while he went back to examine the damage done to his carriage. Meanwhile, Pip took advantage of the situation to scramble up the nearest tree where she perched on one of the branches. When Lisette looked up and saw her she gave her a very sweet smile, but Miss Froom exclaimed loudly, 'What on earth do you think you are doing, miss? Get *down* this instant! Get *down*, I say! Mr Barraclough, tell that child to get off the tree. Look at her! I must protest—'

'Protest all you wish, Miss Froom, it won't do you any good,' he said impatiently. 'I have more urgent things to do than listen to you at the moment. If you can't control the child, then I suggest you leave her up there. She's perfectly safe.' Then, turning his back on her he shouted, 'Jem! Jem! Where the devil are you? How bad is it?'

Scarlet-faced, Miss Froom drew a deep breath, pursed her lips, and sat down on a nearby tree trunk. 'Sit here with me, Lisette,' she said coldly. 'And you may take that silly smile off your face. I do not find your sister's disobedience at all amusing.'

'She's not really disobedient, Miss Froom,' said Lisette earnestly. 'Pip always looks for somewhere to perch. She likes being high up. Papa used to call her his little marmoset…' She bit her lip. 'She…she used to make him laugh…'

'That may be, but if I am to be responsible for her that child will have to behave like a young lady, not a street entertainer's monkey! My previous charge, the Lady Araminta, was younger than Philippa when I first started to teach her. You would never have found her up a tree, she was a model of good behaviour. But then so were all her sisters and brothers. The Marchioness, their mother…'

Both girls sighed. They had known Miss Froom for a mere three days but they had already heard more than they wished about the Marchioness of Ledbury and her perfect family.

After Miss Froom had finished on the subject of the Ledburys she turned her attention to Lisette. 'Try to act like a lady, Lisette! Put your feet together and sit up straight. That is better. Now! You may list for me the kings and queens of England in order of succession. We needn't waste time while we are waiting to continue our journey.'

'I…I don't know them.'

'You don't *know* them?'

'Not…not like that. In a list.'

'William the Conqueror,' shouted Pip. 'He shot an arrow into Harold's eye!'

Miss Froom ignored her. 'Then you will have to learn. What about the prophets of the Old Testament?'

'The prophets? Er…J…Jeremiah…'

'In order, if you please!'

'I…I can't do things like that, Miss Froom. It's not the way Mama taught us.'

'I see.' Miss Froom's tone suggested that she thought poorly of Mama's methods.

'Her lessons were fun, and we learned a lot!' said an aggressive voice from above.

'My methods of instruction are directed towards the acquisition of knowledge, not fun,' said Miss Froom coldly. 'Lady Ledbury fully approved of them. At the age of ten the Lady Araminta could recite all the…'

'The Lady Araminta sounds a dead bore to me,' muttered Pip rebelliously. 'And so does the Marchioness of Ledbury.'

'*What* was that, Philippa?'

'Look, Miss Froom! Edward is coming! I think the carriage is ready,' cried Lisette hastily. 'Come down, Pip, dear. We shall soon be on our way.'

Mr Barraclough reported that the pin had been replaced, and they could now complete the last three miles of the journey to Wychford. 'So, we'll be off! Into the carriage with you! Miss Froom?'

They set off once again. But the silence was oppressive. Mr Barraclough looked sharply at Miss Froom's pursed lips and pinched nostrils, and then at Pip. 'Is there something wrong?' he asked.

'Philippa is a very rude, undisciplined, ill-mannered little girl,' said Miss Froom sharply.

Pip sat upright, looking mutinous, and Lisette put a restraining hand on her arm. 'She didn't mean to be rude. She's tired, Edward. It's been a long day. I am sure she is sorry. Please forgive her, Miss Froom.'

There was silence. Mr Barraclough said, 'Miss Froom?'

'I do not mind so much for myself, though it is not what I am used to,' said Miss Froom stiffly. 'But when an ignorant little girl criticises the family of as great a nobleman as the Marquess of Ledbury, whose family goes back hundreds of years—'

Mr Barraclough, too, had heard his fill of the Ledburys. It was his private opinion that the Marchioness would have done better to pay less attention to her children and more to her husband. Ledbury's *amours* were the gossip of London. But he said, 'Yes, yes, it is absurd. You should not regard it, Miss Froom. In future you must try to guard that unruly tongue of yours, Philippa. Now, do you see the house?'

Chapter Three

They had just passed through some gates. Ahead of them was a long drive that wound round a lake. Pip leaned out dangerously and shouted with excitement, 'I can see it, I can see it! Edward, it's *lovely*! It's got funny little windows—and look! Barley-sugar chimneys and a tower! Can I have a room in the tower? Please let me have a room in the tower!'

Lisette peered round. 'What a beautiful colour it is in the evening sun,' she said. 'And just look at the trees! Green and scarlet, brown, gold—they're glorious! I think we shall like living here. What do you think, Miss Froom?'

Miss Froom had not recovered her humour. She threw a glance at the house. 'I doubt very much that I shall,' she said repressively. 'I know these old houses, though I have fortunately never had to live in one before. This one looks like all the rest—dark and damp. And those windows will let in the draughts.' She stared disapprovingly at Pip's lichen-stained skirt and tumbled curls, and surveyed Lisette with a frown. 'I can also see that I have a great deal of hard work before me before I achieve the standards I expect in my pupils.'

Mr Barraclough observed the excitement in Pip's face slowly die. He looked at the shadows in Lisette's eyes and said abruptly, 'I am sorry you find the prospect of teaching my nieces so repulsive, Miss Froom. They've had—we have *all* had—a difficult time of late. You were engaged to be responsible for their education, but until their aunt and uncle arrive from the West Indies I had hoped that you would see to their happiness and welfare as well.'

'Discipline and hard work bring happiness, sir,' said Miss Froom. 'That has always been my philosophy, and children are the better for it.'

Mr Barraclough regarded her with a thoughtful frown, but said nothing as the carriage came to a halt in front of shallow steps that led to a massive oak door. He ushered the girls and their governess into a large stone hall, where Mrs Dutton, the housekeeper, was waiting to welcome them.

She took Miss Froom and the girls on a tour of inspection while Edward went into the library, but after a short while the two girls came back alone and joined him there.

'That was quick!' he said. 'Where's Miss Froom?'

'She…she said she would lie down for a little,' said Lisette. 'She has the headache.'

Pip ran to her uncle and grasped his arm. 'Edward! Edward, please, please send her away. I don't like her! She's horrid!' she said fiercely.

'What's all this? Have you been rude to Miss Froom again?' asked Edward sternly.

'She deserved it! She said I had to sleep in a horridly poky room next to her so she would know what I was up to. But I wanted the little corner room! The one in the tower. Why couldn't I have the tower room?'

Their uncle looked harrassed. 'That's not my sphere, Pip, and it's a very poor reason for this tantrum! Or for being rude again.'

'It wasn't that! It wasn't that at all! She…she's cruel!' Pip threw herself on the sofa and burst into tears. Edward swore under his breath and looked on with a frown as Lisette took the child in her arms and comforted her. What the *devil* had he done to deserve this? He had always prided himself on the ease with which he could handle any woman in practically any situation. But this one tired, lost, little girl defeated him. Confound Julia! Why the *hell* did she have to break her leg just at this particular time! And what was Henry thinking of to send the girls over without her? He looked at his nieces and his mood softened. With a sigh of resignation he sat down beside them and said, 'What was it, Lisette? Tell me the whole. Is it true that Miss Froom was so disagreeable?'

Lisette said quietly, 'I'm afraid so. Miss Froom isn't at all a kind person. When she refused to let Pip have the tower room, Pip got angry and said that Mama would have wanted her to have it. Miss Froom said…she said she didn't doubt it. That Philippa was a spoiled little girl and the sooner she learned who was now in charge of her the better.'

'Miss Froom is tired after the journey. Pip can be confoundedly trying…'

'She said more than that, Edward. She said that our mama… She said that our mama was dead and wasn't coming back. And that if Pip carried on being such a naughty little girl she wouldn't go to heaven to see her mother again.'

'She said *what*?'

'That Mama was dead. It's true, of course.' Lisette

looked down at the child in her arms. 'It was cruel of her, though.'

Edward Barraclough looked grimmer than ever and said with formidable calm, 'That settles it. Your aunt and I have made a mistake. Take Pip into the morning room, Lisette, and stay there with her. One of the maids will bring a drink for you both. You needn't concern yourselves any further with Miss Froom.' He strode to the door.

'What are you going to do?'

'The carriage is still harnessed up. It can take her to Kingston tonight, and she can take the London stage tomorrow.'

'No, Edward, you can't send her off into the night like that.'

'I can and will! I'll have that woman out of the house before she says another poisonous word to anyone.'

'No, you can't do that. It's too late. She mustn't be asked to stay alone in an inn. You must let her spend the night here. Send her away tomorrow.'

Edward scowled. 'You're just like your mother—too tender-hearted for your own good, girl.'

'Please, Edward! Miss Froom may be unkind, but we ought not to be the same.'

Edward was about to refuse, but he looked at Lisette's face and his expression softened. He said reluctantly, 'Very well. She can stay the night. Now off with you. I want to speak to Miss Froom.'

Miss Froom departed the next morning with pursed lips, a month's salary and a carefully worded letter for her agency. Pip was beside herself with glee, but her uncle was not so happy.

'Stop that war dance, Pip and try to think what on

earth we're to do now! We're in a mess! Who the devil will look after you now that Miss Froom has gone? I can't leave you alone here, but I shall have to go to London occasionally.'

'To see that lady?'

Edward coloured angrily. There had been an unfortunate incident in the hectic rush of the past two days when Pip had accidentally seen him with Louise. What was worse, she had overheard a footman's comment about her. It was not the sort of thing that should happen and he had been both furious and ashamed. He said now as sternly as he could, 'I've told you to forget that lady, Pip. You're not supposed to have seen her. If I hear you mention her again, there'll be serious consequences. Understood?'

'Yes. I didn't like the look of her much anyway. So why do you have to go to London?'

'I have business in London,' he said curtly.

Lisette, the peacemaker, saw that her uncle's patience was rapidly wearing thin. She said to Pip, 'Edward looks after our money, Pip. Not just his own but all the family's. And he has talks with important people at the Foreign Office in London. He really does have to go back sometimes.'

Pip was unabashed. 'All right, Edward. You'll have to send for another governess, then. But choose a young one! A pretty one!'

Edward shook his head and said with decision, 'On no account! You're too much of a handful, midget. I'll choose someone with her mind on her work, not some pretty flibberty-gibbet whose sole aim is to set her cap at the first eligible bachelor who happens along. She'd be more nuisance than she's worth.' He sighed and went on, 'I'll write off to the agency today, but it will be at least a week before we hear anything. And then there'll be interviews… It means I shall have to postpone some important meetings, but it can't be helped.'

Lisette followed him out of the room. 'Edward, I'm sorry we're such a burden to you,' she said. 'I'm sure we could manage without a governess for a while. I can look after Pip.'

Edward's habitually sardonic expression softened into a rare smile. Much as he chafed at the restraints that had been forced on him by the care of his two nieces, he was very fond of them both. Lisette's sadness worried him. She was too young to be so serious. 'Pip needs a firm hand and a lot of attention,' he said gently. 'And I want you to have fewer things to worry about, not more.'

'Pip will always listen to someone she likes. She still misses Mama and Papa. She needs kindness as well as firmness, Edward.'

'Leave it to me, Lisette. I'll make sure I find someone who will know how to deal with her. Not another Miss Froom, I promise.'

The following Tuesday, blissfully unaware that the Barracloughs had already taken up residence, Lady Octavia Petrie said goodbye to her father and Cousin Marjorie, took up her groom, and set off for Wychford with a sense of excitement out of all proportion to the event. Apart from one stop to rest the horses, she wasted no time, and when she arrived at the gates of the house the hour was still comparatively early. She looked up the drive, which led away curving and twisting through an avenue of trees. It was very strange. She felt a tug of recognition, a stirring of adventure. The place seemed to beckon to her…

'Take the gig back to the inn in the village, Will,' she said making up her mind. 'It isn't far to the house and it's a glorious day. I'll walk the rest of the way. You can fetch me in a couple of hours.'

When the groom demurred Octavia said impatiently, 'Don't be such an old woman! I shall be perfectly safe. Mr Walters has engaged a full staff for the house, including a housekeeper. I can't believe there'll be any villains among them, can you? Off you go!'

Octavia watched Will's familiar figure disappear down the road, then walked through the gates. The weariness of spirit that had dogged her for months slowly lifted as she walked up the drive, and she was filled with a sensation of release, a feeling that she was in an enchanted world. She smiled. Perhaps she was under the spell of the Witch of Wychford! On either side were magnificent old trees, some of them with branches hanging low, their foliage touched with gold, scarlet and brown with glimpses of a deep blue sky above. Here and there a bright midday sun flashed and sparkled through the leaves, dazzling her with fairy gold. She walked on towards the house, gazing about her with delight. It was as if she had drunk a glass of champagne, or been wafted off to a land of fairy tales... She nearly jumped out of her skin as a voice from above said,

'He won't have you!'

Octavia stopped and looked up. The sun blinded her and it was a moment or two before she could make out an elfin figure perched on one of the branches. 'I beg your pardon?'

'He won't have you. You're too young and pretty.'

'How very kind of you to say so!'

'He said you'd be more trouble than you're worth.'

'Did he, indeed? How was he to know that? Though I'm not sure I fully understa—'

'He's looking for another Miss Froom, but I wish he'd have you. You look far more interesting.'

'Er…thank you again. I think.' Octavia pulled herself together and made an effort to begin a more sensible conversation. She asked, 'Forgive me, but may I ask who you are?'

'I'm Pip. Philippa Barraclough.'

'*What?*'

'It's rude to say ''what''. Miss Froom got very cross with me for saying it.'

'But…but what are you doing here?' stammered Octavia. 'You're not supposed—'

'You mean I should be inside? On a glorious day like this?'

'Oh, no! That's not it. No sensible person would want to be inside on a day like today. That's not what I meant—'

'I'm exploring. We've only been here a few days, and yesterday I explored the other side of the house. It's a beautiful house. Have you seen its chimneys?'

Octavia gave up trying to be sensible. She was enjoying this bizarre conversation. It all seemed to be part of the madness of the day. 'No,' she said. 'Will you show them to me?'

A little girl dropped out of the tree. Black curls tumbled over a pointed face. The child was thin, but crackled with energy and spirits. Great grey eyes, sparkling with life, gazed at Octavia, examining her with critical interest. What she saw seemed to satisfy her. 'Come on!' she said, and set off.

Octavia laughed. 'Right!' she said and followed.

Pip suddenly stopped. 'Look!'

Octavia obediently looked, then gasped with pleasure. On the other side of a small lake lay Wychford, a rose-red house nestling among lawns and trees, its windows twinkling in the sun. Its somewhat crooked timbers and a small round tower to one side gave it a lopsided, slightly quizzical look. A friendly house, an enticing house…a magic house. And on top… 'Barley-sugar sticks!' she cried.

Pip looked immensely pleased. 'I knew you'd recognise them,' she said. 'Oh, I *do* wish Edward would have you! He's at his wits' end, you know.'

'I'm sorry to hear it. Why is that?' asked Octavia.

'Because we've lost our governess. The last one. But I wouldn't be rude to you.'

'Is that why she went? Because you were rude?'

'No. Edward dismissed her. Sent her away without a character,' said Pip with relish. 'She was unkind. Lisette didn't like her, either, and she usually likes everyone.'

'Lisette is your sister?'

'Yes. She's much older than I am. I'm ten. Do you believe in lists?'

'What kind of lists? Laundry? Shopping? Christmas presents?'

'No! Lists of facts to learn—the kings of England, for example.'

'Definitely not!' said Octavia firmly. 'That's a very boring way to learn anything.'

'I *knew* you were all right! I must go and find Edward. He simply *must* engage you!'

'As what?'

'As our governess, of course. That's why you're here, isn't it?'

'Oh, no! I—'

But Pip had darted off like a dragonfly.

'You mustn't be annoyed with Pip.'

Startled yet again, Octavia swung round, and began to wonder if she really was in a fairy tale, and this the enchanted princess. Standing behind her was a girl with one of the loveliest faces Octavia had ever seen. She had black hair like her sister, but her eyes were a deep purple-blue, the colour of violets. Every feature was perfect: a generous brow, a beautifully straight nose, delicately modelled cheekbones, rose-petal complexion, softly curving lips... The girl looked shy, and bore an indefinable air of sadness. The impulse to comfort her was almost overwhelming. A faint flush stained the girl's cheeks as Octavia stared.

'I...I didn't mean to startle you. I'm sorry. Only I'm sure Pip didn't mean to be rude. It's just that she sometimes forgets her manners when she is in a hurry. My name is Lisette. Lisette Barraclough.'

'I'm Octavia Petrie. How do you do.'

They exchanged curtsies. 'Won't you come in?' Lisette asked. 'I'm not sure it will do any good, Edward seems determined to have someone older, and he seldom changes his mind. But I'd like you to meet him.'

Octavia was not sure what stopped her from telling Lisette the truth about her visit to Wychford. Every canon of good manners demanded it, but she held back, intrigued by the situation, and highly interested in the two girls—the one so bright and spirited, the other so lovely, and so sad. So she said nothing as they set off up the drive.

'I expect you're wondering why we need another governess,' said Lisette. 'Edward engaged someone in London—someone who was very highly recommended to my aunt by the Marchioness of Ledbury.'

Octavia had met the Ledburys. No wonder Pip didn't

like Miss Froom, she thought. No one who had the approval of such a self-satisfied windbag as Lady Ledbury and her awful children could hope to please a lively spirit like Philippa Barraclough!

Lisette went on, 'But hardly two days had passed before it was clear that Pip and Miss Froom would never get on, so Edward sent her away.'

'Without a character. I heard.'

'Is that what Pip told you? I'm afraid she was just romancing. Edward gave her a perfectly good reference.'

Octavia nodded. 'I rather thought that might be the case. But what did your aunt have to say about it?'

'She's not here. She broke her leg and is still in Antigua. She won't be able to travel for some time, so there's only Edward here to look after us at the moment, and he is a very busy man. That's why we need someone else so urgently.'

'I see. In that case, wasn't it rather hasty of your uncle to send Miss Froom away?'

'Perhaps. But once Edward makes up his mind about anything he does things right off. He would have sent Miss Froom away the first night we got here, even though it was very late. He can be quite ruthless when he chooses. But I persuaded him to wait till the morning.'

Octavia began to dislike 'Edward'. 'Poor Miss Froom! To be sent away so summarily—'

'Oh, no! She really wasn't at all kind, Miss Petrie. But he did give her a month's salary and saw to it that she was taken all the way to London.'

'I suppose that helped. But do tell me. Who is "Edward"? Mr Barraclough?'

'Yes. He's our uncle, but he told us years ago to call

him Edward. We are a great burden to him. At least for the next eight or nine weeks until our aunt arrives.'

'I see.'

Lisette fell silent and Octavia was left to her own thoughts. The situation was becoming clearer. The two girls were not the Barracloughs' daughters, but their nieces, and an accident had delayed Mrs Barraclough's return to England. A governess had been engaged, but Edward Barraclough had decided to get rid of her, and was now looking urgently for someone else until his wife arrived. For about two months... Just two months...

They had reached the lawn in front of the house.

'Miss Petrie, would you care to wait here for a moment? There's a seat in the shade over there. Or shall I take you inside? Edward asked me to deliver a message to our housekeeper, and I should really do it straight away. It will only take me a minute.'

'I think I should like to stay here,' said Octavia. 'This is all so beautiful...'

'You think so, too? Miss Froom said the house looked dark and damp.'

'Did she? Then the house didn't like her,' said Octavia without thinking. 'That's why she had to go.'

Lisette gave her a puzzled look, but didn't stay to ask what she had meant. She ran across the lawn and into the house, and Octavia was left to contemplate her inheritance... It was quite extraordinary—Wychford seemed to be smiling! How could a house smile? Of course it couldn't! It was just that the window-panes were twinkling in the sunlight.

She had a sudden vision of her aunt's gipsy-black eyes staring at her, then turning to rest thoughtfully first on her father, and then on Lady Dorney, last spring.

What had been in Aunt Carstairs's mind? Here at Wychford Octavia suddenly saw what an excellent thing it would be if her father and his cousin decided to marry. They had always been close, and Lady Dorney was a caring, loving woman who needed companionship and someone to look after. Yes, it would be ideal. But it would never happen. Papa was too set in his ways—it simply wouldn't occur to him to ask.

The windows were still twinkling, still reminding her of those black eyes. What a strange house it was! Octavia's thoughts returned to her father. What if Lady Dorney could be persuaded to take her place for a while—two months, say? It might occur to her papa that his Cousin Marjorie was more comfortable to be with, more patient, easier to talk to, someone nearer to his own generation….

Two months. Would it be long enough? She was sorely tempted to try. She liked these Barraclough girls, and felt she could do something for them, especially as their uncle seemed to be something of a martinet. Should she go along with their assumption that she was a prospective governess?

Octavia jumped up and took a firm hold of herself. Twinkling windows, gipsy-black eyes, marriages, pretending to be a governess—where was her common sense? It was a mad idea! Her day of freedom had gone to her head! She would go inside to meet Edward Barraclough, and would inform him of her true identity before the mistake went any further. As Lisette approached her across the lawn the sun seemed to go in and Wychford's window-panes were dull. There was an air of reproach about the house and Octavia had an absurd feeling of guilt.

* * *

Lisette led her through the oak door and into the hall. Octavia kept a firm hold on her imagination as she looked about her. The house was not huge and the hall was of manageable size, with a large refectory table down the middle and a fireplace at each end. It had a superb plaster ceiling and two massive, symmetrically placed, brass chandeliers. A handsome oak staircase led to the upper storey, with a gallery leading to the bedchambers. But Lisette led her through the hall and on into a room at the far end. This was some kind of parlour or morning room, and it was reassuringly normal. A fire burned invitingly in the hearth, and the furniture was obviously meant for comfort rather than style. Octavia was invited to sit down.

'I…er…I don't think I will yet,' said Octavia. 'Not before I see your uncle.'

The door opened and Pip burst in. 'Here she is, Edward!' she cried. 'Please say she's suitable!'

A tall, broad-shouldered man followed her into the room. Though he was younger than she had imagined, he looked…dangerous, with an uncompromising chin and a hard mouth. He was quite handsome, though his nose looked as if it might have been broken in a fight. Black hair, clear grey eyes, and a tanned complexion. A small scar lifted the outer corner of one eyebrow and gave him a faintly devilish look. His expression was not welcoming. Oh, yes! thought Octavia. If this was a fairy tale, then here was the ogre!

Mr Barraclough stopped and gazed at her for a moment, coolly assessing her. Octavia became conscious that her person was slight, and not very tall, that her dress was unimpressive, that one or two of her honey-gold curls had escaped from her bonnet and were now tumbling over her shoulders. She flushed angrily under his gaze and wished she had taken time to tidy herself. As he came towards her his stride was arrogantly athletic, his air one of impatience.

'Edward Barraclough,' he said curtly. 'May I have your name?'

'Certainly, sir. I am Octavia Petrie.'

'Well, Miss Petrie, I don't know how you heard so quickly about the post of governess here, but I'm afraid you've had a wasted journey. You're not at all what I'm looking for.'

'You are quite wrong—'

'Am I? Whatever you may have said to charm my niece, give me one good reason why I should employ a woman who arrives on my doorstep—'

'I don't wish—'

Mr Barraclough swept on. 'Arrives on my doorstep without warning, hoping to be engaged on the spot.'

Octavia forgot her embarrassment. 'I should have thought that was exactly what you required, sir,' she said tartly. 'From what your nieces say, you need someone rather urgently. Or am I mistaken?'

Mr Barraclough stopped. He looked at her again, this time speculatively. 'No, it's true that we need someone…' After a pause he said slowly, 'Perhaps I *was* wrong. Perhaps you're not the pretty featherhead you look. You sound mighty sure of yourself.'

'*Featherhead!*' Octavia took a deep breath. 'Really, sir! I assure you I am far from being a featherhead. Nor, unlike others I have met, am I a *block*head! Permit me to tell you—'

Mr Barraclough interrupted her yet again, but to Octavia's astonishment, instead of taking offence at her words, he laughed and nodded in approval as he said,

'That tone was fierce enough… And you're quick. There might be more to you than I thought.'

Octavia replied, 'I can be much fiercer than that, I assure you, sir! Not that I wish—'

'Edward, do say she may stay! *Please*!' called Pip from her perch on the window-sill. 'She doesn't believe in lists. She wouldn't need to be fierce with us. I'm sure I could behave well if *she* was my governess.'

'It *is* only for two months, Edward.'

Lisette's intervention seemed to give Mr Barraclough pause. He looked at Lisette sharply. 'You'd like her to stay, too? It isn't just because you're sorry for her?'

Lisette shook her head and said emphatically, 'I think she would be absolutely right for us.'

Octavia could see that Mr Barraclough was impressed by Lisette's words, and decided that it was high time she said something. 'I'm sorry, but I must tell y—'

'What are your qualifications?' he asked. 'I suppose you have some?'

Octavia was once more annoyed by his tone. He could do with a lesson or two in good manners himself, she thought. 'I think I may say that I am qualified to teach the necessary skills,' she said coldly, remembering all the expensive tutors and governesses insisted on by her mother, her sojourn at a highly exclusive Seminary for Young Ladies. 'But that's not the point—'

'I suppose I'd be satisfied as long as you can keep them safe and happy, and under control. Can you do that? You wouldn't have to teach them very much. Lisette is to come out next year, but I expect her aunt will see that she knows how to behave in Society.'

'I do know something of that, too, but—'

'This would be the very highest society, Miss Petrie. I wouldn't expect or ask you to cope with that. I don't suppose Mrs Barraclough would want you to teach Lisette the manners of some Dame's School or other. She would want better.'

While Octavia was choking at hearing a Seminary that had been patronised by the cream of the English aristocracy described as 'some Dame's School,' he went on, 'Well, I suppose we could try you. If you'll come into the library I'll give you the terms and so on. You'll find the salary generous, but the appointment is only for a short time—eight or nine weeks at the most. You do know that, do you?'

'Your niece did say something of the kind. But I didn't come—'

'Good! Then it's settled. Come through to the library.'

Am I never to be allowed to finish a sentence? Octavia asked herself. This Mr Barraclough absolutely *deserves* to be deceived! She looked at the two Barraclough girls, Pip nodding her head and almost falling off her perch with excitement, Lisette smiling for the first time since they had met, her wonderful eyes glowing with pleasure. Gipsy-black eyes hovered at the back of her mind…sparkling window-panes… To her astonishment she found herself saying, 'Very well, sir,' and meekly followed 'the ogre' into the library.

Chapter Four

At the end of her interview with Mr Barraclough Octavia fervently hoped that Lady Dorney had been sincere in what she had said. She wasn't sure whether she had succumbed to the force of Mr Barraclough's powerful personality, or to the equally powerful force of this strange house. But to her bewilderment she found she had agreed to come back in four days' time, complete with suitable references, to take up duties as a governess companion to the Barraclough girls. The 'ogre' had proved to be more accommodating than she would have imagined—or perhaps more desperate. After she had explained that she would like to keep an eye on an elderly relative who lived some distance away, she was promised two days a month, together with the use of the gig.

However, Mr Barraclough had made it all too clear that he was still not convinced that she could manage. This poor opinion of her abilities so annoyed Octavia that, as she took her leave of the Barracloughs, she swore to herself that she would prove him wrong if it was the last thing she did!

She refused the girls' offers to accompany her down

the drive, and set off in good time to be at the gate when Will Gifford came to pick her up. Having committed herself to a totally mad impersonation, she wanted to make sure it was carried through without any hitches, and Will and the gig were a potential giveaway. Most chance-met governesses did not leave in a well-cared-for gig with a groom who treated them with the deferential familiarity of an old servant!

Perhaps 'impersonation' was not the word—escapade was more like it. After all, she was not impersonating anyone else, and she had given Mr Barraclough her real name, if not her proper title. And though she had never sought employment of any kind, she was fully competent to look after two girls for two months, whatever their uncle thought. She would earn the very generous salary he had promised her…

But she still couldn't understand why on earth she had agreed to do it! The house must have bewitched her. She stopped, turned and looked at it again. Wychford was once again sparkling and smiling in the sunlight. Perhaps there was more to the stories about the house than she had realised? Perhaps Aunt Carstairs *had* been the witch she and Harry had thought her! Why *had* she left her house to Octavia? Had she seen her goddaughter's restlessness, yet understood Octavia's reluctance to marry simply to escape from Ashcombe? It was possible.

But even the Witch of Wychford couldn't have foreseen the Barracloughs and their problem. Or…could she?

As Octavia walked on down the drive she was thinking of the last time she had seen Aunt Carstairs. They had said their farewells and the footmen were waiting

to assist the old lady into her carriage. But just before
she got in her aunt had turned round to take Octavia's
hand and say, 'Be patient, child. Rescue is at hand.'
Then, as the carriage prepared to drive off, she had put
her head out of the window and added with a crow of
laughter, 'There's even a hero in prospect, though you'll
take time to recognise him.'

Octavia was turning these words over in her mind
now as she drew near the gates of Wychford. A hero?
Not among the Barracloughs, that was certain! Edward
Barraclough was not only already married, he was the
opposite of all her ideals. Dark, abrupt, discourteous,
and not much gaiety about him… Anyone less like Tom
Payne would be difficult to imagine! No blond prince
among the Barracloughs, then. So where? Perhaps one
of the local neighbours had a son… But how could she
meet him if she was an employee, a governess at Wychford? Octavia gave a sigh. Surely Aunt Carstairs could
have managed better than this! But as Will Gifford
drove up she laughed out loud. She was beginning to
believe her own nonsense!

Octavia got back to Ashcombe in daylight and, wasting no time before setting her plans in motion, invited
Lady Dorney to have tea with her in private. 'It's an
age since I saw Papa so happy, ma'am,' she began as
they sat down in her parlour. 'You are so good for him.'

Lady Dorney looked at her with amusement. 'I'm
glad to hear that. But I believe I know you too well to
think it an idle remark,' she murmured. 'Tell me, what
plans are you hatching in that pretty head of yours? I
don't believe you invited me here just to pay me compliments. Incidentally, you, too, look happier—excited
even. What happened today?'

Octavia hesitated, then launched into an account of her adventures. When she reached the point where Edward Barraclough said that she wasn't the featherhead he had thought, Lady Dorney was so amused that she nearly dropped her cup.

'So when did you tell him that, far from being an indigent governess in search of a post, you were the daughter of the Earl of Warnham, and the owner of the house he was renting?'

'I didn't. I haven't.'

'*What?* Why on earth not?'

Octavia took a breath and said defiantly, 'I've agreed to begin as their governess in four days' time.'

'But how can you possibly manage that? Rupert would never agree! To say nothing of pretending to be something you are not! No, no! You can't do it, Octavia!'

'I could. With a little help from you, ma'am.'

'Your papa will never consent.'

'I wouldn't ask him. I would tell him that it was as he feared—Wychford needs further attention than I thought, that I need to spend some time seeing to it. It's not quite a lie, ma'am!'

'It's not the truth, either! What do you think he would feel if he learned that his daughter was working as a governess?'

'I don't suppose he ever will. At the end of two months I'll come back here and take up my old life again. But I wish I could explain to you… Those children *need* me, ma'am.'

'So does your father. How will you persuade him to do without you?'

'Ah! That's where the favour comes in.'

'Tell me!'

'Well, you did say that you'd like to stay longer this time. And if you were here Papa wouldn't miss me nearly as much. Our housekeeper is perfectly competent, and the servants are all familiar with the routine of the house…'

'If you are suggesting what I think you're suggesting, the answer is no, Octavia! I won't do it! Take charge of this house? Certainly not!'

'You needn't take charge, exactly—just *be* here. I could come back regularly to see that everything is working, though I'm sure it won't be necessary. *Please* say you will, ma'am!'

Lady Dorney said somewhat coolly, 'You realise, I hope, what I would be risking? Rupert and I have always been good friends. He would hardly believe it if he found out that I had helped you to deceive him. He would certainly be distressed. It might well mean the end of our friendship!'

'It won't! I swear it won't. I just have a feeling… Cousin Marjorie, please do this! I know I am asking a lot. I can't even explain why it is so important to me. Perhaps it's the escape I've been looking for. Please help me!'

Lady Dorney hesitated, started to speak, then stopped again. Octavia waited in silence. At last her cousin said, 'I've tried to persuade you so often to escape that I suppose I can hardly refuse to help you now. And I haven't actually made any plans for the autumn, nor for the winter either. I don't imagine I'll be missed at Lutworth…' She sighed, then sat up and said with decision, 'Very well! I'll do it! I'll stay for two months. But I think I am as mad as you!'

With Lady Dorney's help Octavia was on her way back to Wychford less than a week after her first fateful

visit there. Will Gifford was once again her companion
on the journey, but this time he would return to Ashcombe without her. At the back of the gig was a small
valise with a selection of Octavia's simplest dresses.
Her hair was severely drawn back under an unadorned
bonnet, her cape was of drab grey cloth plainly cut, and
her gloves and boots serviceable rather than elegant.
Lady Octavia Petrie, youngest child of one of the richest
families in the south of England, and heiress in her own
right of a handsome estate, had been replaced with simple Miss Petrie, newly engaged governess-companion
to the Misses Barraclough.

A casual observer would not have known just how
nervous she was. Her outward demeanour was composed and quietly confident. But the spirit of adventure
had not disappeared. Inside Octavia was an unholy mixture of anticipation, apprehension, surprise at her own
daring, and exhilaration at her escape. Two months.
Two months to find out what she really wanted of life.

If anything, Wychford seemed more welcoming than
ever. The day was overcast, but as the gig approached
a fleeting ray of sunshine was reflected in those extraordinary windows. The house was smiling its quizzical
smile. Lisette was hovering on the lawn, clearly waiting
for her arrival. And as Octavia stepped out of the gig,
Pip climbed down from the nearest tree. They took her
over, Pip leading her to the door like a small tug in
charge of a clipper, Lisette giving orders to the housekeeper.

'We've given you a room near mine,' said Pip. 'Not
exactly in the tower but nearby. Did you know that the
old lady who used to live here was a witch? Mrs Dutton

wasn't here then, she lived in the next village, but she says all the villagers here were frightened of Mrs Carstairs.'

'Really?' As they went through the oak doors Octavia once again had the strange feeling that the house was enfolding her, welcoming her. 'I think she must have been a good witch, Pip,' she said, smiling. 'Wychford is a friendly house. Don't you agree?'

As a daughter of the Earl of Warnham Octavia had been accustomed all her life to the deference due to her rank and her wealth. But it was not difficult now for her to maintain her 'disguise'. She was neither arrogant nor conceited, and she had more than her fair share of charm. Her normal, easy, matter-of-fact manner served her very well with everyone at Wychford. Everyone, that is, except the master of the household. She was still very much on trial as far as he was concerned, and more than once Octavia found herself biting back an unbecoming response when he made one of his critical remarks.

Fortunately he was frequently away on short visits to London. She learned that there had been three Barraclough brothers. John, the eldest and father of Lisette and Pip, had inherited a wealthy plantation on Antigua. Henry, the second son, also had land in the West Indies and was still over there. But Edward Barraclough, the youngest, had had little taste for plantation life, and when he had inherited a fortune made in banking by his uncle he had travelled the world. Now he apparently intended to settle permanently in England. At the moment he was attending meetings in the Foreign Office, advising the experts there on affairs in the Americas.

There had been some sort of plan for Lisette to marry

the son of one of their neighbours in Antigua. But John Barraclough had suddenly changed his mind and decided to bring both girls over to England, where Lisette would be presented to London society. They had been busy with arrangements for the trip, when tragically both parents had been killed when their carriage had gone off the road, and the girls had been left orphaned. Their guardians, John's surviving brothers, had decided to carry out John's wishes, which was why they were now in England. But, the day before they left Antigua, Mrs Barraclough had slipped and broken her leg, and the girls had had to sail without their aunt. So the present plan was that the girls should live at Wychford in the care of a governess-companion until Mrs Barraclough could join them all there.

Octavia pieced this all together from what she learned in her first week at Wychford. Not from Lisette, who tended to be somewhat reserved, but from her sister. Discretion was not a word in Pip's vocabulary. Once she had decided that Miss Petrie was a friend, she confided everything she knew of her family's affairs quite freely.

One fine autumnal afternoon, after a morning's work in the schoolroom, Octavia and Pip were walking in the woods behind the house. Lisette had stayed behind to finish a book she was reading.

'You know, Miss Petrie, I think Uncle Henry was quite glad when Aunt Julia broke her leg,' announced Pip.

Shocked, Octavia stopped short and looked at her. '*What* was that?' she asked.

'I said that I think Uncle Henry was glad Aunt Julia had broken her leg,' Pip repeated patiently.

'But that's a dreadful thing to say, Pip! How could he be?'

'It meant that he had to stay behind to look after her. Uncle Henry didn't want to come to England, you know, and Aunt Julia's broken leg meant he had to stay in Antigua a bit longer.'

'But…I'm not sure I understand. If your Uncle Henry was so reluctant to leave the West Indies, why was it necessary for him to come at all? Surely your Aunt Julia and Uncle Edward would have been enough?'

'That's what Uncle Henry wanted. But Aunt Julia wouldn't hear of it. She said Edward couldn't be trusted to do the thing properly without the rest of the family to keep an eye on him.'

'Tell me, if you call your uncle ''Edward'', why don't you call your aunt ''Julia''?'

'Oh, we couldn't! She's *much* older than he is! She looks a bit like Miss Froom.'

'Really?' Octavia was surprised. Older than he was, and looking a bit like Miss Froom? It seemed a most unlikely wife for Edward Barraclough.

Pip went on, 'She and Edward don't like each other very much. It's easy to tell when people don't. They're always *extremely* polite to each other.'

Octavia pulled herself together and decided it was more than time for a proper governess to stem these confidences. 'Philippa, you should not tell me such things. What happens between husband and wife is not for the outside world to know.'

'What do you mean?' Pip looked puzzled at first, then bent over in a fit of giggles. 'Miss Petrie! You don't think… You don't think Aunt Julia is married to *Edward*, do you?'

'Of course I do! Isn't he?'

Pip went off into another paroxysm of giggles. 'He'd rather die! He said so! Aunt Julia is Uncle *Henry*'s wife! And I once heard Edward telling Papa that he would never know why Uncle Henry had married such a sour-faced prune!'

Octavia bit her lip and managed to say severely, 'Philippa! You must not, you really *must not*, repeat things like that, especially not to me! I'm sure your uncle would be very vexed to know that you had heard his words, and even angrier to know you were repeating them! Or even talking about him at all!'

'Would he?'

'Of course he would!'

'Then I won't say any more. I like Edward. But let me tell you this one thing. He isn't married, Miss Petrie. Lisette is sorry for him. She thinks he must have a broken heart, but I think that's rubbish. Some of the prettiest ladies in Antigua made a fuss of him, but he never paid them any attention. I was glad, I didn't like any of them much. I want him to marry someone nice.' She looked confidingly up at Octavia. 'You would do very well, Miss Petrie. I'd like Edward to marry you. You'll have to set your cap at him.'

Octavia gasped. What would the child say next? Choking back another urge to burst into laughter, she said sternly, 'That's enough! You must never let me hear you use such a vulgar expression again, Philippa! Where on earth did you pick it up?'

'What's wrong with it?'

'To accuse someone of setting her cap at someone is not at all the thing. It's not only vulgar, it's unkind. You mustn't use the expression.'

'Edward used it. When we were talking about governesses. He said he didn't want some pretty flibberty-gibbet whose sole aim was to set her cap at the first eligible bachelor who happened along. I don't think he meant himself, though he's very rich, you know. Lots of people have set their—' Pip caught sight of Octavia's frown and corrected herself. 'Have tried to make him like them. Why don't you want to?'

Repressing a mad impulse to tell the child that Edward Barraclough would be the last man she would ever consider, Octavia forced herself to think as a real governess would. The child's capacity for verbatim reporting was amazing, but she would have to be taught to keep such things to herself. 'I can see that you've been left to your own devices for too long, my girl!' she said firmly. 'You need a little discipline. Oh, don't look like that! I'm not a Miss Froom. But you'll have to learn to keep gossip and the things people say when they're not thinking strictly to yourself. It's called good manners.'

Pip sighed. 'I'll try to do as you say, but it's very hard. Lisette thinks Edward needs a wife, and you would be so suitable! I'd like you for my aunt—you're much nicer than Aunt Julia.'

'Philippa! What have I just said?'

'That I mustn't gossip. But that wasn't gossip, it was just an opinion! You would be good for Edward! You're prettier than any of the ladies in Antigua. And much prettier than the lady he visits in London. Though he must like her a lot. He gives her lots of presents.'

Octavia gasped. What else would the child come out with? And what had Edward Barraclough been thinking of to let her see him with someone who, from the sound of it, was quite possibly his mistress?

'I assure you, Philippa, that even if it were possible I would not consider marrying your uncle under any circumstances whatsoever!' she said emphatically. 'And we shall now finish this conversation and return to the house, where you will spend the rest of the afternoon improving your mind! Come!'

They turned to go back. Edward Barraclough was just walking towards them. He was only a few yards away, and looking more than usually sardonic. He could not have helped overhearing what she had just said.

'Mr Barraclough!' Octavia felt her face grow scarlet as she stammered, 'We didn't see you, sir...'

'Edward!' Pip launched herself at her uncle. 'We thought you were in London! What are you doing here?'

'Looking for Lisette. I have a letter from Antigua for her, but I couldn't find her in the house. I thought she would be with you, Miss Petrie.'

With a considerable effort Octavia mastered her confusion and said politely, 'Is she not in her room, sir? We left her there reading.'

'She isn't there now. I suggest you find her as speedily as you can. How long is it since you left her to her own devices?'

Octavia coloured again, this time with anger. But she said calmly and carefully, 'About an hour, sir. I left her, in her own room, with a book she said she wished to finish. It did not seem to me to be a very hazardous occupation.'

Mr Barraclough nodded. 'And if she had stayed there we should not now be looking for her. But she didn't. Nor did she answer when I called. Where do you suppose she is, Miss Petrie? While you have been... exchanging confidences with Philippa, my other niece has been unsupervised for over an hour.'

'Don't be angry with Miss Petrie, Edward. Lisette's safe. I expect she's sitting in the sun on the top of the tower. She likes it there.'

'On top of the…' Octavia picked up her skirts and began to hurry back to the house. Mr Barraclough overtook her after just a few paces. By the time she had reached the foot of the stairs to the tower he was already coming down, followed by Lisette.

'Why are you annoyed, Edward?' she was saying in a puzzled voice. 'It is perfectly safe up there! The parapet is high and the roof is sound.'

'I called you. Why didn't you answer?'

'I didn't hear you.' Lisette had reached Octavia. 'Miss Petrie, I'm sorry! I didn't mean to give you a fright.'

'It's all right, Lisette. I was anxious for a moment or two, but I should have known you are too sensible to do anything rash. Your uncle was worried when he couldn't find you. Did you finish your book?'

'Yes. And then I sat in the sun and fell asleep. That's why I didn't hear his call. Don't be angry with me, Edward!'

'I'm not angry,' he said abruptly. 'I was worried when I couldn't find you.'

Lisette shook her head at him. 'You needn't be,' she said. 'I'm quite safe here. Why were you looking for me?'

'I have some letters from Antigua for you, including one from your Aunt Julia. If you and Pip will come down in a few minutes I'll deliver them. I'd like a word with Miss Petrie first.'

Octavia looked at Mr Barraclough's frown. 'I think you'd both be better for a tidy up,' she said with a smile at the girls. 'The tower may be safe, Lisette, but it isn't very clean. And Pip's clothes always need attention! Tidy yourselves up before you come down.'

As she followed Edward Barraclough down the stairs,

through the hall, and into the library she wondered what he would say. It would not be pleasant, she was sure. He had almost certainly overheard her words to Pip, and she steeled herself to be ready to apologise for them, though she was not at all clear what she could possibly say. But his attitude towards her supervision of Lisette was unreasonable, and if he were to accuse her again of neglecting her duties she would find that difficult to accept without protest.

She was surprised therefore when he invited her to sit down. He stared at her for a moment, then walked to the window. Without turning, he said abruptly, 'I suppose you think I was too hard on you.'

'About Lisette? Well…'

'You needn't hesitate, Miss Petrie. I believe I know what you think of me. But that is of no concern at the moment. I wish to explain why we are so careful of Lisette.'

'Sir?'

He came over and sat down at his desk. 'I'm not sure how much you've heard of our family history, though I imagine Pip has told you everything she knows by now. She seems to have taken a decided fancy to you.' Mr Barraclough's tone implied that he did not share Pip's feelings. 'She isn't too much for you?'

'I don't think so, sir. She is a delightful little girl. And a highly intelligent one.'

'Hmm! You seem to have her confidence at any rate. She's brighter than Lisette, of course.'

'More lively, certainly. But Lisette is utterly charming. She will be a great success in Society.'

'And what would you know of that?' he asked derisively.

Octavia bit her lip. She had spoken without thinking.

Governesses would not normally be able to judge how Society would receive their pupils. But she recovered and said quietly, 'Her beauty, her gentleness and concern for others, must endear her to anyone who meets her, here or in the greater world.'

'You've read too many novels. I hope you're not stuffing Lisette's head with such nonsense. In my experience, gentleness and concern for others are not the qualities looked for in the ladies of society. Nor are they often found—' He stopped as Octavia drew a sharp breath. 'You wished to say something? No? Then I'll continue. Lisette's beauty will be a great asset, but she has a more reliable key to success, the most important one of all. Wealth, Miss Petrie. Money. She is a considerable heiress. That is what will make her a success in Society.'

Octavia could not let this pass. 'I would not wish to stuff *anyone*'s head with romantic nonsense, sir. But neither would I wish to give any young person as cynical a view of the world as the one you have just expressed.'

'Yes, yes, I dare say. But your experience is somewhat limited. What if I were to tell you that, young as she is, Lisette has already been rescued from an unsuitable association?'

This was a surprise. Lisette had never mentioned anything of the sort. 'I suppose I would have to believe you,' Octavia said slowly. 'This was in Antigua, I take it?'

'Of course. The son of one of the neighbours thought that marrying my niece would be an easy way to make himself rich. Ricardo Arandez has a great deal of address, and Lisette, as you may have observed, is too ready to believe what people say, too ready to like them.

Her father was the same. Arandez persuaded him to consent to a betrothal. Fortunately Lisette was still very young, so, though John agreed, he insisted it should not be official before she was sixteen. By that time his eyes had been opened to Arandez's true character.' He smiled grimly. 'I made sure of it. John withdrew his consent, and Lisette was saved from what would have been a disastrous marriage. Ricardo Arandez is a scoundrel.'

'Was she in love with this man?'

'Of course not! The girl was far too young to be in love.'

Octavia thought of Tom Payne and smiled. 'Is one ever?'

Mr Barraclough surveyed her. 'This is just what I feared. Miss Froom would have taken my point immediately, but you are still trailing clouds of romantic folly. Miss Petrie, let me make myself clear. Your task is to look after Lisette, and that includes guarding her from undesirable acquaintances until her aunt is able to take over from you. It is highly unlikely that Arandez will find his way to Wychford, but if he or any other potential fortune hunter appears on the scene, I wish to be told of it immediately.'

'The risk here is surely slight, but I will certainly promise you that. However, I hope that doesn't include acting as some sort of jailer, watching her twenty-four hours a day?'

'No, no. I admit I overreacted to her disappearance this afternoon. My excuse is that I had just heard from my sister-in-law, who is somewhat too protective of our nieces, and always ready to accuse me of not looking after them well enough. I suppose I was still under the influence of her letter.' He fell silent.

Octavia waited a moment, then said, 'Is that all, sir?'

'What? Oh, yes. Ask the girls to come in, will you?'

She went to the door. As she opened it he said, 'By the way, Miss Petrie!' She stopped and turned. 'I know it is almost impossible to silence Pip, but I should prefer you not to discuss my affairs with her. However…I am relieved to know that I am safe from your attentions—whatever the circumstances!' He sat back in his chair with a smile of satisfaction as she blushed and hurried out of the room.

Chapter Five

Still grinning, Edward reached out and pulled a letter towards him. It was from his sister-in-law. Just as he would have expected, it was full of the usual mixture of pointed remarks about his life style, instructions about the girls and dire warnings. What she would say when she learned that he had got rid of Miss Froom and replaced her with a green girl he hardly liked to think. But this time at least Julia had some justification for her fears. She had heard that Ricardo Arandez had left Antigua and was on his way to Europe. She was afraid he might have ideas about meeting Lisette again…

Edward Barraclough sighed. Life at Wychford was not as awful as he had feared. In fact it was occasionally quite pleasant. But, much as he loved his nieces, he wished to heaven he had not been called upon to fill the gap left by Julia's accident. Playing nursemaid to two vulnerable girls was no occupation for a grown man. There seemed to be no end to the problems, and meanwhile his personal life was suffering a marked decline. Louise was not a woman to tolerate neglect for long, and his most recent visit had been something of a failure. He had found her boringly possessive. What concern was it of hers how he spent his time away from her? He hadn't told her how, of course, but she would never have believed him if he had! That he was living in the depths of the country with two young girls and a dowdily dressed young woman! She would have found the very idea ridiculous. And so did he! But that didn't give his mistress—his *mistress*, for God's sake!—the right to know where he went and what he did when he wasn't with her! She was lovely enough, but her voice could get unpleasantly shrill. He was starting to lose patience with the old doddards at the Foreign Office, too, and beginning to think he was wasting his time on them. When would they learn to leave eighteenth-century politics behind, and step into the nineteenth century?

There was one bright spot in all this. Though he didn't particularly want to admit it, Miss Petrie seemed to be a success, for all her youth and prettiness. Edward smiled again as he thought of her confusion when he had teased her a few minutes ago about her remark to Pip. Her cheeks had been bright red. Serve her right! No man liked to hear himself spoken of with such scorn, even by a dab of a governess!

No, that was wrong. She might be small, but she wasn't a dab of anything. An intriguing young woman, Miss Petrie. The girls really liked her, and the servants all treated her with genuine respect. What was her background? She had brought a letter with her, but after a quick glance through he had put it away without bothering to study it more closely. He unlocked a drawer, took out a folder and opened it. The letter of reference was on top, and he picked it up and read it. It was from a Lady Dorney of Lutworth Court, who seemed to be a woman of intelligence and education. Edward remembered meeting Gerard Dorney a few years before. This was clearly his mother. Lady Dorney's letter recommended Octavia Petrie without reservation, praising her patience, her efficiency, her trustworthiness, her high standard of education… All the virtues. It made the girl sound so worthy! A Miss Froom without the sourness. So very dull.

And yet he had the distinct impression that Miss Petrie was far from dull. He was not quite sure why. She dressed quietly enough, with no attempt to attract. If he had not seen those honey-gold curls that had tumbled about her shoulders at their first meeting he would never have known they existed. Miss Petrie wore her hair in a firmly disciplined knot, or even under a cap. She was not particularly tall, and her figure, from what he had seen of it, was slight. Apart from her forget-me-not blue eyes, he would not have said there was anything interesting or attractive about her to a man whose taste ran to women like Louise Kerrall. For a moment he tried to think of Louise as he had last seen her, petulant but still seductively lovely…but the image of Miss Petrie kept getting in the way.

Miss Petrie wasn't dull. She was quick-witted and amusing. And there was something about that small figure: the imperious turn of the head, the straight back, the slender neck. Her carriage was graceful, her manner unassuming, but Miss Petrie was neither humble nor respectful, not underneath. Like Pip, she had a mind of her own, and though she was more skilled at disguising it, she was no more prepared than Pip to give way without argument.

Edward Barraclough was intrigued. Perhaps he should spend more of the time he was forced to spend at Wychford in getting to know his nieces' governess! He told himself with a grin that he would be perfectly safe. No risk of being caught. He had heard it from the lady's own mouth—Miss Petrie wouldn't consider him as material for a husband, not under any circumstances! What was more, she had sounded as if she meant it. For a moment Edward Barraclough was tempted to prove her wrong, but he rejected it instantly. It might well be an interesting exercise, but one did not seduce governesses—not if one were a gentleman.

As a result of these musings Mr Barraclough began to pay more attention to his nieces' progress at Wychford. He found Miss Petrie's methods of instruction unconventional—certainly by Miss Froom's standards. But to his surprise they were in fact quickly making up for lost ground. It was true that laughter was quite frequently heard coming from the room set aside for their morning lessons, but, when he stopped to listen, it always subsided after a moment and was followed by a period of eager discussion, then silence, or questions and answers. Sometimes Miss Petrie read aloud to them. Her voice was beautiful—warm, low in pitch and slightly husky.

When the weather was suitable the governess took her charges into the grounds in the afternoons, and Edward made an effort to join them occasionally. He discovered that lessons were not confined to the mornings in the schoolroom. The girls might not realise it, but they were learning a great deal more while they enjoyed themselves outdoors. Artists, music, scenes from history, a comparison of the plants to be found in the West Indies with those they found in the grounds of Wychford—these and many other topics were taken up to be discussed, dropped if they proved dull, or pursued the next day if they were interesting. At first Miss Petrie seemed inhibited by his presence, but as she grew more used to him he discovered that she used him quite ruthlessly to expand the scope of their discussions, and he was closely questioned by all three about his travels.

Each girl had a notebook for records. Lisette was their botanical recorder. Her exquisite line drawings of leaves, trees and late-blooming flowers were carefully dated and kept in a large folder. Some of them had been turned into delicate watercolours. Pip was more interested in animals and buildings. Her book was filled with bizarre sketches of birds, mice, insects, windows, gable corners, gargoyles and, of course, chimney pots. But the measurements and notes underneath were neatly kept, and checked by Miss Petrie.

And always, at some point in the walk, there would be a game, or some form of more energetic exercise. Pip needed no encouragement, but even Lisette was persuaded to run or skip.

Attracted by the sound of laughter and shouts, Edward came out one afternoon to find them behind the house, enjoying a particularly energetic ball game. All three, including Miss Petrie, were chasing about the lawn. Lisette was doing her best to dodge her governess and throw the ball to Pip. It was a lively, noisy scene, but when Miss Petrie saw him approaching, she left the girls to carry on by themselves and made frantic attempts to tidy herself up. She was still in the middle of twisting her hair into its usual knot when he joined her. Her cheeks were flushed and she was breathing quite fast. She looked about the same age as Lisette. He was amused at the air of challenge about her as she said,

'Good afternoon, sir. You've surprised us.'

He nodded a greeting. 'Miss Petrie. Allow me to congratulate you on your turn of speed. I doubt Miss Froom could have dodged about as nimbly.'

'I suppose you disapprove, Mr Barraclough?'

'Of what?'

'Of our unladylike behaviour.'

Edward looked at his two nieces and shook his head. 'I haven't seen them as happy as this since they came to England, especially not Lisette. No, I don't disapprove.' He laughed at her expression. 'Do I appear to you to be such an ogre, Miss Petrie?'

'Og…ogre! N…no, sir! Of… of course not!' she stammered. 'Excuse me, I must call the girls in. They must change before they get cold. Lisette! Pip!' She gave him a curiously embarrassed little nod and walked away to where Lisette and Pip were playing. He was impressed to see how they ran to her, took her by the arms, one on each side, and towed her in towards him. They greeted him with their usual affection, but when Miss Petrie ordered them into the house they obeyed her.

'You've done well, Miss Petrie,' he said as they followed the girls at a more sedate pace. 'I think I made the right choice of governess after all.'

'Choice, sir?' she said with a sceptical look. 'It was my impression that you thought me a last resort!'

'I thought you far too pretty. Tell me, why do you screw your hair into that hideous knot? Your honey-gold curls are far more becoming.'

Mr Barraclough had spoken without thought. The minute the words had left his mouth he regretted them. The girl was bound to be embarrassed by such a personal remark from her employer. But Miss Petrie did not flush in embarrassment or lose her composure. Her eyes were suddenly no longer forget-me-not, but ice-blue, and she froze him with the sort of look he would have expected to receive from a duchess in a London drawing room. 'Not, however, to a governess,' she said coldly. 'Excuse me.' She increased her pace towards the house.

He caught her up at the door. 'Forgive me,' he said. 'That was an unpardonable piece of impertinence. Please accept my apology.'

She hesitated, still with that film of ice around her, 'Very well, sir. But if you will excuse me I must see to your nieces.' She gave him a slight curtsy and started for the stairs.

Edward went to his library and flung himself into a chair. What a fool he was! Why the devil had he made such a stupid remark? Though…it wasn't as stupid as all that, said a small voice inside. Miss Petrie did look prettier with her hair loose. He dismissed the thought as irrelevant. Miss Petrie was a governess. A *governess*. One did not make such remarks to a governess. One reserved that sort of compliment for a flirtation with one of Society's beauties, or for one's mistress perhaps.

Confound it, why was he in such a state about it? He had apologised, hadn't he? The girl was not even the type he admired! Things had come to a pretty pass when a dab of a governess could make him feel presumptuous for passing a perfectly harmless comment about her hair. Who the devil did she think she was?

Edward got up and strode out of the room, shouting for his groom. He was in a thoroughly bad mood. Perhaps a good gallop through the fields would improve his temper.

* * *

From her window Octavia watched Mr Barraclough ride off. He looked displeased. She sighed. It was not surprising he was angry. Her response to his remark about her hair had been the conditioned reaction of Lady Octavia, daughter of the fourth Earl, not one to be expected of Miss Petrie, the governess. Miss Petrie might be embarrassed, but she would take more care not to offend, especially as her master acknowledged his fault almost immediately, and apologised. The truth was that she had been confused, surprised by her pleasure at what he had said. She had received many a compliment in her time and very few had affected her in the slightest. Why had Edward Barraclough's remark pleased her so? He was not at all the type she admired. His remark had not been particularly polished. Why had she been pleased? She had no idea. No idea at all! She turned away from the window and walked about the room impatiently.

She must take care. This situation was exactly what Edward Barraclough had feared when he had been reluctant to engage her. Too young and too pretty—that had been his objection to her. A featherhead! Well, she had proved she was no featherhead, but he probably now regretted having relaxed his guard, having complimented her on her work with his nieces. Octavia gave an impatient sigh. It had taken a lot to overcome this prejudice of his, and now it looked as if her efforts had been wasted. They would be back on their old footing when they next met.

She came back and sat down by the window. The past weeks had been so enjoyable. The Barraclough girls were everything she had thought, responsive, affectionate, and each in her own way imaginative. She loved teaching them. And recently she had seen a different side to Edward Barraclough. He no longer quite seemed the ogre she had thought him. Since he had taken to joining them on their afternoon walk he had seemed to be more human, with an unexpectedly strong sense of humour, often with a fine sense of irony behind it. Somewhat to her surprise she had enjoyed his company. Yes, Edward Barraclough was definitely more interesting than she had first thought him.

Had she shown him this too freely? Had he begun to think he might find a little extra amusement here to lighten the time he was forced to spend at Wychford until his sister-in-law could relieve him? A gentle flirtation with the governess? Octavia stopped short and stood in the middle of the room. The thought was highly unwelcome. If that was the case, the sooner Mr Edward Barraclough was shown how wrong he was the better! A break was called for. She would speak to him the next day, and claim the free time he had promised her. And when she got back she would make sure she had her behaviour under better control.

Her suspicions increased when Mr Barraclough sent a request that she and Lisette would join him at dinner that night. Till now, if he was at home in the evening at Wychford, he had always dined by himself. Why had he decided on a change tonight? She was inclined to make some excuse, but Lisette begged her to give her her support.

'You *must* come, Miss Petrie! I wouldn't know what to say or do without you there to help me!'

'That is nonsense, Lisette, and you know it. We dine every night, you and Pip and I, and your manners are always perfect.'

'I'm sure to forget them if you're not there. I love

Edward, but he's sometimes so intimidating, especially when he talks about politics and things. And this is the first time I've dined downstairs. I shall be so nervous I shan't be able to say a thing. No, you must come. Please don't send your excuses!'

So Octavia gave in, helped Lisette choose a dress, then went to her own room to see what she could find for herself. There wasn't a great deal of choice. Acceptably plain day dresses for Wychford had been comparatively easy to find, and the addition of a pretty shawl or scarf was enough to make them suitable for the evening meal with the girls. But most of her more formal dresses were either too frivolous, or too obviously rich. Not one was really the sort of thing a governess would wear. In the end she had brought a gown in dark grey mousseline, which she had worn during the period of mourning for her mother. It was cut comparatively high in the bodice with sleeves down to the elbow, and its train was small enough to escape notice. This she put on, together with a wide lace collar that had belonged to her mother. She had dressed her hair in its usual knot, and added a small cap of the same lace. Octavia would not admit even to herself what a temptation it had been to allow some of those famous curls to escape.

When the time was right she collected Lisette, and they went down the stairs together. Edward Barraclough was standing at the foot. For a moment he watched them without smiling. Octavia's first thought was how distinguished he looked in evening clothes. Her second was that however well the trappings of civilised society suited him, they could not disguise what he was. There could not be a greater contrast between the memory of her light-hearted, fair-haired, blue-eyed first love and this dark, powerful, successful man with his scarred eyebrow, and more than a touch of ruthlessness about him.

The top of the stairs was dimly lit, and Edward at first did not see Miss Petrie. She was standing half-hidden behind Lisette, wearing a dark dress that made her practically invisible. Then she moved and he saw the touch of white at her throat. Her hands came up to straighten the girl's shoulders, and give them an encouraging pat, then they started down the stairs together. Lisette was dressed in white, her dark blue eyes glowing like stars, her cheeks faintly flushed with excitement. Edward was filled with pride and pleasure. Apart from her amazing beauty Lisette looked like any normal, slightly nervous, sixteen-year-old girl. The air of sadness that had surrounded her ever since her parents' accident had almost gone.

His attention turned to Miss Petrie. She was wearing a grey dress with a white lace collar. Her hair was drawn back severely under a small cap. The effect was one of quaker-like modesty, but in spite of that she had such an indefinable air of distinction that anything less like a little dab of a governess could hardly be imagined. What *was* it about her?

Edward pulled himself together. The invitation to this dinner was for Lisette's benefit. He wanted to see how his niece's social education was faring under Miss Petrie before his exacting sister-in-law appeared. Julia would complain bitterly if Lisette's manners had fallen off. Besides, after this afternoon's contretemps, he was curious to see how Miss Petrie herself behaved in more formal situations.

'Lisette, that dress becomes you very well.'

'Miss Petrie chose it for me, Edward. And she helped me to choose what to put with it. I'm glad you like it.'

Edward turned to Miss Petrie. 'Shall we go in to dinner?' he said coolly.

It was not long before Edward realised that Lisette's manners could not be faulted. Moreover, he suspected that Miss Petrie's standards were every bit as high as those of his rigorous sister-in-law, if not higher. He could hardly believe that the two elegant creatures gracing his dinner table were the same two females who had been racing about the lawn that afternoon! At first Lisette was nervous in this new and formal situation and said little. But Edward noticed how Miss Petrie gradually drew her into the conversation, speaking of things the girl knew about, asking her about life on Antigua. After a while Lisette had regained her confidence and was talking quite naturally.

Edward turned his attention to the governess. She puzzled him more with every meeting. He was not surprised at her efforts to show Lisette in a good light, but the manner in which she had done it, the confident ease, her poise, were impressive. And though she was dressed modestly, a closer look had told him that the lace she was wearing had cost someone a pretty penny. What *was* her background? Lady Dorney's letter had been enthusiastic, but apart from the mention of care for an elderly relative it had not gone into any detail about Miss Petrie's family. It was time he tried to find out. Lisette was talking of the afternoon's game.

'You looked as if you were all enjoying it immensely. Who taught you, Lisette?'

'Miss Petrie. She knows a lot of games. She used to play them with her brothers and sisters.'

'Do you come from a large family, then, Miss Petrie?'

'Quite large, sir. But I was the youngest.'

'The eighth, perhaps? Since your given name is Octavia.'

'There were originally eight of us, yes. One of my brothers was killed at Waterloo.'

'Along with a great many others. That was a hard-won victory, indeed. What regiment was he in?'

'The Fifty-Second.'

'A crack regiment! You must be proud of him. Is yours an Army family, then?'

'I wouldn't say so. Stephen was the first of my brothers to join the Army,' she said briefly. But before he could ask any more she went on, 'From what you have told us, you were in India during the Waterloo campaign?'

'Yes, I spent some time in Madras.'

'That must have been an interesting experience. Is life there as hard as they tell us?'

With the unwitting aid of Lisette, who asked quite a lot of questions, Miss Petrie led the discussion away from herself and towards his account of life in India. He suspected this was not by chance, but if it had been deliberate the change of subject had been deftly done. However, he did not allow her to put him off for long. As soon as there was a break in the conversation he said, 'Tell me, Miss Petrie, how did you come to know Lady Dorney?'

There was a slight pause, then she replied, 'She is acquainted with someone for whom I have worked.'

'As a governess.'

'No, I believe I told you—I was looking after an elderly gentleman.

'And why did you decide to leave him?'

'I haven't left him altogether, Mr Barraclough. We both needed a change for a short while—that's why this position suits me so well. At the moment he has someone else to see to him.'

'I see. And Lady Dorney is a friend of his, perhaps?'

He saw how she shifted restlessly under his questions. 'She is a…a distant relative,' she replied after a pause.

'Is she a friend of yours, too?'

'I would like to think so. She…she is somewhat older than I am, and has lived a different sort of life.'

'How different?'

Miss Petrie gave him a straight look. 'Lady Dorney is a wealthy widow,' she said abruptly. 'And very well respected. She was the first person I thought of when you asked for a reference. Is it not satisfactory, Mr Barraclough? I could find others.'

'That will not be necessary. The letter is very complimentary. And I've heard of the Dorneys.'

'Good!'

There it was again, the touch of tartness, the hint of challenge! Most servants would be stammering with relief. But not Miss Petrie!

She went on, 'In fact, Mr Barraclough, I'd like you to release me for a day or two in the near future, in order to visit Ashcombe. I think we agreed that I could visit my family occasionally, and I haven't yet been back at all.'

Edward wished, he was not quite sure why, that he could think of a good reason to refuse, but there was none. 'Of course!' he said. 'I shall be in London tomorrow, but I think I can arrange to be here for a few days after that. Will the weekend suit you?'

'Miss Petrie! Why do you have to go? Pip and I will miss you!' cried Lisette.

'It won't be for long,' her governess said with a smile. 'Forty-eight hours at the most. The weekend will do very well, Mr Barraclough.'

'But—'

'Don't try to put Miss Petrie off, Lisette. She may have more than an elderly relative to see. A beau, perhaps?'

'Have you, Miss Petrie?'

'Governesses don't have beaux, Lisette. Those are for beautiful young ladies who are to make their début next spring.' This was said with an affectionate smile at Lisette. The smile faded as she turned to Edward. 'I hope Mrs Barraclough's injury will not prevent her from travelling to England for much longer. Is there any further news?'

Edward decided to concede victory for the moment. He would postpone further delving into Miss Petrie's background to another occasion. He said calmly, 'From what I've heard, matters are proceeding normally. My sister-in-law is reasonably strong, and very determined. She will come as soon as she can, I'm sure. Are you so anxious to be free of us, Miss Petrie?'

'Not at all, sir,' she replied politely. 'I have agreed to stay for two months, and I shall. After that—'

'We shall have to see.'

'As you say, we shall have to see. And now I think it is time for us to leave you to your cigars and port, sir. Lisette?'

'Are you not going to gossip in the drawing room till I join you?' he asked with a mocking smile.

'I think not.'

He found her quietly decisive air a challenge and asked, 'What if I insist?'

'Then we would have to agree, of course. But you wouldn't be so unreasonable! I'm sure you are pleased with Lisette's conduct tonight, but she isn't used to such late hours.'

Edward looked at Lisette and saw that she was having difficulty in keeping her eyes open. He laughed. 'You're right! And you're right about something else. I *am* pleased with Lisette. I congratulate you on your management of her, Miss Petrie. Miss Froom herself couldn't have done better. Goodnight.'

Lisette went to her uncle and put her arms round him. 'Goodnight, Edward,' she said sleepily. 'And thank you for a lovely evening.' She went towards the door. Her governess made to follow her.

'Miss Petrie!'

'Sir?'

'You must tell me more about your brother some time. Or shall I volunteer to take you to Ashcombe?'

Her eyes widened briefly, then she said composedly, 'That won't be necessary, Mr Barraclough. You've already promised me the use of your gig, and I can easily drive myself. I wouldn't dream of taking up your time. Goodnight. Thank you for a pleasant evening.'

He walked to the door with her to see her out. The top of her head barely reached his shoulder. But there was no shortage of spirit and pride in her carriage as she went gracefully up the stairs, the train of her dress trailing behind. A very unusual governess, Miss Petrie!

Chapter Six

Octavia had a hard time with her younger charge the next day. Pip was furious that she had not been included in Edward's invitation to dinner, and none of Octavia's attempts at consolation had any effect on her. When Lisette added to her sister's grievances by telling her that they were about to lose Octavia's company for two whole days, she took the news very badly indeed. She was rude during morning lessons, refused to eat her meal at midday, and later wandered out into the grounds in the afternoon before the others were ready.

Octavia decided not to pursue her immediately. Pip was basically sensible. She wouldn't come to much harm in the short time before they joined her, and a brief period in her own company might help to cure her of her megrims. So it was a few minutes before Octavia and Lisette set off round the lake to the woods at the other side. The leaves were turning fast, and their colours were more brilliant than ever. Lisette was enchanted and she and Octavia spent longer than they had intended gathering specimens to press in her notebook.

The afternoon had been fine when they left the house, but now clouds were gathering and the air was noticeably chillier. Their light jackets and thin muslin dresses were hardly enough to keep them warm, and after a while Octavia decided that Pip had been given long enough to recover her temper. It was time to seek her out and go back inside.

They knew better than to look for her along the paths or in the bushes. Pip would always choose to go upwards into a tree. But after a few minutes' scrutiny of all Pip's favourite trees, and increasingly loud appeals to her, it became clear that the child was deliberately hiding herself. Octavia was getting both angry and anxious. Large spots of rain were beginning to fall, and Lisette was shivering. She took off her own jacket, and, ignoring the girl's protests, put it round her shoulders. Then they went on, searching further and further away from the house. Eventually they caught a glimpse of bright red high up in one of the trees that overhung the far side of the lake.

Octavia was furious. The trees on the edge of the lake had been declared out of bounds, as were any but the lower branches of all the other trees. Pip had broken two of Octavia's cardinal rules. But this was no time to vent her anger. The rain was falling faster, and all three of them getting very wet. Pip must not be made nervous or upset. The descent from the tree would be difficult enough in these conditions. She kept her voice as calm and as matter-of-fact as she could manage.

'Good!' she called. 'I wondered where you had got to. Are you feeling better? Ready to come down? You must be getting very wet up there. I think it's time we all went in.'

'Aren't you cross with me for climbing this tree?' demanded Pip. 'I was sure you would be.'

'Then why did you do it?'

'I wanted to make you sorry! And I'm not coming down till you say you won't go away!' said Pip defiantly, adding, 'Miss Froom wouldn't have left us alone for two days, and I don't think you should.'

'Making me cross with you won't help matters. I might be tempted to stay away longer!' said Octavia.

'Besides, you won't be alone,' pleaded Lisette. 'Edward will be here. You like his company, don't you, Pip?'

'Edward doesn't like mine! He invites other people to dinner, but not me.'

'Edward *loves* your company! Look how much time he spends here at Wychford, even though he's such a busy man.'

Pip shook her head obstinately. 'No, he doesn't! He didn't want to bring us to Wychford at all.'

Putting more authority into her voice, Octavia said, 'Philippa, I'm too wet to be cross, and poor Lisette is cold. I'm getting a crick in my neck looking up at you. Let's talk about all this on *terra firma*.'

'I don't know where that is!'

'Yes, you do! It's the ground. Come down, Pip. We'll go back to the house and have toasted muffins in front of the fire. That's better than a boring dinner.'

Pip loved muffins. She hesitated, then got up and began to move along the branch. Her foot slipped on the wet surface, and Octavia, standing helplessly below, caught her breath. But Pip had hold of a nearby branch and had managed to steady herself again. Still clutching the branch she looked down. 'I...I can't!' she said uncertainly.

'Of course you can, Pip! You climbed up, didn't you? You can climb down again.'

Pip edged along a few more inches, then, just as she

reached the trunk of the tree, she slipped again. For a heart-stopping moment it looked as if this time she really would fall. But she saved herself once again, and with what looked like a huge effort twisted round and sat down against the trunk. Her voice rose as she wailed, 'Miss Petrie! I...I can't! It's too slippy. I can't!'

Octavia's heart sank—this was what she had feared. Pip's fit of royal temper had taken her high up into the tree. But now she could see the dangers. She didn't lack courage and under normal conditions would have tackled the climb down with only the slightest of hesitations. Now, however, she was cold and wet, and probably hungry too. She was quite literally stiff with fright.

'Miss Petrie!' came a scared little voice from above. 'Miss Petrie, what am I to do? I'm afraid!'

Octavia turned to Lisette. 'Run to the house! Get help. I'll stay here. Quickly!'

Lisette threw a frightened glance up at her sister. 'Oughtn't I to stay?'

Octavia said forcefully, 'You can run more quickly than I can. *Go!*' To her relief Lisette obeyed the command, and ran off without more protest.

Octavia had already made up her own mind what she had to do. Lisette had to make her way all round the lake to get back to the house, and meanwhile Pip would only get colder and stiffer. If she was left by herself for too long she might even make another effort to climb down, and that could be disastrous. A quick examination of the tree showed Octavia that she had climbed many more difficult ones in her youth. Though she might be small, she was nimble. Her long skirts would get in the way, however... She took off her stockings and used them as a kind of sash to hitch her dress up above her knee. As she put her shoes on again, she called, 'Stay where you are, Pip! I'm coming up to join you!' Then she braced herself and set off up the tree. The rain ran down her face and into her eyes, but she ignored it, concentrating on finding her way through to the frightened child above her. It was an enormous relief when she found herself near enough and secure enough to take Pip into her arms and settle with her against the trunk. They were both cold and wet, but there they would have to wait for help. Getting Pip down by herself was completely beyond her.

Edward had returned unexpectedly early from London and was busy taking off his wet hat and cloak in the hall when Lisette dashed in. He took one look at her distraught face and her soaking dress and jacket and exclaimed, 'What's happened? Is it Pip? Where is she?'

Lisette began to sob out a somewhat incoherent story, but, the instant she managed to describe where Pip and her governess were, Edward turned to his groom and ordered him down to the lake. Then, stopping only to give orders to the housekeeper and deliver Lisette into her hands, he followed.

At first he thought Lisette had got the directions wrong. Except for Jem, there was no sign of anyone under the tree she had described. But then he heard a cry. Looking up, he saw what looked like a sodden bundle of clothing tucked into a hollow between the trunk of the tree and one of its main branches. It was Miss Petrie. In her arms he could just make out a red jacket and a tangle of black curls.

'Fetch a ladder,' he rapped out to the groom. 'And some men. And blankets, too!'

Before the groom had gone ten paces, Edward had taken off his coat and was scaling the tree. The rain was still streaming down, and the holds were treacherous. Even as he climbed he was wondering how the devil Miss Petrie had managed to get herself up there.

As he got near them he heard her say, 'Here's Edward, Pip! Isn't that nice?' Her calm voice held nothing but pleasure, but her face revealed the strain she was under as she held herself back into the curve of the tree, the child hugged tightly to her. The effort needed to balance them both must be enormous. They were soaked to the skin and Pip was shivering, her head buried against Miss Petrie's neck, with her hands clutching Miss Petrie's shoulders as if she would never let go. Pip was in such a state of panic that getting her to the ground could be something of a problem. His first job must be to reassure the child.

He paused, smiled up at them both, and said cheerfully, 'May I join you? Or shall I escort you down?' Then he swung himself up beside them.

Pip's face was hidden, and her hands only tightened their clasp. Miss Petrie said, 'I think you ought to make your peace with Pip first, Mr Barraclough.'

'What for?'

'You left her out of your dinner invitation last night.'

'Now, isn't that odd? I didn't think she'd mind it a bit! I thought she would much prefer a muffin tea in front of the fire this afternoon. That's why I've come home early. I was a little put out, I can tell you, when I couldn't find any of you about!'

Pip raised her head and said in a small voice, 'Did you, Edward? You came home early? Just for that? I'd like some muffins.'

'Well, you'd better come down, then, midget! Mrs Dutton won't like to be kept waiting. Hand her over, Miss Petrie, and we'll have her down in two shakes of a monkey's tail. That's right.' Edward's deep, reassuring voice had its effect. Pip allowed herself to be transferred, and Edward gave Miss Petrie a sympathetic smile. 'You'll have to wait here, I'm afraid,' he said, as he moved along the branch. 'But I'll soon be back for you. Look, Pip! There's a ladder waiting, and it's only a little way down to it. Come on.'

Edward half-carried, half-guided Pip down to the ladder, which had been brought by Jem and one of the gardeners. He saw her to the ground and handed her over to his groom. 'Let Jem take you now, midget!' he said, giving her a hug as he wrapped her in one of the blankets. 'He'll take you to the house to get warm. Lisette is there. I have to rescue Miss Petrie.'

Jem set off and Edward turned his attention to the tree again. He had one foot on the bottom rung of the ladder before he saw that Miss Petrie was making her own way down!

'Don't be such a damned fool!' he exclaimed. 'Wait!' He climbed up the ladder and was just in time to see her slip on the last major branch before reaching the top rung. For a heart-stopping moment she hung above him, desperately clutching the branch over her head. He caught her just as her arms began to loosen their hold. With a grunt he hauled her against him and held her fast.

'I thought I told you to wait,' he growled.

'I th...thought your p...priority would be to see P...Pip safely indoors, Mr B...Barraclough, and as I was cold I didn't wish to wait for you to come back.' He could see the effort she was making to stop her teeth from chattering as she went on, 'I can't understand it. I would normally be p...perfectly capable of climbing d...down a tree like this by myself.'

'You're a fool! At the moment you're in no state for gymnastics—you're wet, stiff and cold. We must get you in as soon as possible. I don't want a bedridden governess on my hands. Come on!' He moved towards the top step of the ladder.

Miss Petrie looked down, swallowed, then shook her head. 'You'll have to give me a little t...time,' she said. 'I...I don't think I can at the moment. My arms and legs seem to have turned to j...jelly... It's absurd!'

He looked at her more carefully. Her face was pale and as wet as the rest of her. Her hair, loosened by Pip's clutching hands, was hanging down her back in a tangle of curls. She had a streak of dirt down one cheek and the neck of her gown had been pulled almost off her shoulder by Pip's frantic clasp. It didn't matter. The dress had been rendered practically transparent by the rain, anyway. He noted, without really thinking about it, that she had beautifully slender ankles and a well-shaped leg... And then realised with a shock that she had her dress pulled up to her knees, and her legs were bare! Firmly telling himself that this was no time to be distracted, he cleared his throat and said, 'If I go first down the ladder, can you follow me immediately after? I can quite easily stop you falling if we stay close and go down together. It shouldn't be difficult. The sooner you're indoors and in dry—' he cleared his throat again '—in dry clothes, the better. Can you follow me, do you think?'

She eyed the ground uneasily but nodded.

'Good!' he said.

He climbed down several rungs, then waited until she was on the top steps in front of him, and they slowly descended together. Edward's arms were either side of her hips, his face just above her waist. She may be tiny, he thought, but she was beautifully formed… An enticingly perfect bosom seen just a moment before, a tiny waist immediately below his eyes, the rounded contour of her hips between his arms, those ankles… He hoped that Miss Petrie felt safe, but if she had been able to read his mind at that moment she would be seriously worried, and not about negotiating her way to the ground! The sway of those hips, the shift of her waist as first one foot then the other came down the ladder, the brush of her body against his, were having a surprisingly powerful effect on him! He fixed his mind firmly on the job in hand, and managed to reach ground level without doing anything he might later regret, such as letting the ladder go and putting his arms round the tempting curves in front of him!

He helped Miss Petrie off the last rung, where she stood in a daze, completely unconscious of the state of her clothing. When he turned round Seth, the gardener, was holding out a blanket, and grinning broadly as he eyed her.

Edward snatched the blanket from him and said sharply, 'Stop standing there like an ape, and take the ladder back to the shed! Off with you!' He turned back to Miss Petrie. 'You'd better put this round you. And pull your skirts down!' His tone was curt and she looked at him blankly, obviously not understanding his sudden anger. With an exclamation of impatience he pulled her towards him, undid her rag of a sash to release her skirts, then wrapped her in the blanket himself. She looked so lost and tired, that, before he could stop himself, his arms tightened and he kissed her.

For a moment she stood like a child accepting, even welcoming, his lips on hers. The feeling of her soft, responsive mouth under his was magical. Edward's lips moved, and the kiss deepened and changed in character. The blanket dropped as he shifted and held her more closely, more intimately, his body hard against her... She shivered, then clung to him, perhaps seeking his life-giving warmth.

'Octavia!' he said unevenly, and kissed her again.

The sound of his voice brought her out of her trance. She came to life immediately, pulling her arms free and pushing him away. 'No!' she cried, a mixture of shock and shame in her voice. 'No, you mustn't! I'm sorry if I seemed to be asking you to... Oh, what must you think of me? But I wasn't. I assure you. No!' She looked round frantically for the blanket, picked it up and pulled it round her again. 'You must believe me, Mr Barraclough!' she stammered. 'I'm not like that... Not at all...'

Edward was almost as shocked as she was. It was a long time since he had allowed his feelings to take over to such an extent. Whatever the temptation, he usually remained in complete control of what he was doing. He must put things right immediately. 'Miss Petrie, I didn't mean to...to... I'm the one who is sorry!' he stammered with a lack of self-possession that would have astounded his friends. 'I...I didn't think...and then I seemed to lose my head.... I apologise. Please believe me, it won't happen again, I assure you! Never!'

She gazed at him doubtfully, but what she saw in his face seemed to reassure her. After a moment she looked away and nodded. He went on, still feeling somewhat awkward, 'May I suggest we get back to the house as quickly as we can? You'll be ill if you don't change out of those wet garments soon. Do you...do you need my arm? Or shall I carry you?' He was shocked again as the thought of carrying her, of having her in his arms again, suddenly quickened his pulse. This was absurd! What was happening to him? He was behaving like a raw boy! It was almost a relief when she shook her head, and he could take a firmer grip of himself.

But then, when she had taken a few steps, she stopped. Without looking at him she said stiffly, 'I think I should like an arm to lean on, after all. I'm sorry.' She looked so worn, and so nervous, that he was overcome with remorse. Forgetting his own feelings, he offered her his arm.

The rain had stopped. Together they walked back towards the house. They were met halfway by Mrs Dutton, who had dealt with Lisette and Pip and was now coming to look for their governess. She offered to take over from Edward, but he refused. Miss Petrie's hand was only lightly resting on his arm, but he was proud she had trusted him enough to ask for his help. Besides, it felt strangely comfortable. He didn't wish to relinquish it.

As they drew up to the house a faint ray of sunshine caught the windows of Wychford. It seemed to Edward that they twinkled with surprising brightness in the watery light. The house looked somehow…pleased with itself.

The muffins were served in the small parlour in front of a roaring fire. By the time Octavia came down after changing, the others were gathered round a tea table laden with silver coffee pots, jugs of chocolate, lemonade and, of course, dishes of muffins. It was an attractive scene—firelight reflected on the silver, Pip sitting close to her uncle, Lisette, quite recovered from her anxiety, smiling at them affectionately across the table. Octavia hesitated on the threshold, but Edward Barraclough got up the instant he saw her and led her forward to her place.

Octavia found it impossible to meet his eyes. A short while before, when she had reached her bedchamber and removed the blanket, she had been shocked beyond measure at the state of her dress—torn, almost transparent, and, until Mr Barraclough had released it, she remembered, it had been held well above her knees by her stockings! No wonder he had taken such a liberty with her! Between the display of her person, and the way she had positively *asked* to be embraced, he might well have thought it discourteous to refuse! If he *had* been looking for a flirtation with the governess to while away the time at Wychford, she had just given him every encouragement! She stood in front of her mirror, holding her hands to hot cheeks, and feeling deeply ashamed.

He had been a true gentleman afterwards, she thought, taking the blame on himself, and apologising very convincingly. Perhaps he really thought he *had* been to blame, and wouldn't regard what had happened as encouragement. He had sounded sincere enough in his promise never to repeat it.

But that was no comfort. She knew that inside she had *wanted* him to hold her as he had, *wanted* him to kiss her. What did that say of her? She didn't even like the man!

But that wasn't true. Mr Barraclough might not be the blond hero of her dreams, but she liked him. His treatment of Pip that afternoon had been exactly right. One could do more than like such a man... Octavia drew herself up with a start, alarm bells ringing in her mind. She must not go further with this line of thought. Mr Barraclough might be everything that was admirable, but she had no intention of thinking of him as anything but her employer. In taking this job with the Barracloughs she had deliberately set herself in a different sphere from them, and the distance between Edward Barraclough and herself must be kept while she remained in his service.

She stared at herself in the mirror and wondered what would happen later, when her charade was over. If they met in London next year would she, *could* she attract him when he knew her for what she really was, the youngest daughter of the Earl of Warnham, and the owner of Wychford? He was a presentable and eligible male—there must be any number of ladies in society who would wish to claim him for themselves. Still, she could look quite pretty when her hair wasn't screwed into an unbecoming knot…and her family connections were impeccable.

She gazed at her mirror, but saw a man's dark face there. How strong he was! He had swung himself up that tree with no difficulty at all, and had afterwards saved her from falling. Then, when he had held her, kissed her, she had felt the strength in those arms, the power of his muscular body… Octavia passed her fingers slowly over her lips. He had seemed angry with her, but the kiss had not been at all rough. It had been gentle, tender, comforting. Not at all what she would have expected from a man like Edward Barraclough. Even when the kiss had changed, it had still in some strange way been tender. That kiss… It had aroused sensations inside her which were new and almost frightening. There was danger in such a kiss…

What would it be like if a man had a right to hold you like that? If you could let him take you even more closely into his arms without feeling you had to protest?

For the first time in her life, Octavia considered what it must be like to be married—to a man like Edward Barraclough, say... This gave rise to such a feeling of longing that her eyes widened in shock, and she jumped up, away from the mirror and its dark, enticing images. What was she *thinking* of? One kiss and she was ready to abandon Tom Payne and his like, ready to let her blond hero vanish into the past, prepared to put a...a black-haired ogre in his place? Mr Barraclough was nothing to her! Nothing! How he would laugh if he could see her now, languishing over his image in her mirror! A man of experience like Edward Barraclough would take such kisses in his stride, hardly even notice them. Of course he would forget it!

Octavia pulled herself together with steely determination. The kiss had meant very little to him and it must mean nothing to her! She had been too long at Wychford, a break was definitely called for. And on her return she would make sure to remember who she was—Miss Petrie, a paid companion and governess, and definitely not someone for the master of the house to flirt with!

However, when Octavia went downstairs her meeting with Mr Barraclough went better than she had hoped, and she began to relax again. The muffin tea was in progress, and though he was civil, there was nothing in his manner to suggest that he regarded her as anything but his nieces' governess. She began to think that the episode in the woods could indeed be forgotten.

But after Lisette and Pip had gone early to bed, he asked her to stay behind, and she was in a panic again. When he saw this his face grew grim.

'I see you are nervous. Miss Petrie, what happened this afternoon was a mistake. I am deeply sorry for it, but I had hoped that we could put it behind us. Whatever you may have thought, I meant you no disrespect, and, if you are to continue to act as my nieces' governess, it must be forgotten. Anything less would give rise to an impossible situation. What do you say? Can you forgive and forget, or would you prefer not to return to Wychford after you leave tomorrow? Much as I would regret it, I would understand if that were so.'

Octavia's heart gave a thump. Not to return? No! She must! She must come back. She could not leave…leave Lisette and Pip now! She pulled herself together and said evenly, 'I'm sure I can put it behind me, Mr Barraclough. We had both been under extreme tension, and I believe that we neither of us behaved typically.'

A slight glint, quickly suppressed, came and went in his eyes. 'Quite,' he said.

Octavia didn't like the glint. She went on coolly, 'Perhaps this break will make it easier for us both to forget it altogether.'

'I hope so. Good! But this is not the only matter I must discuss with you.' He paused, frowned, then went on, 'You have done better than I hoped with the girls. They appear to be well taught, and they are certainly happier than they would have been with Miss Froom. But this afternoon Pip was in some danger. The fact that you risked your own safety in order to rescue her doesn't alter that.'

Octavia waited. She was aware that any other employer would have berated her before now. She tried not to flinch as his voice changed and he went on, 'But tell me, Miss Petrie, what the *devil* you meant by letting that child risk her life in such an irresponsible manner? Are there no rules, no precautions for her safety?'

Octavia was miserably conscious that she was at

fault. She had left Pip to her own devices for too long. It was no excuse that she had never imagined the child would be so disobedient. 'I…I am sorry—'

'Why do you allow Pip to climb when and where she pleases?'

'I don't! It's true that I haven't tried to stop her from climbing—she has so much energy, and she does seem to feel a need to be above the rest of us. It's a harmless enough habit, and I'm sure she will grow out of it—'

'Harmless!'

'But I *have* made some rules, Mr Barraclough. Certain trees are banned, and that tree is one of them. Any tree that overhangs the lake is forbidden. And so are branches that are as high as the one she got to today. Pip must have…must have forgotten.'

'Forgotten? Or was it defiance? I gather from Lisette that Pip has been in one of her black moods.'

'That's true. But she was ready to obey me when I found her. She would have come down if she hadn't lost her nerve.'

'If she hadn't fallen into the lake first.'

'Yes,' said Octavia. 'Yes, that's true. I'm sorry! I'll talk to Pip—'

'Don't bother. I had no wish to spoil this evening's muffin party, but I shall talk to her myself tomorrow and put my own absolute ban on high branches and trees near the lake. She won't do it again. But in future I'd like you to keep a closer eye on her when she's out of doors. Your task is to keep the girls safe as well as happy! When Pip is in one of her moods she can be very wilful. It's then she needs the firm hand.' He gave her a sharp look. 'Are you still sure you can control her?'

'Yes, I can! I'll be ready for her if it happens again.

But please don't be too hard on her. I still feel that Pip is best governed by love, not threats.'

He looked exasperated. 'What do you imagine I'm going to do when we have our talk? Beat her into submission?'

'Of course not! But you can be more intimidating than you think to someone so much smaller.'

'I doubt very much I could intimidate you, Miss Petrie, tiny as you are.' He pulled a face and before she could say anything he put up his hand and went on, 'But, as you were no doubt about to remark, that's beside the point. I don't wish to intimidate Pip, merely to make sure she doesn't kill herself! For your information I love my nieces, both of them, and I shall do what I think necessary to keep them safe, without interference from you or anyone. Is that clear?'

This was the real Edward Barraclough, she thought. A hard man, with any softer feelings soon buried and forgotten! She said coolly, 'You make it perfectly clear, sir.'

'Good! In that case we'll forget it, along with all the rest. Now, when do you plan to leave? I'll make sure the gig and groom are available for you.'

'The gig will be enough, sir. I can drive myself.'

'As you wish. Goodnight, Miss Petrie.'

After she had gone Edward Barraclough sat staring at the papers on his desk, without seeing them. Though he would not for the world have admitted it, he was profoundly glad that Miss Petrie was going away for two days, and would indeed have given her a week if she had asked for it! It would give him time to recover. From what? What was there to recover from? After a moment's concentration he decided that he had no idea, only that it concerned his feelings towards Miss Petrie! They were, to say the least, inappropriate! Just now he had had to *force* himself to voice a perfectly justifiable criticism of the way she looked after his nieces. And when she had looked so stricken, he had had a hard job not to get up and reassure her! It was absurd! Ridiculous! Edward moved restlessly in his chair. What the devil was wrong with him? Why was he feeling so confused?

Perhaps it would be better if the damned governess decided not to return at all. No! He rejected that thought as soon as it occurred to him. No! That would never do—it would be most…most inconvenient. That was the word! If Miss Petrie were not to come back it would be inconvenient.

All the same, he was glad to have two days in which he could get over this curious fascination he felt for her. It was not at all reasonable!

Chapter Seven

But Octavia had to put off her visit to Ashcombe. At the muffin party Pip had been quieter than usual, and the next morning she woke up flushed, and complaining of a multitude of aches and pains.

Edward sent for the local doctor, who diagnosed a fever brought on by exposure. Careful nursing would be needed, and he recommended that his patient should be kept in bed for at least a week. When he offered to find a nurse, Octavia shook her head.

'I am well used to nursing,' she said. 'If you are prepared to trust me, I am perfectly confident I could manage.'

'There's no doubt that Pip would prefer someone she knows,' said Edward doubtfully. 'I should be easier in my mind if you were here with her. But aren't you just about to leave us for a while?'

'That can be postponed. I should prefer to stay until Pip is better.'

'That's settled then. But you must tell me if you need help.'

For the first three days Pip was quite ill. A truckle bed was put in the child's room, and one of the maids slept there at night, ready to call Octavia whenever Pip needed her. During the day either Lisette or Octavia sat with her, and Edward came in quite often, too.

But on the third evening Octavia looked up from her sewing to see that Pip's eyes were open and fully conscious. She got up and went over, taking the lamp with her.

'Hello,' she said putting the lamp down on the table by the bed. 'Welcome back. Would you like a drink?'

Pip was held up to sip from the beaker kept by the bed, 'I haven't been away,' she said slowly. 'I've had a headache. But I feel better now.'

'That's very good news.'

'Where's Lisette?'

'She's asleep, I think. She's been looking after you most of the day, and was quite tired. So I sent her to bed.'

'And Edward? Where's Edward?'

'He's been here a lot, too. I expect he'll come in later.'

'Can I get up?'

'Not yet. Perhaps tomorrow or the next day.'

'You're going away. You won't be here.'

Octavia sat on the bed and took Pip's hand in hers. The lamp enclosed them in a little circle of light, leaving the rest of the room in darkness. She said softly, 'I shall stay until you are better, Pip dear. Properly better.'

'I don't want you to go away at all,' said Pip fretfully. 'Mama and Papa said they would only be away for two days, but they never came back.'

'I shall come back, Pip. I promise.'

'But why do you have to go to this Ashcombe place? There's only some old man there!'

'It's not just "some old man"!' Octavia hesitated, looked at Pip's flushed little face, and said gently, 'I wouldn't go if it was just any old man, Pip. He's my father and I love him. I have to see him, just to make sure that he's happy and well. He allowed me to come here to look after…to look after you and Lisette, but he'd be disappointed if I didn't visit him occasionally. You can understand that, can't you?'

'I suppose so… I didn't know it was your papa.'

'I haven't told anyone but you.'

'Couldn't he come here instead? I'd like to meet your papa.'

Octavia smiled. 'He's very old. He couldn't travel so far. I shall be back in two days, you'll see.'

'I suppose you have a lot of brothers and sisters at home, too.'

'Not one! I'm the youngest, and they're all married except one. And he's away in the Army.'

'What are they called?'

Pip was getting sleepy again. It wouldn't do any harm to talk about her family a little. It might send her off. 'Well, there's Arthur—he's the eldest. He has four daughters.'

'As old as me?'

'Two of them are older than you. Then after Arthur come my sisters Gussie, Eleanor and Charlotte. They're all three married with lots of children between them.'

'Are any of them my age?'

'All of Gussie's are older than you. And three of Eleanor and Charlotte's are. The rest are all younger.'

'Go on. Who comes next?'

'There's Elizabeth next. She was married but her husband died. She's been living in France, but I think she's coming back to England soon.'

'How many children has she got?'

'None.'

'Gussie, Eleanor, Charlotte, Elizabeth… Haven't you any more brothers?'

'Apart from Arthur? I did have two more, but Stephen, the elder one, was a soldier and died at Waterloo. Now I only have one other brother, beside Arthur.'

'Four sisters and two brothers. That's quite a lot,' said Pip sleepily. 'Will Edward come soon? I think I'd like to go to sleep.'

Octavia smiled and kissed her. 'He'll be here any minute,' she said.

'He's here now,' said a deep voice out of the dark.

'Mr Barraclough!' Octavia was startled.

'I didn't like to disturb you,' he said as he came further into the room. 'I was interested in your family, you see. Six brothers and sisters! No wonder you know so many games. How do you feel tonight, midget?'

'I'm better, I think. Miss Petrie says she won't go away till I'm properly better, though. And she's promised to come back.'

'Good!' Edward Barraclough's eyes rested on Octavia for a moment. 'I'm pleased she feels she can.'

Octavia felt her cheeks grow warm, and was thankful for the dim light. 'If you've come to sit with Pip, sir, I shall go to see that Lisette is asleep. She was very tired.' She leaned over the bed and kissed Pip. 'Goodnight, dearest Pip. Goodnight, sir.'

They followed much the same routine for the next couple of days, but, with the resilience of the young, Pip was soon full of her old spirit. Edward spent a lot of time with her, and Lisette was never far away. After a week Octavia felt she could safely leave them all for two days, and she set off for Ashcombe.

She need not have worried about her father. Lady Dorney's husband had suffered from a delicate constitution and Lord Warnham was having a most enjoyable time comparing a wealth of symptoms and their cures with his cousin. He had missed his daughter, of course, but not nearly as much as she had feared.

'Cousin Marjorie's collection of recipes for tisanes is bigger than my own,' he told his daughter. 'I do believe they have done my health a great deal of good. I hope you can persuade her to stay a little longer, Octavia. We have not yet tried the half of them.'

'She has agreed to stay for at least two months, Papa. She might even agree to stay longer if you wish. I don't believe she has any plans for the winter.'

'Excellent, excellent! We must make sure she stays till the spring. I was very cast down, you know, when I heard about poor Arthur's misfortune, but Cousin Marjorie was a great comfort.'

'What is wrong with Arthur, Papa?'

'His wife has had another daughter, my dear! I warned Arthur, before he married her—the Dawsons always have daughters. But he took no notice. Now the doctors have told him that Sarah cannot have any more children. Arthur has five daughters and no heir!'

Octavia did not particularly like her eldest brother, but this would have been a severe blow to his pride. 'That's very sad, Papa.'

'It is indeed! I feel for him.'

'It's Sarah I feel for,' said Octavia. 'Arthur won't forgive her for this.'

'You realise what it means, Octavia? It's now up to

Harry to carry on after Arthur and I have gone! What do you think of that?'

The Honourable Harry Petrie, youngest of the Petrie boys and something of a daredevil, was Octavia's favourite brother. He was a Lieutenant in the Guards and as yet unmarried.

'Does it mean that Harry will have to sell out?'

'Of course! Arthur has already written to him. Arthur always takes such matters in hand, he is very obliging.' Octavia thought her eldest brother could be better described as officious, but she didn't say so.

'What did Arthur tell him?'

'That Harry must sell his commission and come home, of course. He can't waste any time in settling down and finding a bride.'

'Poor Harry!'

'Stephen shouldn't have gone into the Army. It's a very dangerous occupation. Harry wouldn't have had to sell out if Stephen had lived.'

'No, Papa. But then Harry would be at risk!'

Her father looked at her doubtfully, then decided to change the subject. 'You haven't told me how you are faring at Wychford, my dear. You look very well.'

'We are going along quite nicely, Papa. I think we are making progress at last, though much still needs to be done. I must go back tomorrow.'

'So soon?'

'I'm afraid so, Papa. I hope you don't mind?'

'Oh, you must not worry about me, my dear. I have Cousin Marjorie to talk to. We chat, you know, about our younger days. And she has promised to make me another tisane tomorrow.'

After more talk with her father, it was clear to Octavia that this stay of Lady Dorney's was being a huge success. Lord Warnham was as content as she had ever known him, and by the time she left Ashcombe she was no longer at all worried about leaving him.

In fact, Octavia was rather more concerned about what she would find waiting for her at Wychford, and asked herself if she was being foolhardy to return. She had pondered a lot over her behaviour on the day of Pip's accident, and how it would affect her relationship with Edward Barraclough. He had appeared to think the blame all his, and had seemed sincere in his apology, and in his desire to treat the kiss as a momentary madness, which was to be forgotten. There would be no repeat, of that she was certain. Mr Barraclough had meant what he had said. Certainly his attitude to her during the week that followed had been coolly correct.

No, it was not Edward Barraclough's attitude that worried her—it was her own! She would miss a lot if she were not to return to Wychford. She would miss Lisette's gentle charm and Pip's energetic liveliness. She would miss the quirky house and its funny windows, its lake and its ancient trees. But above all, and this was what dismayed her, she would miss Edward Barraclough's abrasive company. She had dismissed the importance of the kiss—it had been an accident, brought on by the exceptional situation, of that she was sure. She had always been the most sensible, level-headed member of all the family, not at all romantically inclined. Quickened heartbeats, panting breath, the torments of passion—these were for others, not Octavia Petrie. It was very unlikely that she would lose her head again. But this surprising enjoyment of Edward Barraclough's conversation was not so easy to ignore. Not one of the eligible young men she had met during her London season had intrigued her as much.

One other matter worried her. She and her brother Harry, the two youngest Petries, had always been close. If she was not at Ashcombe when he came back to England, he might well come to seek her out at Wychford. That *would* set the cat among the pigeons!

She consoled herself with the thought that it would take some time for Harry to find his way back to Ashcombe. If she was not already back home, she would make sure he got a message to tell him not to come to find her. In the past they had often been co-conspirators—he wouldn't let her down!

This settled, Octavia spent the rest of the journey disciplining her mind into a proper acceptance of her position. She was confident that her two-day absence had rid her of the unsuitable memories of how it had felt to have a man's warm body pressed against hers, of the images of a dark-haired man in her mirror. She was now once again the unromantic, down-to-earth person she had always been. Her duty was towards Lisette and Philippa Barraclough, not their uncle, and between them they would give her all the affection and interest that any reasonable governess could expect.

Edward Barraclough found to his annoyance that Miss Petrie's absence had not cured him. He was looking forward with unreasonable eagerness to her return, and not because the girls had been difficult to look after. The two days had been pleasant enough. But a certain spice had been lacking, and he had come to the conclusion that he missed Miss Petrie!

Though it wasn't easy, he had conscientiously tried to put the unexpected delight of the kiss right out of his mind, as he had promised. If she was to continue to live at Wychford, that was an area that must remain barred, he knew. But there was so much more to it than that...

It was strange. For such a little thing she had made quite an impression on him! He had always been attracted before to dark-haired, dark-eyed beauties, who were accomplished in the game of love. Neither their minds nor their powers of conversation had ever interested him. He would have said it was impossible that he should spend time really talking to a woman, enjoying her company, particularly the company of a *dab* of a woman, with scraped back hair, and features that were not at all striking. What was it about Miss Petrie...?

Was it the way her face changed when she laughed, the way her eyes narrowed when she concentrated, the way she raised one eyebrow to express scepticism, or irony? Was it her willingness to challenge him while somehow remaining perfectly respectful? Or was it the annoying habit she had of managing to make her views absolutely clear while saying nothing at all?

And she wasn't at all a dab of a woman. Her face had a delicate beauty, and though she was small she was perfectly made... Edward Barraclough sat up and shook his head. This was doing him no good at all. He must stop thinking of Miss Petrie and her perfect proportions, and do something to cure himself of this madness. Looking after his nieces was all very well, but the comparatively celibate life it brought with it was not good for any man. No wonder he had strange ideas about their governess! He must spend more time in London, and as soon as the governess returned he would. Though he had to give up the tempting invitations to join his friends' autumn house parties, there was plenty of entertainment still to be had in the capital. He would gamble in the clubs, drink with his friends, and enjoy Louise's considerable attractions. That would soon chase away these confoundedly unsuitable thoughts of Miss Petrie!

So Octavia Petrie was hardly back at Wychford before Edward Barraclough escaped to London, where he plunged into a determined round of pleasure.

It lasted a week. He had done what he had promised himself, sought pleasure wherever and whenever he could find it. He had gambled a great deal, drunk even more and whiled away many an hour with Louise, who seemed to have recovered her desire to please him. But, maddeningly, after just a couple of days, he grew restless. London began to seem stale and dirty, its set patterns of behaviour and conversation artificial and dull. He found himself longing for the freshness of the woods round Wychford, the sound of his nieces' young voices, their spontaneous laughter and games, the liveliness of their conversation, the sight of three figures as they wandered about the grounds, discussing and recording.

Even his hours with Louise began to pall. She was as lovely, as skilled as ever in her efforts to please, but once they had made love what else was there to amuse him in her company? *Her* eyes never sparkled with anger or challenge, only at appreciation of some bauble or other. The delicate arch of *her* eyebrow was never raised in disbelief or scepticism at something he said. She could pout prettily enough, but you never saw her laugh in sudden delight, or risk wrinkling her brow in a real frown. Furthermore—and he wondered why he had not seen it before—Louise was entirely devoid of any real sense of humour.

* * *

He came back on a blustery, cold day at the end of October, but even in the rain Wychford looked welcoming. The windows of the little parlour were lit up with the glow of a fire. He went up to the window and looked in. Three figures were gathered round a table, intent on a board with counters on it. As usual, Miss Petrie was plainly dressed with no attempt to flatter the shapely form beneath. Her hair was scraped back into its ugly knot, too, but the firelight touched it with colour and life and he found himself smiling with pleasure at the sight. He watched how her face lit up with laughter as she passed a pile of buttons over to Lisette and threw up her arms in mock despair.

'Lisette! You wretch!' she cried. 'That was the last of my fortune. I am *ruined*!'

Lisette joined in the laughter, her lovely face quite transformed. But Pip got down and went round the table to give her governess a hug. 'You can have some of mine, Miss Petrie! I've got plenty.'

'You're a darling, Pip, but no, thank you. If you can't pay, don't play. My brothers taught me that from the first. Besides, you'll need all your wealth to beat Lisette. She's on the top of her form!'

'Who's that?' In getting down Pip had turned to face the window. She pointed at Edward. Then she recognised him. With her usual shout of 'Edward!' she raced to the door of the room and out into the hall.

The sight of her employer made nonsense of Octavia's belief that she was a sensible, rational creature, with her feelings well under control. Her feelings when she saw his dark face at the window were neither cool nor proper. Her heart had jumped, her pulse had quick-

ened, and she had caught her breath at a sudden and
vividly explicit memory of their kiss. So much for level-
headed discipline! However, she still had some command of her emotions, and by the time he came into
the room, towed by an ecstatic Pip, her manner was
polite rather than warm.

'You've had a cold journey, I think, sir. Shall I send
for some tea, or other refreshment?'

'It can wait. Finish your game. I don't think I've seen
it before, have I?'

'Miss Petrie brought a lot from her home, Edward,'
said Pip, dragging him over to the table. 'She and her
brothers and sisters used to play with them. It's been
too cold to go out today, so we got them out. Look at
Lisette's heap of winnings! She's ruined Miss Petrie
already!'

Edward picked one of the pieces up. It might be old
and battered, but it had originally been quite valuable.
He put it down again and said, 'That's unfortunate. Let
it be a lesson to you, midget! Now, let me see you play!'

As the two girls got absorbed once again, he drew
Octavia to one side and said in a low voice, 'How has
Pip been? She seems well enough now.'

'I'm sure there's no lasting damage done. But she
has the occasional nightmare when she wakes up crying
with fright, convinced that she's falling.'

'Still? She had one while you were away at Ashcombe, but I thought they would disappear with time.'

'I think they will. It would be better if the weather
improved and she could get out in the fresh air as she
used to. Pip has so much energy—she needs to get rid
of it, but I haven't dared to take her out for long. I've
been trying to give her other things to think about. I've
even been teaching her chess.'

He looked at his nieces. 'And backgammon. Are the chessmen as valuable as the backgammon pieces?'

Octavia stared at him. 'What do you mean?'

'Merely that I wonder about you. Those pieces are old, but they're not ordinary children's playthings—they're made of ivory, and I see some ebony and rosewood over there. Strange toys for the children of a poor parson.'

'Who told you my father was a parson? I certainly never have!'

'I think I just assumed it. You're obviously a woman of education, but you have to earn a living. You obviously like caring for others. A parson's daughter seemed to fit. Your family would appear to be eminently respectable.'

'Indeed they are, sir,' said Octavia.

'What is your father, if not a parson—a schoolteacher?'

'No. He…he has been an invalid for years. Before that he…he looked after an estate.'

'Ah! A land agent.'

'Something of the sort. The…the toys were handed on from a family who lived in the local manor house.' Octavia felt very uncomfortable. She was getting deeper and deeper into a mesh of half-truths. She had brought the games with her from Ashcombe without thinking of their value, merely as a means of keeping the girls amused during the colder weather. Now Edward Barraclough was quizzing her, and his questions were getting too close to home! It was time to change the subject.

'Did you enjoy your stay in London, sir?' she asked.

'Not altogether,' he replied. 'Do you know the city?'

Here she went again! 'I…I stayed there for several

months,' she said, 'but it was some time ago. I expect
it has changed a lot. Have you heard recently from your
sister-in-law?'

Edward frowned. He glanced at his nieces, who were
intent on the game, and led her away to the other end
of the room.

'I think Julia may well arrive in England earlier than
expected,' he said quietly. 'She is very concerned about
a former neighbour of ours—I think I told you about
him. Ricardo Arandez. It seems he has followed us to
Europe.'

'You think it is to see Lisette? Perhaps he loves your
niece more sincerely than you thought?'

'It's her fortune he loves.'

'But what can he do? I thought you told me that her
father had withdrawn his consent? He must surely know
that Lisette would never act against authority! Pip
might, but Lisette never!'

'I would agree with you, but the situation is not quite
so simple. After my brother died, Arandez managed to
convince Lisette that he had relented and wished her to
marry him after all.'

'And this wasn't true?'

'Of course not! Once John had decided that Arandez
wasn't suitable, that was it. He wouldn't change his
mind.'

'Then…then why does Lisette believe differently?'

He sighed. 'I see I shall have to tell you the whole.'
He threw a glance at the two girls. 'But not here. Come
to the library.'

Once in the other room he invited her to sit, and
began. 'Ricardo Arandez is plausible enough. My
brother John saw that Lisette liked him, and eventually
promised that if, when she was older, she liked the fel-

low well enough to marry him, he would give his consent. There were advantages to the match—the Arandez estates border on ours. However, John soon came to realise that Arandez was not the sort of son-in-law he wanted, and withdrew his promise. Right?'

Octavia nodded.

'Then John and his wife were killed. Before the week was out Arandez was at the house, claiming that he had spoken to John the night before he died, and that John had regretted his change of mind. The promise of a match between Lisette and himself had been renewed. We didn't believe him. It was all too opportune. Henry and I sent him away, and told Lisette to forget him.'

'Wasn't that a little harsh? The poor girl was already in some distress. This Arandez might have been able to comfort her.'

'Comfort her! Hear me out before you judge, Miss Petrie! Arandez waited till I had left Antigua and then he approached Lisette in secret. From what Lisette told my sister-in-law, he showed her a letter from John saying that he wished her to marry Arandez as planned. We all think it was a forgery, though no one other than Lisette ever saw it. But it was enough to convince Lisette. She was prepared to defy her family and run off with him. Fortunately Henry saw them, and Arandez was sent packing.'

'Did it never occur to any of you that Lisette might be in love with this man?'

He uttered an exclamation of impatience. 'I've told you before, Miss Petrie! Lisette is far too young to be in love with anyone! Arandez used the fact that she was distraught and vulnerable after her parents' accident. She saw him as someone to cling to, that's all! She was *not* in love with him!' He saw her sceptical expression and went on more seriously, 'And it wouldn't matter if she was. Neither Henry nor I would ever allow her to marry Arandez!'

Octavia was not at all convinced of Lisette's indifference, and her heart ached for the girl. Her air of sadness might not be due solely to her parents' death. However, she saw little point in pursuing the subject for the moment. Instead she said, 'So you think your sister-in-law will be here earlier than expected?'

'She will if she can. I'm afraid Mrs Barraclough has no great opinion of my ability to look after our nieces, Miss Petrie. With some reason, I fear.'

'I disagree. She can't have seen you with them!'

He looked surprised, and said, 'I'm touched. Compliments from you are rare indeed!'

'I mean it. Look at the way you've just cut short your stay in London.'

'Er…yes. Yes, indeed! Though I have to confess that London is very boring in the winter months. I was not at all sorry to leave. Life at Wychford can be far more interesting.'

Edward had clearly spoken without thinking, but Octavia felt her face grow scarlet and looked at him accusingly. For a moment he looked blank then he smiled ruefully. 'I meant no harm, Octavia,' he murmured. 'I've done my best to forget as I promised. Don't make it difficult.'

'I…I don't know what you mean,' she said bravely.

'I meant, Miss Petrie, that we *both* need to keep a firm control of our memories. That is, if we are to continue to live under the same roof without the sort of scandal I would wish to avoid.'

Octavia's nerves were stretched to the limit. His sudden appearance, her efforts to counter his questions about her family, her sharp sympathy for Lisette, and now the discovery that the attraction between them was as strong as ever—it was almost too much! She called on all her reserves of pride and said coldly, 'You have no reason to fear scandal from any actions of mine, sir.' Then she turned away from him and went back to the table.

The game was finished, Lisette had won.

Octavia avoided Edward Barraclough for the next two days. It wasn't difficult. He took the girls to visit friends in Guildford the next day and readily accepted her excuses when she refused his invitation to accompany them. It was almost as if he was relieved. The day after that he was closeted in the library for most of the day, and eventually came into the parlour, frowning at some papers he had in his hand. The girls were playing chess, and Octavia sat by the fire, keeping an eye on their progress and sewing.

'Are you cross, Edward?' Lisette asked.

'No, I'm curious, that's all.'

'What about?'

'This house. I've been looking through every paper connected with our tenancy, but nowhere can I find the owner's name.'

'Isn't it Mr Walters?'

'No, he is merely the agent. The house was left to a niece of Mrs Carstairs, but I have no idea what she is called. All our dealings have been with Walters, and his signature is on every single document. I think Miss Carstairs, or whatever her name is, must be very shy. It's a pity. I should have liked to talk to her about her aunt. Perhaps I'll write to Walters to ask him if she would meet me.'

Octavia jumped. She knew that Walters would never divulge her name without her permission, but this sudden announcement had been a shock.

'Is something wrong, Miss Petrie?'

'Nothing, Mr Barraclough. I pricked my finger, that's all. It's nothing.' He regarded her closely, and Octavia was glad of the excuse to keep her head bent.

'Do you know anything about the house, Miss Petrie, or Mrs Carstairs's niece? Ashcombe is not that far away.'

Keeping her head bent, Octavia said carefully, 'Mrs Carstairs was something of a legend in the county. But…but we none of us knew she had any intention of leaving Wychford to her niece. The niece certainly never visited her here, as far as I know.'

'I see. Then I shall write to Walters. By the way, I'm taking the girls to Guildford again tomorrow. Mrs Allardyce has arranged dancing lessons for her own daughters and has suggested that Lisette and Pip share in them. Do you wish to come?'

'I think not. The girls' lessons have been a little neglected recently, and I should be glad of a chance to prepare some exercises for them.'

'As you wish,' he said, turning away. The girls protested, of course, but Octavia refused to change her mind. A day on her own, an opportunity to talk firmly to herself, seemed very desirable.

After Edward Barraclough and the girls had left for Guildford, Octavia spent some time preparing work for the next week. Her heart was heavy. Julia Barraclough might arrive quite soon, and from what had been said she was not the easiest of people to please. If the formidable Mrs Barraclough was not to be disappointed in the governess her brother-in-law had chosen, then they would all need to concentrate during the coming days. Otherwise her arrival might well betoken Octavia's departure. In any case, Octavia's time at Wychford would not last for very much longer. Two months was the original contract, and she had already been with the Barracloughs for well over half that time.

She worked steadily during the rest of the morning without any noticeable improvement in her mood. In the afternoon she dressed herself warmly and went out into the grounds. Perhaps a walk before the Barracloughs returned would clear her melancholy. The ground was wet and soft underfoot, though at least the rain had stopped, and the air was fresh. She walked briskly down the drive. When she turned the corner she saw a solitary rider coming towards her and recognised him with a shock.

Chapter Eight

'Harry!' cried Octavia. 'Oh, my goodness! Whatever are you doing here?'

The tall, fair-haired young man dismounted and enveloped her in a vast hug. His riding cape swung open to reveal the uniform of a Lieutenant in the Guards. 'What a way to greet your long-lost brother, Tavy! I expected better than this, I can tell you!'

'But…but where have you come from?'

'From Ashcombe, of course. I thought I'd stay a few days with you here, and have a look at your house. You're a lucky dog! From what I've seen so far it's a fine place! Fancy the Witch of Wychford leaving it to you!'

'B…but what did Papa tell you?'

Her brother looked puzzled. 'Why, that you were staying here putting the house in order. I didn't stay long to talk, I was too annoyed with him. Did you know that Arthur says I have to leave the Army?'

'I heard something of the sort, yes.'

'What I want to know is why the *devil* has Arthur any say in it?'

'I told Papa you'd take it badly. You're right, Arthur's too much of a busybody, but then he always has been, and now Papa has started leaving everything to him to do. It's the succession he's worried about, of course. You heard Sarah had another daughter?'

'Hang the succession! What do I care about the succession? I wouldn't do anything Arthur ordered me to, I can tell you. If it was just Arthur I'd stay put. But Father agrees with him. He wouldn't even listen to what I had to say, so I thought I'd come and find you. Although you don't seem as pleased to see me as you should!'

He sounded offended. Octavia gave him an affectionate hug and kiss. 'Harry, of course I'm glad, very glad to see you! How could you think otherwise? It's just… We have to talk. I have things I must tell you.' She pulled at his sleeve. 'Come away from the drive. They could be back at any moment.'

Her brother looked at her with suspicion, but didn't resist. 'Who are "they"? You look pretty worried, Tavy. What have you been up to?'

Octavia led Harry and the horse a short distance back from the drive along one of the rides that led into the wood. Fortunately, none of the groundsmen were about. As quickly as she could, she gave her brother the full story of her adventures at Wychford, omitting only certain personal and unnecessary details.

Harry had never been slow. In no time he was in full possession of the facts and highly amused.

Octavia gazed at him in exasperation and exclaimed, 'You're a dolt, Harry! Why are you laughing? Do you realise what would happen if they found out who I am?'

'Well, I can't answer for Barraclough, but if it were me I'd throw you out on your ear! Or can't he do that to his landlady?' Harry went into another paroxysm of laughter.

'Harry!' Octavia tried to stamp her foot, but failed in the soft ground.

'Well, what were you thinking of? It's a bit of a lark, perhaps, but I would have said you were past that kind of caper.'

'I've told you! I didn't mean it to be a caper! But the house…those girls… I was so tempted to stay here. You've no idea how I wanted to get away from Ashcombe!'

Octavia went on to tell him of her frustration, her boredom with her life at home. Harry was instantly sympathetic and said so. 'But all the same, there must have been some other way, Tavy. You've put yourself in a pretty impossible position with the Barracloughs. What are they like?'

Octavia stopped and listened. In the distance could be heard the sound of hooves, the crack of the coachman's whip and the crunch of wheels on gravel as a carriage turned in through Wychford's gates. She said nervously, 'If we're not very lucky you may find out sooner than you thought. That's Edward Barraclough's carriage arriving back from Guildford. Pull your cape around you. That scarlet uniform can be seen for miles. And keep quiet. They mustn't see us together. They mustn't see you at all!'

Octavia waited tensely, then breathed a sigh of relief as the carriage passed safely by. She turned to her brother. 'I'm sorry, Harry, but I'll have to go. If Pip can't find me in the house she'll come looking for me, or send Lisette.'

'But what am I to do? We haven't had any time at all together! There's much more to say. Dammit, we haven't seen each other for more than two years! Be reasonable, Tavy! Can't I come with you up to the house?'

'No! What could I tell Edward Barraclough? He's far too quick to be taken in by any story. He'd suspect something the minute he saw you.'

'We aren't very alike. I could pretend to be a friend.'

'You're not to come up to the house, Harry! In fact, I'd like you most of all to go back to Ashcombe and wait for me there.'

'What, hang about Ashcombe for another three or four weeks? There's no chance of that! I have to be back with the regiment well before then. Look, I'll go to Ashcombe for tonight, but only to leave my uniform behind, and collect some other things to wear. Tomorrow I'll get a room at the inn in the village here for two or three nights. We can see a little more of each other. Don't worry! I won't use my own name. I'll be Harry… Harry Smith.'

'That's not very imaginative.'

'Harry Smith is a great hero to anyone in the Army, my girl. He fought all through the Peninsular campaign, and at Waterloo.'

'I see…' said Octavia, her mind elsewhere. 'Harry, if you want to be a hero, *my* hero, you could do something absolutely vital for me. I have an urgent message for Mr Walters, and I've been racking my brains how I could get it safely to him. If you would agree to deliver it on your way it would solve my problem. Tomorrow if possible. His chambers are in Guildford.'

'Guildford! That's miles out of my way!'

'*Please*, Harry! It would take one worry off my mind if you would. I don't think for a minute that Mr Walters would do anything without consulting me first, but it's better to be sure. Mr Barraclough can be very forceful.'

'I suppose I could come back via Guildford... What's the message?'

'It's just that Mr Barraclough wants Mr Walters to arrange a meeting with Mrs Carstairs's niece. That's me, of course, and it's impossible. But tell Walters he must be sure *not* to give my name, or tell Mr Barraclough who I am. Understand? Walters is not to give in. Can you remember it? There isn't time to write it down.'

'My dear sister, I've carried longer messages than that, and more important ones, too.'

'Not to me they weren't. Harry, you're a darling! And now I *must* go! I'll see you the day after tomorrow. I teach the girls in the morning, but I'll meet you here at three. Don't come earlier, whatever you do! If the weather is good the girls may come out for a walk with me before that. If I see you when I am out with them, I shall ignore you.'

She hurried back to the house, suffering from a mixture of feelings. It was wonderful to see Harry again, but she was not at all sure she wanted him so close. Wychford village was small, and there was bound to be speculation about what such a handsome young man was doing there all alone. But, thanks to Harry, she had at least found a way of warning Mr Walters. Octavia sighed. Life at Wychford had started out so simply. Now it was getting more complicated by the minute!

The girls were full of excitement about their dancing lesson, and insisted on taking Octavia to the music room to show her the steps they had learned. Even Pip, who had been rather scornful, was enthusiastic. Days of confinement to the house had left her with a good deal of surplus energy, and she had enjoyed the activity, especially the more lively steps of the dances.

'Edward, you must help me to show Miss Petrie what we did!' she cried. 'Lisette, you play the piano!' Laughing, her uncle allowed himself to be dragged into the centre of the room, where he bowed and took Pip's hand, then set off round the room with her. They were an unevenly matched pair, to say the least, since Pip was not half her uncle's height, and danced with all the grace of a grasshopper. But her uncle treated her with the polish and courtesy due to a belle of the ball. This was Edward Barraclough at his best, thought Octavia, watching them both rather wistfully.

'Now you must try!' said Pip, after they were back. She led her uncle up to Octavia and put their hands together. 'Edward will show you how.'

'I...I think I know the steps, Pip. Your uncle has had enough, I'm sure.'

'Do dance with Edward, Miss Petrie!' called Lisette. 'Just a few steps—I'd like to see it done properly.'

'Miss Petrie?' asked Edward Barraclough, raising one eyebrow. 'May I have this dance?'

The contrast between that eyebrow and his excessively formal tone made Octavia laugh. She entered into the spirit of the thing. 'Why, thank you, sir,' she said with a graceful curtsy. 'Of course!'

He led her to the centre with a flourish, and bowed. Lisette struck up another country dance and they went twirling round, watched by a fascinated Pip.

Nothing could have been more closely chaperoned or more decorous. They were not dancing a quadrille or a waltz, but a harmless country dance with little close bodily contact. They did not even exchange a significant glance. But at none of the great balls she had attended in London had Octavia ever felt as she did in the music room at Wychford, dancing to Lisette's piano—exhilarated, in harmony with her partner, tinglingly aware of his touch, however slight. They went round twice, at the end of which she decided she had better stop. She curtsied and said, 'I think Lisette will be satisfied, sir.'

'Perhaps so, but I'm not,' he murmured as he bowed.

Octavia blushed, and looked at him reprovingly. It was a mistake. Mr Barraclough had such an engaging glint in his eye that she was strongly tempted to smile back at him. This would never do. She said severely, 'I think Pip looks as if she's had enough excitement for today, Mr Barraclough. Shall I see if Mrs Dutton has anything to suggest for supper?'

Octavia was unable to sleep that night. After tossing and turning for some time she sat up and stared at the circle of light cast by the small lamp by the door. It had been put there at the time of Pip's illness, and was now lit every night, in case Pip had another of her nightmares. But she didn't really see it. Instead she saw a dark face, the lift of a scarred eyebrow, the charm of a man's smile, the glint in his eye…

Octavia sighed deeply. The feeling she had for Edward Barraclough did not seem to be influenced by rational arguments. Just when she thought she had mastered it, it had sprung to life again at the mere touch of his hand in a country dance! She had seldom felt so alive, so aware of a man's presence. But it would not do! This was a passing phase, it must be! She must take a firmer grip of herself…

And now, just when she needed all her strength to master these new sensations, Harry had come to complicate matters even further. His presence in Wychford was bound to increase the danger of discovery. When she next saw him she must persuade him to go back to Ashcombe, even if it meant that she had to ask Mr Barraclough for another two days' leave of absence in order to meet him there. And she didn't wish to leave Wychford at all, even for two days. Time was getting so short...

Her anxious thoughts were cut short by a cry of fright from next door. It was followed by another, and another. Forgetting all her problems, Octavia leapt out of bed, and flung her wrapper round her. She snatched up her lamp and made her way to Pip's room. Pip was asleep, but was seriously disturbed, tossing in her bed, whimpering, her arms flailing about as she vainly tried to find something to hold. The child was having one of her nightmares. Octavia hastily set the lamp down, sat on the bed and took her in her arms.

'Hush, Pip, hush! I've got you. I'm here, my darling, I've got you safe.'

Pip's eyes opened, and she stared blindly at Octavia. Then recognition came and she buried her head against Octavia and wept, 'Miss Petrie! Oh, Miss Petrie, I was so frightened...'

'I know,' Octavia said, holding the child even more tightly. 'But you're safe now. It was only a dream, Pip. See? You're here in your little tower room, and I've come from next door to make sure you're all right. There's nothing at all to worry about, darling.'

Pip stayed still for a moment, then she lifted her head and gazed round. What she saw seemed to reassure her and she smiled. 'That's right. I'm safe in my tower room. And you're here. I'm so glad Edward chose you, Miss Petrie.' She nestled more closely into Octavia's arms, her eyelids drooped, and in less than a minute she was peacefully asleep again.

Octavia rested her cheek against Pip's hair. The child was so easy to love. What a wrench it was going to be for both of them when she left! She settled back against the pillows and her eyes closed....

Edward had not been fully asleep, either, but just dozing off when Pip cried out. His room was some distance away and at first he thought it was an owl or some little creature in the woods. But after a few minutes it occurred to him that the sound might have come from Pip's room. He lay there listening, but heard nothing. The house was in silence. All the same he decided that he would get no rest till he had made sure she was all right. Picking up his dressing gown and belting it round him, he strode swiftly along the landing to his niece's room. Here he stopped. The door was open, and through it he could see Pip's bed bathed in the light of a small lamp. Octavia Petrie was half-sitting, half-lying against the pillows, holding Pip in her arms. They were both asleep. Edward paused. He was in something of a dilemma. He had no wish to wake either of them, but though Pip was half under the blankets, Miss Petrie was on top, and lying very awkwardly. She would be cold and stiff when she woke.

He entered the room cautiously and stood by the bed. The ring of light shone on a face surrounded by loosely tied, honey-gold curls, resting lovingly on Pip's black mop. Miss Petrie was breathing gently, the rise and fall of her bosom clearly visible under her thin wrapper. It was one of the most touchingly, innocently seductive sights he had ever seen... Determinedly, he looked away, round the dark room for a blanket or something

else to put over her to keep her warm. When he turned
back to the bed he saw that her eyes were wide open
and she was looking at him.

'Don't worry,' he whispered. 'I was merely fetching
something to put over you. You'll get cold.'

She shook her head. 'Pip is sound asleep. I think I
can leave her.' She twisted round, carefully pulled the
covers up over Pip, then turned to stand up. She gave
a cry of pain which was instantly suppressed.

'What's wrong?'

'My…my leg! It's gone to sleep…'

'Here, let me!' Edward gave her his hand and helped
her to stand. 'You shouldn't have—'

'Don't talk here!' she said. 'We mustn't wake the
child.' She took a step to the door and gasped, nearly
falling as her leg gave way under her. Edward swept
her up and carried her out of the room without saying
a word. Then he set her down on the landing and carefully pulled Pip's door to.

'Can we talk here?' he asked in a low voice.

'I suppose. But there's nothing to say. Except to
thank you for helping me. I would have been very stiff
tomorrow.' She smiled up at him.

Edward could not help himself. His arms went round
her and he held her very gently to him, one hand holding her head against his chest. 'My dear Octavia,' he
said. 'What am I to do?'

She let her head stay for an instant, then moved to
look up at him gravely. He was touched to see that there
was no sign of fear in her eyes. The feel of her silken
hair and her slenderness in his arms were sending his
senses rocketing, yet he was determined to justify her
trust in him.

'You have no idea how much I would like to take

you with me back to my room—' he put a finger over her lips as she started to protest, and went on '—and yet I won't even try. That isn't for us.'

'That's good,' she whispered, 'because I would resist with all the strength I have. I won't be any man's mistress, however much—' She stopped.

'Go on!'

'No! I won't. I can't! This is wrong.' The instant she tried to remove herself from his arms he let her go, though the temptation to pull her back and kiss her was almost overwhelming. 'Goodnight, Mr Barraclough.'

'Octavia!'

'My name is Petrie, sir. Miss Petrie. I am a governess. Goodnight!' Before he could stop her she had gone into the next room and shut the door.

He went back to his room, but didn't even bother getting into his bed. Instead, he sat up and wrote some letters till morning came.

Edward went again to Guildford the next day, but this time he left the carriage behind and rode. He wished, he said, to discuss some matters with Mrs Carstairs's lawyer, who had his chambers there. In truth the ride through the countryside was almost more important to him than the meeting with Mr Walters. Edward was in a most unusual state of confusion, and he hoped that fresh air and exercise would help to clear his mind. But as he rode to Guildford, he was quite unaware of the glorious colours of the trees in their autumn foliage, the work going on in the fields to prepare them for the autumn ploughing.

He was struggling to come to terms with new and unwelcome thoughts. Before his nieces had come to England he had led the life of a wealthy bachelor, interested in his work, but always free to rove the world as he chose, to take up residence in London, Paris, Vienna, in the town or in the country, wherever he wished, without reference to any other person. It might be thought a selfish life—his sister-in-law certainly considered it so—but Edward had never cared for anyone else's opinion enough to let it interfere with his pleasures. He had counted himself fortunate to have reached the age of thirty without any of the usual entanglements—wife, children, obligations to others... His chief enemy was boredom.

And then because of Julia's accident he had been forced to accept responsibility for two young girls, orphans in a strange country. Though he had always been fond of his nieces, he had regarded their arrival as an imposition, an interference with his life of leisure. During the past weeks they had amused him, worried him, exasperated him, even occasionally annoyed him. But he had missed them when he had gone to London, and when the time came he would hand them over to Julia with real regret.

But they had brought with them Octavia Petrie, and this was now becoming a major problem, one that could not simply be handed over to someone else. The plain fact was that he could no longer persuade himself that his feelings were a temporary aberration. He suspected that they might well prove to be a real and permanent threat to his peace of mind. What was he to do about it?

Of one thing he was quite sure. Even if he had been ready to consider marrying—which he certainly was not—he would not think of marrying Octavia Petrie! He had never liked the Cinderella story. He had known men who had married women out of their sphere, and both

partners had usually ended up very unhappily. Octavia
Petrie was the last of a brood of children born to a
respectable, probably not very wealthy, professional
man. She had been brought up simply, quietly, in a
remote country village. How could she possibly cope
with life in London?

No, marriage to anyone was out of the question, but
marriage to Octavia Petrie was especially so! He must
not think of her as anyone other than his nieces' governess. Indeed, if the girls had not been so fond of her,
and if the end of her time with them had not been so
close, he would have sent her away immediately. But
to do so without cause, merely because he feared temptation, would be unjust. He must be strong and fight it
out till she went.

Satisfied that he had reached the only possible conclusion, Edward rode on with a heavy heart to Mr Walters's chambers. He arrived early and was kept waiting
for a minute or two while the lawyer finished dealing
with another client. When this client emerged, Edward
was surprised to see he was a handsome young man,
obviously from his bearing a soldier. A rare sight in the
stuffy rooms of a country lawyer! But Edward's momentary interest in the young man was forgotten as soon
as he entered the inner room.

Here he met with a setback. His confidence that he
could persuade any lawyer to do anything he wanted
proved to be misplaced. Mr Walters was everything that
was amiable, but he absolutely refused to divulge the
name of his principal.

'The lady's family are among my oldest clients, Mr
Barraclough. They are very protective of the owner of
Wychford, and indeed, I cannot myself see why you
wish to approach her. I do not think she had a great

deal to do with Mrs Carstairs during the latter's lifetime. So you must forgive me, but I very much regret that I am unable to oblige you.' He spread his hands apologetically and sat back.

Edward frowned, then shrugged his shoulders. 'I'm disappointed. It seemed such a small thing to ask. However, I suppose I have to accept what you say, though I think the family are being very unreasonable. One might almost be led to think the woman an imbecile.'

The lawyer gave a chuckle. 'I assure you that is far from being the case. She is eminently sane. But tell me, what do you think of Wychford? I've always thought it an odd sort of house.'

'It's delightful,' said Edward. 'My nieces love it. They will be sorry to leave it next spring. But I expect my sister-in-law will want to take them to London soon after she arrives. They'll need a little town bronze.'

'Quite! Well, if there is nothing else…?'

'Nothing.' Edward's tone was abrupt. He added, 'If your client should relent, you know where to find me. Good day, Walters.'

He went out, feeling that, one way and another, the world was not on his side!

It was as well that Octavia did not know that Edward Barraclough had actually passed Harry in the lawyer's chambers, though neither had recognised the other. She had been on tenterhooks ever since that morning when her employer had announced his intention of seeking out Mr Walters in Guildford. It was difficult to concentrate on French grammar, or a review of the Counties of England together with the Seats of the Aristocracy to be found in them, when she was so anxious, and her lessons suffered as a consequence.

But this was not by any means the greatest of her worries. Her immediate concern might be the possible encounter in Guildford, but the turmoil in her mind had a deeper cause. In spite of her brave words the night before, it was Edward Barraclough's scruples, not her own, which had saved her. The impulse to put her arms round his neck, to draw his head down to hers had been almost overwhelming... Perhaps she ought to acknowledge the truth, at least to herself. Octavia Petrie had at last fallen in love. And with a most unsuitable man.

Moreover, by her impulsive and stupid actions on her arrival at Wychford, she had put herself into an entirely false position. What would happen if Edward Barraclough discovered how she had deceived him? Harry had said straight away that he would throw her out on her ear if he were Edward Barraclough, and she rather thought that Mr Barraclough would feel the same. Her only hope was to remain undetected until she left. Then perhaps she could join the Season next year and meet the Barracloughs on her own ground. And perhaps, just perhaps, Edward might forgive her.

That was, of course, only half the story. She had no idea of what he really felt about her, though she was aware of his resistance to the idea of marriage. But granted she could meet him on level terms, she was sure she had a chance. He did like her, and there was certainly a strong attraction between them...

Octavia saw the girls looking at her curiously, and returned to discussing the castles, courts and great houses of England's aristocracy.

Pip wanted to go out in the afternoon, and quite rightly said that the weather was perfectly suitable. Octavia had to agree, though she made Pip promise not to climb anything at all. The three of them wrapped up and set off round the back of the house, away from the main drive. Octavia wanted no encounters with Mr Barraclough on his return from Guildford! Pip was delighted to be in the open air again and ran about under Octavia's watchful eye for quite some time. But then she started to flag, and made no objection when Octavia suggested going back. Lisette, who had stayed to help entertain Pip, asked if she might just spend a few minutes by herself, looking for some specimens for her sketch book. Octavia hesitated, then gave in. There was still plenty of light, and, unlike Pip, Lisette was naturally cautious. She could hardly come to harm. So she made Lisette promise to follow them in after a quarter of an hour, and took Pip to get warm by the parlour fire.

Lisette was only slightly late, but came in with flushed cheeks and sparkling eyes, looking as if she had been running. Octavia wondered if the girl knew how stunningly beautiful she was. She thought not. Lisette was essentially a very modest young woman, and would have no idea of the impact her looks would have on the polite world. She might well find it difficult to cope with the admiration and attention that she would surely attract. Octavia made up her mind there and then, that, whatever happened between herself and Edward Barraclough, she would make certain she was in London during the next Season. The doors of Society's most exclusive hostesses were always open to Lady Octavia Petrie. After all, she was related to half of them! She must make sure that Lisette had the success and the support she deserved.

Chapter Nine

Lisette was even quieter than usual over tea, and Octavia asked her if there was something wrong.

'Oh, no, Miss Petrie! I was just thinking about… about this afternoon.'

'Did you find many specimens?'

'What? Er…no. Not many. The leaves are beginning to look faded, and I couldn't find anything else worth bringing in. I might find some more tomorrow.'

'We'll see. I hope you aren't sickening for something, Lisette. You look a little feverish.'

'Please don't worry about me. I feel very well, Miss Petrie.'

In fact, Lisette would have found it difficult to describe what she really was feeling! Guilty, nervous, excited, apprehensive… And all because of a chance ten minute encounter that afternoon with the handsomest young man she had ever seen. She fully intended to tell Miss Petrie all about it eventually, but just for the moment she wanted to keep it to herself. She gazed into the fire lost once again in the memory of that afternoon…

* * *

She had gone round to the front of the house and wandered off the drive up one of the paths through the wood. Suddenly she came face to face with a tall, blond young man. She was startled, but not really frightened. He looked harmless enough, though very handsome, and strangely, he seemed as shocked as she was. Lisette was quite reassured. After a moment during which he appeared to be trying to find his voice he stammered, 'I…I'm sorry. I didn't mean to frighten you. I…I was just w…walking in the woods. Where…where did you come from?'

It was such a ridiculous question that Lisette laughed. 'I live here,' she said.

'At…at Wychford?'

'Yes. I'm Lisette Barraclough. These are private woods, you know.'

'Are they? Yes, of course!' The young man appeared to be a little distrait, and Lisette began to wonder if she was wise to linger.

'I…I must go back,' she began. 'My governess is expecting me.'

'No! Don't go! You must forgive me if I seem a bit bowled over. It's just that I've never before met anyone as lovely as you.'

He blurted this out so straightforwardly, so simply, making no effort to come any nearer, that Lisette was both disarmed and deeply embarrassed. 'Please,' she said, holding her hands to her cheeks, 'you mustn't say such things. I don't know how to take them.' Then, feeling very shy, she went on, 'Tell me instead where you come from. Are you staying in the village? Or are you a neighbour?'

'I'm staying in the village for a few days. Visiting a…a friend. My name is Smith. Harry Smith.'

'Like the famous soldier?'

'You know of him?'

'Yes, I do! I've read a lot about him. How brave he was, and how he rescued a young Spanish girl, and then married her…it's such a romantic story! Oh, yes, I know quite a lot about Harry Smith—the other one, I mean.'

'That's wonderful!' The young man gazed at her in admiration. 'He's one of my own heroes. That's why—' He stopped short. 'Look, I'm not going to let you believe something that isn't true. Not you. My name isn't Smith at all, though it is Harry. There's a good reason for it, but I can't tell you at the moment. Please don't let it put you off me.'

Lisette gazed at him doubtfully, but he looked so anxious that she smiled. 'I believe you. But all the same, I can't stay. I have to go, really I do. I promised I wouldn't be long.'

'Meet me tomorrow!'

'I couldn't! It wouldn't be proper.'

'Oh, hang being proper! No, I don't mean that exactly…' He shook his head in exasperation. 'I don't know how to put it. You must think I'm an idiot! You see, I've never been in this situation before. But I must see you again. Just a few minutes. Please!'

Lisette was strongly tempted. Her experience of young men was not wide, but this one seemed much nicer than any she had met before. 'I'll try,' she said at last. 'It'll have to be in the afternoon. I have lessons in the morning.'

'At two?'

'Here?'

'Here. You'll come? That's wonderful!'

* * *

'Lisette!' Lisette came back with a guilty start to the parlour. Miss Petrie was looking worried. 'You were miles away just then. I think you must have caught something,' she said and added decisively, 'No more walks for you until we're sure you're not sick.'

'No, no, I'm very well,' Lisette exclaimed in fright. 'Really I am!' And she set about convincing her governess that she was, with such success that there was no further talk of remaining indoors the next day.

The next afternoon Lisette begged to be allowed to look again for specimens for her notebook. Miss Petrie readily agreed and suggested that they all three of them set off straight away. 'I shall have to be back before a quarter to three,' she said. 'I have things I must do.'

'I could go alone if it is inconvenient,' said Lisette eagerly.

'Thank you, but I'm quite sure your uncle would not like me to leave you to look after Pip while I do other things,' said Miss Petrie with a smile. 'No, Lisette, we'll go now. There's plenty of time.'

Lisette was unused to subterfuge. The last thing she wanted was to have Pip on her hands when she went out to meet her exciting new acquaintance. It was only half past one. With luck, she thought, she could arrange to have a little time to herself, when she could slip away.

She was luckier than she deserved. Pip wanted to stay close to the house, where most of the leaves had already faded or even vanished, and when Miss Petrie saw Pip's sister looking longingly over to the other side she suggested that Lisette had ten minutes to herself again. 'No more, mind!'

Lisette sped off back to where she had met 'Mr

Smith'. He was waiting for her. She was suddenly overcome with shyness.

'Hallo,' he said. 'I'm jolly glad to see you—I never really thought you'd come.'

'I…I…er…I shouldn't have. My governess would be so disappointed in me if she knew I was meeting you.'

'Rubbish! Tavy is a good sport. She wouldn't mind a bit!' he said heartily.

'Tavy? You mean Miss Petrie? You know her?'

'Oh! Er… Well, as a matter of fact, I do. In fact, she's the one I've come to Wychford to see. Only it's a touch difficult.'

'You're a friend of Miss Petrie's? Is that why you wanted me to meet you again—so that I would agree to give her a message or something?' Lisette was too young to hide her hurt.

'Oh, Lord, no!' Harry said hastily. 'Not at all. You mustn't believe—'

'What else am I to believe?'

Harry stared at her in dismay, and Lisette suddenly felt she wanted to get away. 'I think I'll go,' she said stiffly. 'They'll be looking for me.'

'No! Don't go like this! It's not what you think at all! Look, I'll tell you something, but you must promise to keep it a secret.'

'What is it?' said Lisette, still rather stiff.

'My real name is Petrie. Harry Petrie. Tavy is my sister.'

'Your *sister*?' Lisette felt a smile spreading over her face. 'Really? Are you the one in the Army?'

'She's talked about me?'

'Only a little. But why does it have to be a secret? I'm sure my uncle wouldn't mind your coming up to the house to visit her.'

'I'm sure he won't—when one or two things have been sorted out. But you'll have to take my word for it. It's got to stay a secret for the moment.'

'You're not in any kind of trouble, are you?'

'No! No, I promise you. It's more that Tavy doesn't want him to know about me. Yet. The situation is a touch delicate, take my word for it. Do you think you could do that? Keep it all a secret?'

'Oh, yes! I suppose it's really rather exciting. I'm so glad you told me—Miss Petrie is the nicest governess I've ever had.'

Harry started to chuckle. 'I'll tell her that, she'll be pleased. She's had enough experience of governesses herself.'

'What did you say?'

'Governess*ing*! I meant governess*ing*! She's had a lot of experience. Er…when can I see you again? Can you get away tomorrow? At the same time?'

'I'll try.'

He looked at her, hesitated, then said awkwardly, 'I'd like to know you a lot better, Lisette. I've not met anyone like you before.'

Lisette looked down. 'Thank you. I haven't known anyone like you. Perhaps, when Miss Petrie has told my uncle that you're her brother, we could meet properly. But I think I must warn you. Edward is very strict. He doesn't really wish me to make any new friends before I come out next year.'

'Then it's perhaps better he shouldn't know about me till next year. Then I'll come to London and we can be officially introduced.'

Lisette was doubtful. 'I shall be mixing with all sorts of people in Society,' she said awkwardly. 'I don't somehow think we'll visit the same places in London.'

Harry started to say something, then seemed to stop himself. 'We might,' he said with a mysterious look on his face. 'Meanwhile, we'll make do with what we've got, shall we?'

Lisette nodded. 'I'll come tomorrow at the same time,' she said. 'Goodbye, for now.'

'Goodbye, Lisette! You'd better leave it to me to tell Tavy that you know about her and me. She's going to be a little annoyed at first.'

Harry watched her as she sped through the trees back to his sister. He felt guilty at betraying Octavia's secret to her pupil, and his sister would have every right to be more than a little annoyed! But he couldn't have let Lisette carry on thinking he was interested in someone else! And she seemed to take it in her stride. She wouldn't tell. What a darling girl she was! If he could be sure of winning Lisette Barraclough, he might listen to his father and settle down after all! The temptation to tell her who he really was, the son of the Earl of Warnham and acceptable anywhere in London, had been very strong. But he had stopped himself just in time, and he was glad. He had betrayed enough of Octavia's secrets. Besides, it was a bit of a lark passing himself off as the brother of a poor governess! It hadn't seemed to make any difference to Lisette. He rather thought she quite liked him. For a moment Harry was lost in happy contemplation of a rosy future with Lisette Barraclough. Then he came back to the present. As soon as he saw her he would tell Octavia that Lisette knew they were brother and sister. He mustn't leave her in the dark. Harry went off to walk discreetly in the woods and wait for three o'clock.

But his honest intentions were foiled. Octavia didn't

appear at three. Harry waited for an hour, then had to accept she had been prevented from coming and went back to the inn.

While Harry was waiting in the woods Octavia was in the library with her employer, who had taken her there to inform her that Mrs Barraclough would be arriving at Wychford the next day. She received this news with a sense of foreboding. Nothing she had heard of the lady encouraged her to think she would approve of Edward Barraclough's decision to dismiss Miss Froom and employ someone so much younger. Octavia was sure there would be changes, though she was not at all afraid that there was anything wrong with what she had taught the girls. In spite of Pip's illness they had done well. So much so, that when she saw how intrigued Pip had been with the dancing lesson, she had relaxed her academic routine, and had taught them some of the ways and manners of Society. This was, of course, in direct conflict with what Edward Barraclough had told her in their first interview. But he wasn't aware that no one could have had a more intensive, or more highly polished training than the Lady Octavia Petrie!

'I seem to have lost your attention, Miss Petrie.'

Octavia jumped and dropped Pip's jacket, which she had been carrying when Mr Barraclough had called her in. 'I'm…I'm sorry,' she said in confusion, picking it up. 'Please excuse me! This news has come as something of a surprise.'

'I did not know myself before an hour ago.'

'I was going over in my mind the differences Mrs Barraclough's arrival might make to my routine with your nieces. I imagine she would want to take over some of their training?'

'Training? What training? Do you mean their lessons? Mrs Barraclough would hardly wish to do any teaching!' His tone was cool. 'I have no idea of the state of her health. She was presumably well enough to travel, but I have no further information. Unless she is seriously incapacitated she will almost certainly wish to take over the running of the house and so on, and I shall hardly be needed. After the end of the week I shall expect to spend much less time at Wychford.'

Octavia looked down. It was better so, she told herself. It must be better for everyone!

His hard grey eyes rested on her hands, which had a painfully tight hold of Pip's jacket, and he echoed her thoughts. 'Though my sister-in-law's sudden arrival is inconvenient from many points of view, it has come at a good time for me. For us. I have decided that the less we see of each other the better, Octavia,' he said quietly.

She nodded. 'Of course. I know things can be... difficult between us. And I would not wish to embarrass you...'

'Embarrass!' He got up and stood gazing out of the window. 'It's not a question of embarrassment! Don't think I've dismissed what I feel for you so lightly! But I refuse to insult you by asking you to be my mistress, and, since I have no intention at the moment to marry, any other relationship is not possible. I intend to avoid you as much as I can. It is the only rational solution.'

Octavia felt a sudden surge of rage. *Any other relationship is not possible...I intend to avoid you...* Had she been the governess he thought her, this would have been cruel! No discussion, no regret, no attempt to comfort. Only a calm, rational decision, taken without reference to any feelings the poor creature might have herself. No options for governesses! The man was a monster!

For a moment she was strongly tempted to throw his 'rational solution' in his face, tell him who she really was, that she was more than his equal in rank, and probably more familiar than he was with the upper echelons of true Society! What was more, she owned the house he was living in! But two things stopped her. One was that though she was proud of her breeding, it was not in her nature to boast of it. But what moved her far more powerfully was the idea that he might misunderstand her motives for doing so. He might even think that she was pleading with him, hoping that, with the barrier of rank removed, he would declare his love for her on the spot. And that would be intolerable! She would not do it, not on any account! He could wait till he met her in London, and then he could *grovel*!

The thought of Edward Barraclough grovelling to anyone was so absurd that her lips twitched in an involuntary smile. He had turned round in time to see it.

'That amuses you?' he said.

'Not at all, sir. I think you are being very…sensible.' Try as she might, she could not help letting a touch of bitterness in her voice.

'My dear, I wish—'

'There is really no need for another word, sir. May I go?' she asked, standing up with determination.

He lifted his shoulders and let them drop. 'Of course,' he said sombrely.

Octavia was so angry and unhappy that she had difficulty in keeping her patience with the girls for the rest of the day. At dinner she sat quietly, carefully keeping strictly to what a governess might be expected to say and nothing more. It was not an easy occasion. Edward's face was like a thundercloud, and Lisette was not behaving normally, either. She was always quiet, but there was an air of abstraction about her that Octavia would have found strange if she had not been so preoccupied with her own thoughts. Pip had been allowed to join them, and she, too, was quieter than usual. The prospect of her aunt's arrival had subdued even her lively spirit. After dinner Octavia saw Pip to bed, then pleaded a headache and escaped with relief to her own room.

But not very long after there was a tap on the door and Lisette came in. 'I'm so sorry about your head,' she said. 'I asked Mrs Dutton to make up a tisane. It's here. It might help.'

Octavia was sitting in her chair by the window. She took the tray and put it down on the table. 'Thank you, dear,' she said, making an effort to smile. 'You're such a thoughtful girl, Lisette.'

'Miss Petrie, I must talk to you. I have a confession to make.'

Octavia shut her eyes. It probably wasn't anything serious, Lisette was too well behaved. But she had had enough of crises today.

'What is it?' she said, trying to sound sympathetic.

'I like your brother a lot,' said Lisette. 'Too much!'

Octavia's eyes flew open, her headache forgotten. *'What?'* she asked. 'Say that again, Lisette, I can't have heard you properly. You like...?'

'Your brother Harry. I like him. And I ought not to.'

Octavia shut her eyes again. It was too much! She really did not want this!

'Miss Petrie?' Lisette's voice was worried.

It was not going to go away by itself. Octavia pulled

herself together and opened her eyes. 'My brother, Harry,' she said slowly. 'You've met him? When? How?'

'I thought you knew! He said he was going to tell you when he saw you this afternoon.'

'I didn't see him this afternoon. Lisette, are you telling me that you met my brother and didn't say a word to me about it?' said Octavia, beginning to get really angry. She had thought she had had enough for today. And now even Harry had let her down. She was surprised and disappointed. How dared he approach Lisette! And, having done so, how *could* he have betrayed his sister to her!

'I met him yesterday when I was gathering leaves in the drive. It was an accident. I didn't know then that he was your brother, of course, though he seemed very nice.'

'I'll have something to say to that brother of mine,' Octavia began ominously.

'No, don't blame him! He was polite and perfectly respectful. Though I don't suppose Edward would approve...'

'I am quite *certain* that Edward wouldn't approve!' said Octavia with complete conviction. 'What's more, nor do I, Lisette!'

Lisette gazed at her in astonishment. 'I thought you'd be pleased! Are you saying he's not good enough? I was afraid Edward might think so, but not you.'

'That has nothing to do with it! Even if...if Harry were the...the son of an earl, I still shouldn't approve of your meeting him like this. It is not right.'

'Well...that's just it, Miss Petrie. There's something I have to ask you about. Something I must confess.'

'You mean...*this* wasn't what you wanted to confess?' Octavia passed a hand over her brow. 'What else is there? What is it, Lisette?'

'Do you think it's very wrong of me to like Lieutenant Petrie? Or wicked of me to want to meet him again when I'm really betrothed to someone else?'

'Betrothed to someone else?' Octavia forgot her headache. 'What do you mean?'

'Before I came here I was promised to someone on Antigua, Miss Petrie. It was my father's last wish that I should marry him.'

'I...I don't understand,' Octavia said carefully. 'I thought your parents wanted you to come to England?'

'They did! I don't understand it either! But Ricardo assured me he had spoken to Papa the night before he died, and that Papa wished me to marry him straight away. He even showed me a letter from Papa. Do you think my father's last wishes ought to be sacred? Ricardo said they ought to be.'

'I...I think your father would want you to be happy, Lisette. Did he tell you himself that he wanted you to marry this Ricardo?'

'No. I thought he wanted me to come to England, as you said. That's what Edward and Uncle Henry say, and they're my guardians now. It was just the letter...'

Octavia paused. 'I don't think you should give too much importance to that letter,' she said slowly. 'You have only Ricardo's word for when it was written, or what was said that night. If he was desperately in love with you, he might have stretched the truth a little in order to persuade you to defy your uncles. He knew you wouldn't have done so otherwise. But...what about you? What do you want?'

Lisette shook her head. 'I don't know! I would have

married Ricardo on Antigua. But now.... I don't know. It's different here. Do you think I'm betrothed?'

'That's easy to answer! I'm quite sure you aren't. You're in the care of your uncles until you are twenty-one, and you can't be betrothed without their consent!'

Lisette broke into a smile. 'So you don't think I'm wicked for wanting to see your brother again?'

'No, I don't. But I don't think you should meet him, all the same.' Octavia leaned forward. 'You've asked for my opinion, Lisette, and I shall give it to you. Your guardians are quite right. It would be very wrong to let you get too fond of *any*one, before you've had a chance to sample the world outside. I assure you, it's not a question of social sphere, or eligibility, or previous promises. Anyone who loved you would do all they could to save you from making such a mistake.'

Lisette nodded and looked down. 'I'm not to see Lieutenant Petrie again.'

'Not before you go to London. After you've been introduced to Society, it might be different. You might meet him then. It's only a few months away.'

'But...it isn't very likely, is it? We shan't move in the same circles.'

Octavia took Lisette's hands in hers. 'I'm *sure* you will meet my brother in London! Trust me. But until then I want your word that you will not try to see him here again. Do I have it?'

She waited until Lisette gave a reluctant nod, then went on, 'Thank you. And just think, Lisette. You told me once that when your uncle has made up his mind he doesn't usually change it. If he should catch you with Harry at the moment, I'm sure he would be so angry that he would banish Harry, and forbid you to see him ever again. Is that what you want?' She waited while this sank in, then continued, 'Of course you don't. But once you are out, after the beginning of the Season, he might be more prepared to listen to you. Be patient, Lisette. Things might turn out better than you can hope.'

'Can't I even say goodbye?'

'I'll see Harry and explain. It's really too risky, my dear. Your aunt could arrive at any time tomorrow, and you will be expected to be there to welcome her. Besides, there'll be more people about. I'll slip down to the inn tomorrow morning to see Harry and make sure he understands. Don't look like that, Lisette! Remember my promise!'

The next morning was full of disturbance and bustle. Mrs Dutton was seriously put out at Mrs Barraclough's sudden decision to come earlier than expected to Wychford, and spent all morning organising extra staff, discussing menus and making sure the best bedroom was ready for her new mistress. As she came out of her room, Octavia was surprised to find the housekeeper urging two of the men to take care with a large chair that was being carried up the narrow stairs to the room above Pip's.

'I believe it belonged to Mrs Carstairs, Miss Petrie,' explained the housekeeper. 'Mr Barraclough says it was in the top tower room when he first came to visit Mrs Carstairs, and he wants it taken back there. Apparently she spent most of her time up there when she was still well enough. The chair's an ugly old thing, but I'm told she loved it. She had it brought down to her bedchamber when she was ill. But it can't stay there. Mrs Barraclough is going to use that room, and the master doesn't think his sister-in-law would like it. So the chair is to go upstairs again.' From Mrs Dutton's expression she could well have done without the extra work!

So that room on the top floor of the tower had been a favourite of her aunt's? Octavia could well imagine it! She had only once taken a quick look inside it, and had been very intrigued. It was a strange room with a slanting ceiling and windows on nearly every side. The views were wonderful, and the tables and shelves were crammed with objects of all kinds—books, pictures, miniatures, ornaments, souvenirs… She had promised herself that she would go back one day to have a better look at it, but the room was normally locked, and Edward Barraclough kept the key. She had somehow never found a way of asking him for it. Today was obviously not the right time. Besides, she had things of her own to do, including a visit to the inn for her talk with Harry.

It was later than Octavia had hoped when she finally managed to slip away from the house to the inn, where she asked for Mr Smith. To her relief the inn was empty of company and she was alone as she waited for her brother in its small parlour. Harry had clearly not been expecting a visitor so early. He came downstairs, shrugging on his coat and, at the same time, making a vain effort to tie his cravat.

Octavia shook her head at him. 'Where's your man?' she demanded. 'He should be doing this!'

'Don't be a fool, Tavy! I'm in disguise, remember? I sent Crocker back to Ashcombe! What the devil are you doing here at this hour?'

'Here, you'd better let me do that,' she said, looking with a critical eye at his efforts. 'I can talk while I do it. I can't stay long. They're expecting Mrs Barraclough today, and I ought to be there. But I had to see you.

Why did you have to tell Lisette that you were my brother?'

'She thought I was your lover, or something! I couldn't let her believe that, Tavy! She would have been put off before she'd even begun to know me! I was sure you'd understand.'

'You shouldn't have been speaking to her at all, Harry Petrie! But that's water under the bridge now. There are more important things to say. I've come to stop you from making a big mistake.'

'If you mean to warn me against Lisette, then I tell you you're wasting your time! She's the loveliest thing I've seen in my life, and I intend to marry her!' Harry said belligerently.

'And I wish you good luck in that, though you might have competition! But you'll still need her uncle's consent before you could—or do you intend to fly off to Gretna with her?'

'Of course not, dammit! What an improper suggestion!'

'Then you'd better listen to me. I know Edward Barraclough. He's very protective of Lisette, and would *never* consider you suitable if he found you were having clandestine meetings with her. And I wouldn't blame him! She's only sixteen years old, for goodness' sake! I'm surprised at you. What were you thinking of?'

'We met by chance the first time. And then… It was the only way I could get to know her, Tavy!'

'Rubbish! It would sink every hope you might have about the girl if her uncle were to find out. Harry, I mean what I say. You mustn't try to see Lisette again, not here in Wychford. She's too young and too innocent to know any better. But you—you're certainly old enough to know what you're doing, and it's wrong!

What sort of man will Edward Barraclough think you are if he finds out that you're persuading his precious niece to misbehave like this?' Harry, looking slightly shame-faced, said he hadn't thought of it that way.

Octavia's voice softened. 'I know you haven't. But if you'll take my advice, you'll be patient. I've promised Lisette that I shall make sure she'll meet you in London, and you must wait till then. Once she has been presented to Society, then you can plead your case with her. Not before.'

'But she's so beautiful! Tavy, you don't know what it's like to be in love. I'd give up the Army and settle down like a shot if I could be sure it would be with Lisette Barraclough.'

This was a new Harry. Octavia was impressed in spite of herself. She said gently, 'Then you must bide your time and take your chance. You might well win. But don't spoil it by pursuing her now.'

'What will she think? I promised to meet her this afternoon.'

'I've made sure she understands the situation. She knows I'm talking to you. Trust me, Harry!'

'I suppose I'll have to,' her brother said glumly. 'It's clear you don't want me to meet her at the moment.'

'Much as I love you, I can't let you. I would stop you if you tried. And now I must hurry back. Leave here as soon as you can, Harry. I shall probably see you in a week or two at Ashcombe! Meanwhile, behave!' She hugged him. 'Smile! Three months isn't long! Think of what Papa will say!'

He grinned at her then. 'He'll be amazed! The last time I saw him I wouldn't hear of staying at home, and now…'

Octavia laughed and kissed him. 'Look after yourself,

my dearest. Things will turn out right, you'll see. For you, at least. Goodbye!' She turned and hurried out of the inn.

She and Harry had been so absorbed in their conversation that they had failed to notice an important-looking carriage that had stopped briefly outside, long enough for the driver to ask for directions, and had then carried on. Julia Barraclough was arriving at Wychford.

Chapter Ten

Julia Barraclough had sharp features, and narrow hands and feet of which she was inordinately proud. She thought it showed her breeding. She affected an aristocratic drawl, too, though her comments were usually as sharp as her nose. She was suspicious of everything her brother-in-law had done, including not only his choice of governess, but the freedom he had then granted her. She had not been very long in the house before she was making her views plain.

'Where is this Miss Petrie?' she demanded, after Edward and the girls had greeted her. 'I expected her to be here to give me an account of her work! Where is she?'

'I think Miss Petrie went out for a walk, Aunt Julia,' said Lisette, timidly.

'Out for a walk? What was she thinking of? Her employer is due at any time, and the governess goes out for a walk! Did you know about this, Edward?'

'Not exactly. But I don't find it a matter of concern, Julia. Miss Petrie is very conscientious. You arrived rather earlier than we expected, you know. She probably thought she would give you time to have a rest and a talk with the family, before you took up the reins. You can talk to her at dinner.'

'At dinner? Surely you do not allow the servants to dine with the family?'

There was a slight pause before Edward said in an even tone, 'Miss Petrie is hardly a servant. And the girls benefit considerably from her conversation at the table.'

'We shall have to make other arrangements now that I am here. I have no wish to be edified by the conversation of a country bumpkin!'

'That is a pity. I'm not quite sure how to arrange matters to satisfy you. As long as I am at Wychford, Miss Petrie will continue to dine with us,' said Edward courteously but firmly.

'Well, that won't be for very long, will it?' Julia said sweetly. 'But…did I hear you say 'girls'? Does that mean Lisette *and* Philippa? I do hope you haven't allowed Philippa to join you for dinner! She's far too young to be down in the evenings. She should be in the nursery with the governess. Miss Froom would have understood that, of course. A most superior woman, from all accounts. She was for many years governess to the Ledburys, you know. Dear Daisy Ledbury was quite upset when I told her you had let Miss Froom go.'

'Have you met Miss Froom?'

'Of course not! But I met Lady Ledbury in London while I was passing through, though I didn't meet her husband. He was staying with friends in the country.'

'You surprise me. However, Miss Froom was, in my opinion, completely unsuitable for my nieces. We were all glad to see the back of her.'

'That's right, Aunt Julia! Miss Froom was a horror!' cried Pip, unable to hold her tongue any longer. 'And you mustn't say things about Miss Petrie! Miss Petrie is the best governess you could want!'

'She has apparently failed to teach you to be quiet until you're spoken to, Philippa!'

'Miss Petrie likes to hear what I say!'

Lisette took Pip's hand. 'Shall I see if Miss Petrie is coming up the drive, Edward?'

'Do!' said her uncle with relief. 'Your Aunt Julia would probably like to have a rest. Tell me, Julia, are you completely cured?'

Lisette and Pip made their escape.

'It's going to be awful,' said Pip gloomily. 'I'd forgotten what Aunt Julia was like. She hasn't even brought Uncle Henry with her. He's not much but he's a lot better than her.'

'Uncle Henry wanted to stay in London for a few days longer,' said Lisette. 'He was going to look for a suitable house for us to rent there. And Aunt Julia was worried about us, so she said she would leave him and come down to Wychford alone.'

'If I were Uncle Henry I'd want to stay in London for *weeks*! I hope he does! Edward said he would leave as soon as Uncle Henry arrived, and I don't know what it will be like without Edward!'

'No,' sighed Lisette.

'Perhaps Miss Petrie would agree to stay a bit longer?'

'I wish she would, but I somehow don't think Aunt Julia will want her to. We shall have to see, Pip. I suppose it isn't too long before we all go to London.'

'Oh, why couldn't things stay as they were? We were so happy at Wychford with Edward and Miss Petrie! I don't want to go to London! I love this house!'

'So do I. Though I'd like to see London...and the people there. But wait! There's Miss Petrie coming up the drive. Pip, you're not to repeat the things Aunt Julia said about her, do you understand? They would hurt her.'

'Well, I won't! Miss Petrie! Miss Petrie!' and with her usual enthusiasm Pip ran off down the drive.

Octavia hugged Pip, then looked to where Lisette was waiting for her. Her heart gave a pang. It was so like the first time she had come to Wychford, and she had met Pip, then Lisette, almost at this very spot. She looked at Wychford. The house looked somehow closed...remote... It was astonishing how it changed with the weather!

'This is nice,' she said, as she came up, with Pip hanging on to her arm. 'I must go for a walk more often!'

'Did you enjoy it?' asked Lisette. It was clear to Octavia, at least, what she meant. Lisette could guess that she had been to see Harry.

'It was entirely successful, Lisette,' she said with a smile. 'It cleared the air completely.'

Pip looked slightly puzzled, but Lisette breathed an audible sigh of relief. She said, 'Aunt Julia arrived while you were out. Her leg seems to be not nearly as bad as we thought.'

'So your uncle will be leaving us soon?' said Octavia, trying to sound casual.

'Not yet. Uncle Henry has stayed in London and Aunt Julia can't manage on her own. He'll come down in a week or so, and Edward will leave then.'

Octavia didn't know whether to be glad or sorry at this news. Of course, things would not in any case be the same with Julia Barraclough there. 'I must hurry,' she said. 'Your aunt will be annoyed that I wasn't here when she arrived.'

'She was,' said Pip. 'Very.' Octavia saw Lisette frown and shake her head at her sister and she laughed.

'Don't worry,' she said. 'I deserve her disapproval. Come on! We mustn't keep Mrs Barraclough waiting any longer.' Octavia started to walk very fast, and, laughing and protesting, the girls tried to keep up with her.

Dinner that evening was once again rather strained. Mrs Barraclough made her disapproval of Octavia's presence at the table very plain by addressing her remarks exclusively to her elder niece and her brother-in-law. Lisette obviously felt her aunt's rudeness even more than Octavia, and was painfully embarrassed. She hardly said anything at all. Octavia remained calm, and responded to such remarks as came her way from Edward Barraclough with perfect self-possession, but did not feel inspired to expand on them. Even Pip was quiet. As they rose after the meal, Mrs Barraclough said coldly, 'I should like to see you in the library, Miss Petrie. In ten minutes, if you please. I should like a few minutes first to talk in *private* with my *family*.'

'Certainly, ma'am. In ten minutes.' Octavia left the room. If this was a foretaste of what life would be like under the new regime, she was not sorry it was to be short-lived! Mrs Barraclough was worse even than she had feared. An overbearing snob! But worse was to come.

In the library Mrs Barraclough gave her a merciless grilling, during which Octavia was forced to reply with less than complete candour. Some of the questions verged on the offensive, and Octavia dealt with these as she thought they deserved, with cool disdain—a reaction that did not endear her to her employer. But just when she had started to congratulate herself on avoiding the pitfalls in Mrs Barraclough's interrogation, her complacency was brought to an abrupt end when Mrs Barraclough suddenly said,

'I think I saw you at the inn in the village this morning. Who was the young man?'

Octavia did her best but she could not prevent the colour rising in her cheeks. 'Did you, ma'am?' she said, playing for time.

'I did, so don't try to fob me off, young woman! Who was he? Does Mr Barraclough know you have a follower in the neighbourhood? I can't imagine he does. It's something I have never allowed among the servants in my household!'

'Mr Barraclough has never asked me what I do in my free time, Mrs Barraclough. But you need have no further worry about the young man in question. I was there to bid him goodbye. He is leaving today.'

'And how long has your affair with him been going on?'

'There has been no affair,' said Octavia, suppressing her anger. 'He has been here for a mere three days. I assure you, Mrs Barraclough, you need not concern yourself with him any longer.'

'That is surely for me to decide, Miss Petrie! I insist on knowing his name, if you please!'

Octavia hesitated, then said, 'Smith. Mr Smith. He is an old friend of my family.'

'Really?' Mrs Barraclough's tone conveyed what she thought of this. 'Well, unlike Mr Barraclough, I do not permit mysterious walks, or secret assignations, Miss

Petrie. For the remainder of your employment here, you will please inform me when you intend to leave the house.'

Octavia took a deep breath. 'Does that include my afternoon walks with the girls, ma'am?'

'Yes, of course it does! Well, I think I have made matters clear. I suppose, since my brother-in-law wishes it, you will continue to sit with us at dinner. At least when he is in residence at Wychford. Not otherwise. But I do not expect you to take part in any conversation. Your views are a matter of indifference, at least to me. Miss Froom would, of course, have appreciated that fact, but then Miss Froom is a well-trained servant and knows her place. That is all, Miss Petrie. I shall see you again tomorrow or the next day, after I've had an opportunity to judge what you have been doing with my nieces. You may go.'

Octavia came out of the library, quivering with suppressed rage. She had never in her life been spoken to in such a manner. What was more, she did not believe that her mother would ever have spoken to any of her governesses so. The woman was a viper, an ill-mannered, ill-bred viper!

Octavia thought she would explode if she didn't get some air. She walked rapidly up the stairs, fetched a thick shawl and slipped out of the side door on to the terrace. The sky was stormy, and a cold wind was blowing. Clouds raced across the face of the moon, sending eerie shadows over the terrace. Octavia hardly noticed any of it as she walked swiftly to and fro in an effort to master her fury, muttering imprecations, kicking a branch blown there by the wind quite unnecessarily out of the way. The branch was hard and her slippers thin. It hurt. She swore, stopped and nursed her foot.

By the time she put it to the ground again she had recovered enough of her equilibrium to start laughing at herself. She had always thought she had the least pride, the least self-consequence, of any of the Petries. She and Harry had always laughed at Arthur's air of self-importance. And here she was, giving way to a fit of fury just because some woman from the Colonies had dared to insult her. Lady Octavia Petrie at her most top lofty!

'If you stand still for very much longer you'll get cold.' The voice came from the shadows at the edge of the terrace. She peered in its direction and could just make out the figure of a man. Edward Barraclough. He went on, 'That was quite a fit of rage. I can guess what—or who, rather—caused it. She's a most unpleasant woman. Don't let her affect you, Octavia.'

'How can I not? She is in charge here.' She stopped and pulled herself together. 'And this is a most improper conversation. You should not be saying such things to me. Mrs Barraclough is your sister-in-law.'

'The history of my battles with Julia is a long one. She is aware of what I think of her.'

'You at least are in the fortunate position of being able to answer back!'

He came towards her. She could now see that he had been smoking a cigar. 'What's wrong? In the past you've quite often obviously disagreed with something I've said to you. I've even been amused at your efforts *not* to answer back. But I don't remember your ever being as angry as this.'

'That's because you have never made me feel like a servant! Mrs Barraclough does. I find it intolerable!'

He looked at her with a faint smile. 'That duchess air of yours is most intriguing, Octavia. Where did you pick it up?'

Octavia said woodenly, 'I don't know what you mean. Sir.'

He shrugged his shoulders and threw his cigar away. 'Julia has an unfortunate effect on a good many people. She is essentially a cold woman with very little imagination. I hope you'll stay with the girls as long as possible. They need you, they need your affection, your warmth.'

He was very close. His body was sheltering her from the wind. The temptation to lean against it was very strong… She made an effort and pulled herself away. 'I'm not sure…' she stammered. 'I'm not sure I can. The two months is very nearly up…' The moment of weakness had passed. 'No,' she said in a firmer voice. 'I can't stay longer. In fact, I somehow doubt I shall last even as long as that! I don't think your sister-in-law approves of me.'

'It's a damnable mess,' he said bitterly. Unconsciously he echoed Pip's sentiments of the afternoon. 'Why does everything have to change? Why the complications? It was so pleasant at first…' He turned again to her. 'I'm off to London tomorrow for two days. Don't let her get you down, Octavia. I expect to see you still here when I return. And now you must go in. Come!'

Julia had disliked Miss Petrie from the start. She disliked the obvious affection her nieces had for their governess. She disliked Miss Petrie's youth and charm. And she particularly disliked the manner in which she, Julia Barraclough, had been made to feel somehow impertinent during her interview with someone who was, after all, no more than a servant! It took a few minutes before she could feel composed enough to walk out of the library and go upstairs to her room. Once there she gazed critically round. What a dreadful place this house was! Old-fashioned furniture, dark rooms, musty passages… Impossible to keep clean! The sooner they could leave and go to London the better.

The maids had been careless. The curtains at the window overlooking the terrace were not quite pulled to, and with a frown Julia went over to close them. Her eye was caught by two figures down below, clearly visible in a patch of moonlight. Julia quietly opened the window in order to see better. Edward and Miss Petrie very close together…too close. Well, well, well! *That* was how Edward had kept himself amused at Wychford! *That* was why he was so eager to have the governess at his dinner table! She leaned further out as they moved to go inside. Edward even had his arm round the woman. Julia's lip curled. Typical! Edward up to his tricks as usual! As for the young woman…!

She jumped back, gasping and spluttering as the rain spout over her window suddenly emptied the contents of its gutter on to her head. This *awful* house! She was drenched with foul-smelling water and spattered with dead leaves. Her cap sodden, her hair dripping down over her shoulders, she yelled angrily for her maid. The girl came running, but stopped, amazed, at the sight of her mistress. Her exclamations were soon cut short, however, and she was sent scurrying round to find more help, towels and hot water. After some minutes of furious activity accompanied by a stream of impatient commands, the maids had bathed Julia and put her to bed with a warm drink. Then they left, thankful to escape, and the room was quiet again.

Julia leaned back against her pillows with a sigh of relief. As she settled down for the night she was filled with a warm feeling of righteousness. Miss Petrie would have to go. Assignations at the inn with 'Mr Smith', an affair at home with her employer... For all her airs the girl was nothing but a light-skirt! Julia looked thoughtful. It wouldn't be easy to get rid of Octavia Petrie. Edward would probably deny Julia's accusations, and he could be annoyingly obstinate. He might well demand proof if she tried to tell him about the episode with Mr Smith. Well, proof was what she would give him, and the inn was the place to start looking for it. She would send her maid down there tomorrow. She blew out her candle and composed herself for sleep.

The next day was a miserable one for Octavia. Edward Barraclough set off early for London, and Mrs Barraclough made excuse after excuse to keep the girls from her. Lessons were suspended, and to keep her occupied she was given set after set of laundry sheets and bills to check. When she offered to take the girls for their usual walk in the afternoon, Mrs Barraclough smiled coldly and said the weather was not at all suitable—she wished to keep them at her side. A fire was lit in the large salon, and the girls and their aunt spent the afternoon there, while Octavia sat alone in the small parlour. It was no consolation to her when the door to the salon was opened and she heard Pip's voice raised in protest. It was followed by an angry order from Mrs Barraclough, the sound of a scuffle, and then the door was slammed shut again. Octavia's heart ached for her charges, but she felt completely helpless. She was also very puzzled. She could tell that Mrs Barraclough had not liked her, but the woman was treating her as if she had the plague! What had gone wrong?

She and Pip had supper in the schoolroom. This was no hardship, but afterwards she spent most of the night lying awake, and got up feeling unrefreshed.

The day was no better than the one before. Mrs Barraclough announced at breakfast that she was taking her nieces to Guildford.

'Good!' said Pip. 'We can take Miss Petrie with us. I want her to meet my dancing teacher.'

'I think not,' said Mrs Barraclough. 'We shall be visiting friends afterwards, and I hardly think they would be interested in meeting your governess, Philippa.'

'But—'

'Be silent!' Mrs Barraclough turned to Octavia. 'I do wish you had managed to teach Philippa how to behave in company, Miss Petrie. She has always been a difficult child, but she seems to have got worse under your regime. We shall have to see what can be done before she becomes quite ungovernable. I have a good mind to leave her behind today!'

'Oh, would you? Please, Aunt Julia!' Pip's eyes were shining and she clasped her hands in supplication. 'Miss Petrie and I could have a day to ourselves, and you and Lisette could visit Mrs Allardyce in peace. Please say you will!'

This was not the response Mrs Barraclough had expected or desired. After a surprised pause she said, 'I prefer to keep an eye on you myself, Philippa. Finish your breakfast and get ready.'

Octavia followed Pip up to her room. 'Pip dearest, you must try to be good today. Your Aunt Julia is strict, but I'm sure she has your best interests at heart. Show her that I *have* managed to teach you something.'

'She doesn't like you. She wants to hurt you.'

'Pip!' Octavia sat down on the bed and held Pip before her. 'If I'm honest with you, will you be grown up enough to understand and not repeat what I say?' Pip nodded. 'You will? Good! I think your aunt disapproves of me, I'm not sure why. There's not much I can do about it. But that's not important. What is important is that she cares about *you*. She wants you to be a success, and she's right. You have to live with her after I've gone, remember, and you'll be much happier if you do your best to understand her point of view. Will you try? It would cheer me up no end if I heard when you all come back this evening that your aunt is pleased with you.' She gave Pip a kiss and pushed her away. 'Now, be off with you! Don't trip over your toes at the dancing lesson!'

Pip ran to the door, then came back to throw her arms round Octavia and hug her. 'Oh, Miss Petrie, I do love you! And I will try!'

'That's good!' said Octavia, and watched as Pip raced along the landing. 'Slowly, Pip! Slowly!' she called, smiling.

The sounds of departure died and Octavia was alone in the house. Even the servants seemed to be hiding. They were probably in the kitchen at the back. It was warm there, and the day was cold. It would soon be winter.

She wandered about the house like a lost spirit, until she found herself, she was not quite sure how, at the foot of the stairs leading to the room at the top of the tower. The room would be locked of course, it always was. She might just have a look… She slowly mounted the narrow stairs and found she had been right—the door was shut. And locked? She gave it a gentle push, and to her surprise it slowly opened. She went in.

A faint fragrance hung in the air, not sweet but herby, dry, intriguing. The chair she had seen being carried up was in front of the fireplace. There was even a fire in the hearth. It was almost out, but there was still a faint glow at its heart. Had it been lit by the servants who had brought the chair upstairs? Had Mrs Dutton ordered them to light it in order to air the room? It had lasted a long time, if that were so. It didn't matter. Whoever had lit it, she was grateful to them. They had probably left the door unlocked, too.

Octavia coaxed the fire into life again, and added one or two pieces of wood from the basket at the side. Then she wandered over to a table full of knick-knacks, and saw that there was a small framed drawing of herself among them. The picture of another little girl held pride of place. She read the writing below. *Theophania Carstairs, born 1770, died 1778*. So this had been Aunt Carstairs's daughter, her only child. Had she left Wychford to Octavia because she reminded the old lady of the daughter she had lost all those years before? A breath of air, like a sigh, wafted through the room. Octavia looked round. The windows looked firmly shut, but the room was high up. It wouldn't be surprising if there was a draught…

She sat down in the chair. So much sadness. With a heavy heart she thought once again about Julia Barraclough and what her arrival meant to Lisette and Pip. Pip was a very special sort of child, but Julia Barraclough was just the sort of person to rouse the worst in her: critical, overbearing, lacking in perception and full of ideas on discipline. Pip would have a hard time before she learned how to live with her aunt. And what would happen to all that lovely spontaneity while she did? Then there was Lisette… Lisette would never rouse her aunt's disapproval, she was always too anxious to avoid conflict, ready to believe the best of everyone. But the freshness, the charm of her gentle spirit, would be lost under Julia Barraclough's dominating personality. Lisette might well become a meek nonentity, even forced into Julia Barraclough's idea of a 'good' match. Harry just might save her if he was given the chance, but there was nothing Octavia could do about that at the moment. There wasn't much she could do at all.

She looked down in surprise when a tear fell on to her lap. She never cried! Octavia Petrie was famous for it—she never cried, not even when she was quite badly hurt. But the tears did not seem to know this piece of family lore. They came faster and faster, and were soon followed by a sob, and then another. Confused and ashamed, Octavia struggled to find her handkerchief. It wasn't there! It was a little scrap of a thing, it probably wouldn't have been much good anyway, but its loss was the last straw. Octavia hid her face in her hands, lay back in the chair and gave way to a storm of tears. It didn't matter that her hands were dusty, that her face would have streaks of dirt on it. Who was there to see?

She calmed down eventually, in some strange way feeling better…the scent of herbs in the room was even stronger… She closed her eyes. The image of a dark man floated in front of her. He was smiling that special smile of his, one eyebrow faintly raised, the glint in his eyes inviting her to share his amusement… Then he was serious again, telling her he loved her, that all would be well… Octavia felt happy again—and very sleepy.

* * *

Edward came back from London to find the house deserted. When one of the servants told him that the family had gone to Guildford for the day, he was quite annoyed, more with himself than anyone else. He should have ignored the strange urge to return that had attacked him in the middle of the morning. There had been no need to hurry back after all!

He wandered restlessly through the house, not quite sure what he was doing. There was an air of expectancy about the place that he could not understand. Eventually he came to the schoolroom. There was nothing of interest there. The schoolbooks were carefully stacked away, the papers on the desk in a neat pile. He turned them over. Laundry lists? Household bills? All noted and recorded in Octavia's handwriting. Edward dropped them back on the desk. What a spiteful woman Julia was! Octavia had offended her in some mysterious way, and she had taken her revenge by giving the governess a clerk's work to do!

How was Octavia being treated today? A visit to the Allardyces would give Julia numerous opportunities to humiliate her—Lavinia Allardyce was almost as great a snob as Julia! Edward stared into space. What the devil was he to do? It wasn't only Octavia who would suffer under Julia. Pip and Lisette would, too, especially when Octavia left. She had done so much for them. Pip was once again the merry little soul he had known in the old days, and the sad look in Lisette's eyes, which had so disturbed him, had almost vanished. For this he was sure he had Octavia to thank. As for himself… Edward swore violently. It seemed he couldn't stop himself from thinking about Octavia Petrie! He knew very well why he had come back early from London. It wasn't the first time it had happened. The truth was he couldn't keep away from Wychford for long while he knew Octavia Petrie was there. And now he had come back to find she was out for the day—what a waste of time!

A window banged shut, startling him out of his reverie. The house was empty, as far as he knew. Did they have an intruder? Edward came out of the schoolroom and looked around, but the house was silent about him. Something told him that it had come from the direction of the tower. High up. He went along the landing to the foot of the narrow staircase that led up to the top and listened. Nothing. All the same… Edward took out his bunch of keys and selected the one that fitted the door upstairs. Then he quietly mounted the stairs.

He found he didn't need his key. The door was slightly open, and through it he could see the light of a fire.

Chapter Eleven

Edward pushed the door further, and bunched his keys inside his fist. If there was an intruder he knew how to deal with him. He went softly in. The fire was glowing, but the room was empty. He stood at the door and the strong, sharp fragrance in the air brought back a vivid picture of Mrs Carstairs as she had been when he first visited her in this very room. She had been lying in that chair over by the fire, and he had hesitated, standing at the door like this. Her black eyes had twinkled at him.

'Come in, come in!' she had said. 'You needn't expect me to stand up for you. It's enough of an effort to get up here at all!' She was thin, but not yet wasted by illness, and her spirit was very much alive. 'Come over here! I want to have a look at you.'

He had advanced into the room. She had nodded. 'Yes. I thought you'd do. I was just thinking up someone like you. I'm pleased to see you again, Mr Barraclough. You're just what I need!' He hadn't quite known how to reply to this, and she had continued, 'You're not fair, of course, but that doesn't matter. I prefer dark men, myself. Do you still wish to rent

Wychford when the rest of your family come over to England?'

Her conversation had always been somewhat odd, but never dull. He had enjoyed it. He had visited her several times after that, but each time she had seemed weaker, until she could no longer get up to the room in the tower, even with the help of the servants. That was when the chair had been taken down to her bedchamber. It had been brought back up here again just the other day.

Edward came further into the room. Then he saw that it wasn't empty after all. Octavia Petrie was lying back fast asleep in the chair. She was so tiny that she had been out of sight from the door. Why hadn't she woken up when the window had banged? He came nearer... She was in much the same position she had been in that night in Pip's bedroom. Then she had been in a night-gown and thin wrapper; today she was fully dressed in a plain blue stuff gown, buttoned to the throat. But the sight was as touchingly seductive now as it had been then. He knelt down beside her and saw the streaks of dried tears on her face. His heart melted and he put a gentle hand against her cheek. 'Octavia!' he whispered.

Her eyes opened, and widened as she saw him. Then she smiled and shook her head. 'I know you're not really here,' she said dreamily. 'It's just my imagination. You're in London. But it's nice to have your ghost to keep me company.'

Some bird outside—a rook or gull, perhaps—gave a cackle of laughter, but they didn't hear it.

'I'm here, all right,' said Edward. 'In the flesh. No ghost could possibly feel the way I do at this moment.' He bent forward and kissed her.

She was still half-asleep, but, after a brief hesitation,

her lips softened and melted under his. He held her face in both hands and kissed her again, more demandingly, and this time fire ran along his veins as he felt her immediate, and passionate, response. He covered her cheeks, her eyes, the tip of her nose, her chin, with kisses, and, slowly undoing the buttons of her dress with trembling fingers, he kissed her throat, her shoulders, the shadow between her breasts… It wasn't enough. He lifted her bodily out of the chair and held her there in his arms. She felt so light, as if a breath of wind would blow her away, and he was suddenly afraid that he might hurt her, or frighten her with the intensity of his feelings. With great reluctance he gently set her down away from him.

For a moment she stared at him in shock and then smiled when she saw what was in his eyes. Lifting her arms, she wound them round his neck and fiercely pulled him back to her, holding her mouth to his. Not one of Louise's expert blandishments had ever made him feel half such a man, so electrically alive, so startlingly aware of every nerve in his body. Never before had he felt such a desperate need to keep himself in control, as he knew he must. Never before had it been so difficult. His arms tightened round her and he pressed her to him, her yielding softness sending desire rocketing through his blood. Heaven forgive him, he must stop this, he must! It would soon be too late.

'Octavia,' he said, his throat dry.

'Don't talk,' she murmured, her lips still pressed to his. 'Talking will spoil it. Kiss me again, Edward! Please kiss me again!'

It was no use! He had to respond. Still locked in a kiss, they sank back in front of the leaping fire, lost to the world. He thrust her dress away from her shoulders, kissing the satin skin of her bared breasts....

A breath of air from one of the windows passed through the room, and Octavia shivered in the cool draught. It was the slightest of movements, but it was enough to bring Edward to his senses.

'I...I mustn't!' he said with a groan. 'God help me, I mustn't! You don't know what you're doing, Octavia. How difficult you're making it for me! This is where it must stop.' He unwound her arms from his neck, and drew her dress up over her shoulders again. Then he got up and pulled her to her feet, almost angrily. She stared at him, dazed. Then her face changed—it was as if she woke up. A look of shocked horror came into her eyes and she bent her head with a sob. Turning away from him, she began to fasten her dress.

'Octavia—' he said.

She shook her head, still not looking at him.

'Octavia!' he said again.

She put her hands to her ears in an effort to shut him out. 'Don't! Don't say anything!' she said hoarsely. 'It happened *again*! I don't know what came over me, I don't *have* such feelings! Oh, God, I'm so ashamed! What must you think of me? How could I have let you...*begged* you to kiss me like that? Allowed you to...to...touch me... Such wanton behaviour... Don't look at me like that! I can't bear it! I can't *bear* it!'

She whirled away from him and ran out of the door and down the stairs as if she was being pursued by demons. He heard the door of her room slam.

Edward looked around him. It all looked so innocent. Not at all like a scene for seduction. And yet it had taken all the strength he had not to seduce Octavia Petrie, here in this very room, even though he was fully aware that it would be wrong. He felt exhausted, battered by a maelstrom of conflicting emotions...

It was some time before he felt ready to leave Mrs Carstairs's room, and even then he still wasn't able to think rationally about what had just happened. Before checking the fire and locking the room, he went round all the windows, examining them for loose catches, or gaps in their frames. There was nothing. The banging window must be somewhere else. He would get one of the handymen to take a look round the rest of the rooms. But...in that case, where had that sobering breath of air come from? Edward shook his head. Whatever its origin, they both had reason to be grateful to it.

It was no surprise when Miss Petrie sent a message to say that she had a bad head and would stay in her room for the rest of the day. Julia, of course, congratulated herself on winning the battle of attendance at dinner.

'These people are all the same, Edward,' she said. 'Give them a little leeway and they will waste no time in taking advantage of you. But they soon knuckle under if you are firm with them. Miss Petrie has had the day to consider her position, and has now realised that she cannot win. I dare say she will not come down to dinner again. Mrs Allardyce had some similar experiences to recount. Governesses always tend to think themselves a cut above the other servants. Did you know that Lavinia Allardyce is distantly related to the Ledburys?' She hesitated and threw a glance at her nieces. 'Lisette, since Miss Petrie tells us she has the headache and cannot, it seems, perform her duties, I should like you to take Philippa upstairs and see her to bed. She is tired after her day out, and I wish to talk to your uncle. You needn't bother to come downstairs again yourself.'

Edward roused himself. 'Not unless you wish to, Lisette. I should like to hear how your dancing lesson went.'

'Perhaps tomorrow, Edward?' Lisette's voice was subdued. 'I think I should prefer to stay with Pip till she goes to sleep. Aunt Julia is right, she is very tired.'

As the two left the dining room and went up the stairs Pip whispered, 'Can I see Miss Petrie, Lisette? I knew if I asked Aunt Julia she'd say no, so I didn't. But I'd like to tell her how well I behaved.'

'I'll see if she's well enough,' said Lisette with a smile. 'I was proud of you today, Pip, and I think it might do Miss Petrie some good to hear about it. Let me ask her first.'

Miss Petrie wasn't in bed, as they had half-expected. The lamp by the bed was lit, but she was sitting in a chair by the window, gazing out into the darkness. But she turned and smiled when she saw Lisette's head round her door.

'Come in,' she said. 'Where's Pip?'

'I'm here!' Lisette held Pip firmly back. 'We're sorry you have a headache again,' she said. 'Would we be too much for you?'

'Never!' said Miss Petrie. 'Come in.'

'Aunt Julia thought you weren't really ill,' said Pip, looking at her governess's pale cheeks and heavy eyes. 'But I think you look *very* ill, Miss Petrie. I think you should get Edward to send for the doctor.'

'I…I don't think that will be necessary, Pip. It…it's only a bad head. Tell me how you did today.'

'I was very good!' announced Pip. 'I was very good all day.'

'Was your aunt pleased with you?'

'She didn't say so. But she must have been. It was very boring at the Allardyces, though.'

'Poor Pip,' said Lisette with a smile. 'She tried so hard. I was really proud of her.'

'I'm glad. I think that deserves a cuddle, Pip darling.'

Pip needed no second invitation. She clambered on to her governess's lap and hugged her. Miss Petrie shut her eyes, and Lisette said quickly, 'I think that's enough, Pip. We've stayed long enough. You've told Miss Petrie about today, now we must let her rest. Come along.' Pip got down reluctantly and allowed herself to be led to the door. Here Lisette stopped. 'Can I fetch anything for you?'

'Thank you, but no. I shall go to bed very soon, and will be perfectly fit and ready to hear more about your day tomorrow. Goodnight, my dears.'

Pip was very quiet as they left to go to her room. Lisette kept her sister company while one of the maids undressed and washed her, then put her to bed. The maid went away, and Lisette came over to kiss her goodnight.

'Lisette,' said Pip in a troubled voice. 'Miss Petrie was crying.'

'I don't think so, Pip!'

'Yes, she was! It was too dark by the window for you to see, but her cheeks were wet. She was crying.'

Lisette hesitated. Then she said, 'I expect it was the headache. Remember how your head ached when you were ill? Let's hope she's better tomorrow. Goodnight, Pip.'

Lisette went out quietly. She hadn't wanted to worry

Pip, but she very much feared that they were about to lose Miss Petrie sooner than they had expected.

Meanwhile, Julia was about to launch her campaign. 'Lavinia Allardyce tells me that Daisy Ledbury is a much wronged wife. Did you know? Ledbury is hardly ever at home, and usually in some very doubtful company. Female company.'

'Well, yes, I had heard something of the sort,' said Edward curtly. The last thing he wanted to hear was gossip repeated from the Allardyce woman. Julia was bound to find some reason to moralise somewhere, and he didn't think he could take it.

'Of course, morals are so slack in England,' she went on. 'Even among persons one might have thought would set an example. Especially to the young.'

'Really?' said Edward in his most repressive tone.

Julia took no notice. 'I had always expected governesses and the like would have a higher standard of behaviour than most,' she went on. 'But apparently it isn't so. Take Miss Petrie, for example.'

Edward stiffened. Julia could not possibly know of the scene in the tower room. Not possibly! Not even any of the servants had been around this afternoon, and Julia and the rest of the family had been in Guildford. So what did she mean? He said coldly, 'If you are about to be unpleasant about Miss Petrie, Julia, then you can save your breath. I know you don't approve of her, though heaven knows why. But I have always been very satisfied with her.'

'I'm sure you have, Edward,' said Julia significantly. 'But did you know she had a lover?'

'A lover? What nonsense is this?'

'No nonsense, my dear. I have made very careful

enquiries. Miss Petrie's lover has been staying at the inn in the village. He left just as I arrived—only two days ago.'

Edward stood up. 'Be careful what you say, Julia! I won't have your poisonous tongue slandering a woman I hold in the highest esteem!'

'Yes, well, that's another story, isn't it? She has obviously caught you in her toils, too.'

By a very narrow margin Edward overcame his inclination to take his sister-in-law by the throat and choke her. The events of the afternoon had shaken him to the depths of his being and he was still very much off balance. He was no nearer to understanding what exactly had happened to him up there in the tower room, but to hear Julia, a woman he had always scorned and disliked, dragging Octavia's name into the dirt like this was more than he would tolerate.

'I don't want to hear any more. I'll leave you to wallow in your own filth, Julia. I don't want to hear it.'

'I can prove it!' Julia's voice stopped him at the door.

He turned round and said slowly, 'If this is one of your fantasies, then by God, I swear I'll ruin you—and your husband, too. It wouldn't be difficult. Your finances are not as safe as you'd like them to be.'

'What an unpleasant thing to say! You sound very fierce. I would be quite worried if I weren't so sure of my facts.' She eyed her brother-in-law with interest. 'It seems you are even fonder of Miss Petrie than I thought. But if that's the case, it's better you should know the truth about her! That woman has been playing a double game, Edward. The day I arrived she was not just out for a walk. She was at the inn, enjoying a little idyll with a certain Mr Smith. Smith! You'd think she could find a better pseudonym for him!'

'Go on,' said Edward grimly.

'I can answer for their meeting—I saw them myself, and she didn't try to deny it. They were alone in the inn, enjoying a very intimate conversation, when I saw them. But there's more to it than that. When I made enquiries I found that others had seen them kissing and hugging each other! She was even seen helping him to dress!' Julia looked at him triumphantly. 'Ask her! I challenge you—ask her who Mr Smith is! Let's see if she tells you.'

Edward stared at her, stunned. Then he shook his head and burst out, 'There's some explanation. There's got to be an explanation! I don't believe that Octavia…that Octavia would do this.' He shook his head. 'I must get out of here. I can't think…' He strode out of the room, through the hall and out into the grounds.

Julia followed him out and watched him striding down the path. She smiled complacently. She was sorry for Edward. Truly sorry! Always so sure of himself, always so ready to criticise others. And now the tables were well and truly turned. It must be quite distressing for him.

Still smiling, she turned to go back inside, but a sudden gust of wind blew the oak door shut in her face. She stared at it in disbelief. Where on earth had that gust of wind come from? *Inside* the house? Impossible! With an impatient exclamation she took the bell pull in her hand and gave it an angry tug. No response. Where were all the servants? Keeping warm in the kitchen, no doubt, and ignoring the needs of their betters! It was cold out here. She pulled the bell again, more vigorously, and the handle came away in her hand. With a cry of pure frustration she threw the thing away and, shivering in the cold wind that had sprung up, she set off round to the kitchen quarters at the side of the house. She would die of cold if she didn't find them soon! Someone would pay for this, she would see to it personally! As for this wretched house...anyone would think it was trying to get rid of her. Well, if it was, she had received the message. They would all leave this ruin as soon as they could, and find a decent place in London. She would deal with the Petrie woman and then set about arranging it... Where *was* the damned door to the kitchen quarters?

Edward walked about the grounds for a while, strenuously resisting any thought of duplicity on Octavia's part. Her honesty, her pride, her sweetness, her wit— all the qualities he treasured in her—were powerful arguments against Julia's accusations. His judgement could not, *could* not have been so wrong! But as his temper cooled, reason started to take over. He reminded himself that Julia would not have made these accusations without very good grounds. She was malicious, but not stupid. There must be, must be a mistake somewhere! He would have to go down to the inn himself, if only to scotch the story.

He set off for the village, convinced he would soon have an explanation. Then he would deal with his sister-in-law as she deserved!

It was getting late, but the inn was still open and the landlord was perfectly prepared to talk. Yes, he had had a young gentleman by the name of Smith staying with him, as nice a gentleman as you could find. And handsome with it. He'd wager the lad had been a soldier, he had the air of one about him. No, he couldn't answer for any visitors, not personally. But Maggie, one of the maids, had seen a young lady at the inn with him. Very affectionate they'd been. He thought she'd said it was the governess from the big house, but he could be mistaken, o' course. Did Mr Barraclough wish to question the girl himself?

Edward was still hoping for a misunderstanding. Octavia had apparently admitted meeting Mr Smith at the inn, but perhaps the maid had been mistaken in what she saw? When the landlord produced her, he put the question.

'Oh, no, sir!' said Maggie, giving him a dimpled smile. 'Most affectionate they were, huggin' and kissin'. They hadn't spent the night together, mind! But it was clear enough to anyone that they knew each other very well indeed—if you know what I mean. And it's true that he was not what you might call properly dressed when I first saw them. No, they was very fond of each other, of that I'm certain sure. Lovely to see them, it was. Him so handsome, and her so pretty, like.'

Edward left the inn and walked back to Wychford in a daze. He went straight to the library and poured himself a large brandy. And another. He couldn't understand it. Every instinct he possessed told him that there was something wrong. Octavia Petrie was honest. That he would swear to! But the evidence… How could she possibly have been so passionately responsive to him, if she was having an affair with another man? How could she have seemed so genuinely distressed, so movingly innocent when she realised how her behaviour must look?

Or was he being incredibly naïve? Had he forgotten that some of the most successful courtesans he had known had the art of projecting an appealing innocence that quickly disappeared once they were in the bedroom. But not Octavia! Dear God, no, not Octavia! He buried his head in his hands, trying not to remember the way she had pulled him to her, pressed herself against him, demanded his kisses. Were those the actions of an innocent? Before tonight he would have said yes, they were! They had been the reaction of an innocent who had till that moment been unaware of her own deeply passionate nature, someone who was experiencing for the first time the wildness, the temptation, of physical love. Surely her shame, her shocked modesty at the end, could not have been faked? But what if it had? What sort of a fool did that make of him?

His doubts grew. With the end of her time as a governess at Wychford fast approaching, had Octavia Petrie attempted to seduce the master into offering marriage? Had she really thought she could do it? If the truth were known, she had come damned close to succeeding, by God, she had!

Edward sat brooding the rest of the night. If this loss of judgement, this loss even of reason was what came of falling in love then he wanted none of it! Innocent or not, Octavia Petrie would have to go. Immediately!

In the morning he asked Octavia to come to the library.

Octavia, too, had spent a sleepless night. It was torture to her to remember her behaviour the previous day. She had behaved like a trollop! It was as if she had turned into another person altogether in that room in the tower, one who had no modesty, no shame, no self-respect! How could she have? Edward Barraclough had always made his position perfectly clear. He had no intention of marrying—neither his nieces' governess,

nor anyone else. And, knowing that fact, knowing that
marriage played no part in his plans, she had allowed
him to take such liberties with her! No, she had not
allowed him, she had *asked* for them, *pleaded* for them.
How could he possibly believe what she said, when she
told him that she was not that kind of person? He probably remembered as well as she did that she had been
just as wanton after he had helped her down from the
tree. It was no use telling him, or herself, that she wasn't
that sort of person. She *was*, where Edward Barraclough
was involved.

It was quite clear to her that now, whoever she told
him she was, however she presented herself, he would
regard her as fair game, an easy prize for the taking.
Governess or great lady, it was all the same, what man
would respect her after such a display of…of mindless
abandon! She knew what people thought of women who
behaved as she had, and it wasn't flattering.

Worse than anything, she was afraid that, if Edward
Barraclough kissed her again, there was no guarantee
that she wouldn't behave in exactly the same way!

There was only one answer. She must remove herself
from temptation, leave Wychford, leave Lisette and Pip,
and go back to Ashcombe.

When Edward Barraclough's request to see her in the
library was delivered she was tempted to leave the
house there and then. The thought of facing him terrified her. But she set her jaw and went down, grimly
determined to see it through. She *deserved* his poor
opinion of her, his contempt. She even deserved any
attempt he might make to persuade her to become his
mistress. But she would not change her mind. Whatever
he said, she would tell him that she was leaving Wych-

ford the next day, as soon as she could arrange some manner of reaching Ashcombe. On one thing she was absolutely determined. She would *not* tell him what her real position in life was. Her family didn't deserve to have their reputation besmirched by her behaviour.

Edward was sitting behind his desk. He looked white and drawn, and her heart, her foolish heart, gave her a pang. He spoke without looking at her.

'Sit down, Miss Petrie.'

She sat, looking at her hands which were folded in her lap. There was a silence. When he spoke again she did not at first understand what he was saying. A complaint from Mrs Barraclough? Was that all? Why this fuss about a complaint against her from Mrs Barraclough? What was new about that?

But when he spoke again her heart gave a thump and she began to feel cold.

'Mrs Barraclough tells me you have had a friend staying at the inn. Is that right?' When Octavia nodded he went on, 'You didn't think to let me know? Or bring him to the house to be introduced? It *was* a man, I gather?'

'He…he was not supposed to come to Wychford. I didn't want him here. I told him to leave as soon as he arrived.'

'But he didn't leave immediately, did he? He stayed long enough for a very affecting little scene to take place.'

Octavia looked up. Had Edward heard about Harry's meeting with Lisette? Was that why he was so angry? She breathed an inward sigh of relief when he added, 'At the inn. You were being very…friendly with each other.'

How ironic! It wasn't Lisette he was angry about at all, but her own perfectly innocent meeting with her brother! Still cautious, she answered, 'I...I...er...we are very good friends.'

She jumped as Edward thumped his fist on the desk. 'Don't try to play with me! The maid at the inn thinks you are lovers!'

Octavia was astounded. 'That's not so!' she said angrily. 'How could you even *think* it? The girl's a liar!'

'Do you deny you were at the inn?'

'No.'

'Do you deny that you met a man there?'

'No.'

'Do you deny that he was only half-dressed when you met him the other day? That you embraced each other?'

'No. But that's because—' Octavia stopped short. Her own hopes of happiness were in ashes, but Harry's still had a chance. But not if Edward Barraclough learned about him while he was in this mood. She went on, 'That's because he had only just got up when I arrived. We were saying goodbye.'

'How very touching! I suppose you were missing him yesterday when you so charmingly invited my attentions. Or had you thought I would be a better prospect? Hoped for marriage, even? How disappointed you must have been when I managed to avoid actually seducing you.'

His voice was suddenly so harsh, his words so cruel, that Octavia could hardly breathe for a moment. This was the man who had held her so tenderly, breathed such words of affection, not twenty-four hours before! Her heart felt as if it was being squeezed by an iron fist. The fact that she had half-expected his contempt didn't make it any easier to bear.

'I understand your suspicions,' she managed to say at last. 'They're wrong, though I can hardly expect you to believe that. But for what it's worth, I give you my word that Harry Smith is not, and never has been, my lover. As for yester—' She choked and had to begin again. 'As for yesterday, I am more ashamed than I can say about my behaviour. You are quite wrong about my motives, but I don't blame you for thinking badly of me. You couldn't think worse of me than I do of myself.'

Edward regarded her in silence. 'You realise that I cannot possibly let you stay here after this?'

'If you are looking for an excuse to send me away, I can spare you the trouble. I could not possibly let *myself* stay here after what happened between us, Mr Barraclough. I...I had hoped to stay with your nieces to the end, but I'm afraid you must explain to them why I must leave as soon as it can be arranged. Try not to destroy their illusions about me.' Her voice wavered. 'I have grown very fond of them.'

He got up and walked to the window. Then he turned and said violently, 'Damn it, why did it have to happen like this, Octavia? For the first time in my life I—' He stopped. 'Never mind! What's done is done. You can go in the gig. Jem will take you. In an hour?'

She nodded and went to the door. He said abruptly, 'I'll explain as best I can to the girls. They'll miss you.'

Octavia couldn't speak. She nodded again and went out.

The windows of Wychford had a number of faces at them as Octavia Petrie left. Julia smiled as the gig went down the drive. She would have been failing in her duty to her nieces if she had allowed that…that harlot to stay on!

Lisette watched with a troubled face. She was old enough to wonder what lay behind Miss Petrie's sudden departure. It was more than her aunt's simple dislike of her, she was sure.

Pip was at the window of her tower room, but she could not see for tears. She hated her aunt! What was the use of being good when you lost one of the people you liked best in the world?

Edward's face was not at the window. He was bent over his papers in the library, determinedly *not* thinking of honey-gold hair, eyes alight with laughter or dark with desire, the feel of a woman's slender body in his arms… With a curse he threw his pen away and stared at his desk. He would master this. He had been perfectly happy with his way of life before he met Octavia Petrie, and he would be perfectly happy with it again. This terrible sense of loss was not to be borne!

There were only three of them at dinner that night. Pip had stayed upstairs. When the meal was nearly finished, Lisette regarded her uncle and said quietly,

'Why did you let Miss Petrie go, Edward?'

'I told you,' he said curtly. 'She found she had some urgent business at home.'

Lisette flinched at his tone, but went on bravely, 'I think that was an excuse. Neither Pip nor I can believe she would leave us so suddenly, not without explaining things to us herself.'

'Leave it alone, Lisette!' her uncle said.

'I think Lisette is old enough to know the truth,' said Julia. 'You should tell her. It will rid the girls of this admiration for a woman who doesn't deserve it.' Edward remained silent and after a pause Julia turned to Lisette. 'We did not consider Miss Petrie a fit person to have charge of you, Lisette. There! I've said it for you, Edward.'

The colour rose in Lisette's cheeks. 'I don't believe that!' she said. 'I think she had to go because you didn't like her, Aunt Julia!'

Edward gazed in astonishment at his gentle, well-behaved niece. Lisette never criticised, never argued with anyone!

Julia's face coloured, though not as prettily as Lisette's. 'Well!' she said. 'It's a fine thing when my own niece can say such things to me! I am more shocked than I can say at your rudeness, Lisette. But I know who is to blame! It is yet more proof of Miss Petrie's bad influence—if any proof were needed! Miss Petrie left of her own accord, but if she had not, I confess freely, I would have dismissed her. It was as well that she did not have the impudence to ask for a reference, for I should not have been able to give her one!'

'Julia, I hardly think—'

'No, Edward, you heard what Lisette said. My own niece, a girl I have cherished like my own child, has accused me of spite. It is only fair that she knows the truth.' She turned to Lisette. 'Your precious Miss Petrie was having a clandestine relationship with a young man, Lisette, and that is something no responsible guardian could condone in a governess. She was even seen kissing him!'

The flush in Lisette's cheeks faded and she grew pale. She asked, 'The young man—who was he? What was his name?'

Edward's eyes narrowed at this strange question. What lay behind it?

'There's no need for you to know—' began Julia.

'Smith,' said Edward. 'Harry Smith.'

Lisette jumped up. 'And you sent Miss Petrie away because of that!' she exclaimed. 'How could you! Oh, how could you!'

'What's the matter, Lisette? What do you mean?'

'Edward! Harry Smith is Miss Petrie's *brother*! You've dismissed the kindest, nicest person Pip and I have ever known, someone we really loved, because she kissed her *brother*!'

Chapter Twelve

Lisette burst into tears and ran sobbing to the door, but Edward leapt up and fetched her back.

'Wait a minute, my girl,' he said sternly. 'You can't say something like that and then disappear. How do you know that Mr Smith is Miss Petrie's brother? Did she tell you?'

'No,' sobbed Lisette. 'He did. His name is Harry Petrie, not Smith at all.'

'This man told you himself? When? When did you meet him, Lisette?'

Julia started to say something, but Edward cut her off. 'I'll deal with this Julia,' he said brusquely. 'This has gone beyond the question of Miss Petrie's behaviour. Lisette has been in my care for very nearly the past two months, and, as her guardian, my concern at the moment is what has been happening to *her*.' He turned his attention to his niece, saw the state she was in, and made an effort to speak more gently.

'Sit down, Lisette, and try to calm down. Do you want a drink of water?' Lisette shook her head, but she did make an effort to compose herself. After a moment Edward went on, 'Tell me, where did you meet Harry

Petrie?' He paused. 'At the inn? Did you…did you ever
see him at the inn?' Lisette shook her head vigorously.

'Where, then?'

'We…we met in the woods. Here at Wychford.'

'Did Miss Petrie introduce you?' asked Julia.

'No! Harry and I met by accident.'

'Harry! You called him Harry, did you, when you
met him in the woods? Fine goings-on!'

'Julia, I would like you to stop interrupting, and allow
me to deal with this. Lisette will tell us the truth in her
own time, I know she will. Please keep quiet. Now,
Lisette, you said you met Harry Petrie in the woods, by
accident.'

'Yes. Miss Petrie didn't know anything about it. I
was collecting specimens for my notebook. It was after
Pip was ill and we went out for an airing behind the
house. Pip got tired and Miss Petrie decided to take her
indoors, but she knew I wanted some leaves and things
for my drawings. So she gave me a quarter of an hour
to look by the drive. There are better ones there.' She
threw a glance at her aunt. 'It was just a quarter of an
hour!'

'Go on.'

'He was in the woods near the drive. He startled me.
But his behaviour was very gentlemanly, and after a
while I…I liked him.'

'What did Miss Petrie say when you told her you'd
met her brother in the woods?'

'I didn't know that he was Miss Petrie's brother! He
told me his name was Smith. Like the hero.'

'She knew, of course. She'd arranged it!' said Julia
with a sniff.

'She didn't! I didn't tell her about it at all at first.
I'm sorry, Edward, I really am. I knew you wouldn't

approve, but I didn't mean any harm! He was perfectly polite and…and respectful.'

'When did you tell Miss Petrie about it?'

'After our second meeting. He told me then that he didn't want to lie to me. His name wasn't Smith, it was Petrie. He was Miss Petrie's brother.'

'Ha!'

'Julia!' warned Edward. He turned to Lisette again. 'What did Miss Petrie say?'

'She was very annoyed. With both of us. She said it was very wrong to meet her brother secretly, and that you would be angry if you knew. And that she would agree with you.' Lisette added sadly, 'She said I mustn't see him again—she wouldn't even let me say goodbye.'

Edward thought for a moment. 'So did you? See him again?'

'Oh, no!' said Lisette. 'Of course not, Edward! Miss Petrie said I wasn't to. She was quite clear about that.'

'Well, it seems to me that very little harm was done, though I am surprised you said nothing about it to me, or your aunt.'

'I was afraid you'd think he wasn't good enough for me,' said Lisette simply.

'You're quite right! Your governess's brother! What a fine match that would be!' said Julia sarcastically. 'Of course, it would be wonderful for him! One cannot blame Miss Petrie for wishing to promote such a wind-fall for her brother.'

'He was just a friend! And Miss Petrie had nothing to do with it! Why are you so unpleasant about her, Aunt Julia? What has she done to make you so unkind towards her? I don't believe for a minute that she would plan anything of the sort.'

'You will allow that I've been about the world a good

bit more than you, my dear. I am considerably older and wiser. Miss Petrie's motives are perfectly comprehensible. It would be a negligent sister, indeed, who would fail to see the advantage to her brother in marrying a girl who is a considerable heiress!'

Lisette stood up twin flags of anger burning in her cheeks. 'Edward, I've told you everything now. I'm sorry for deceiving you. I'm even sorrier that my conduct has caused you to be so unfair to Miss Petrie. But if you will excuse me, I should like to go to my room.'

Edward gave Julia an exasperated look, but merely said, 'Of course you may go, if you wish, Lisette. You've been very honest with us.' He hesitated, then said, 'Try not to blame yourself for Miss Petrie's departure. She had already planned to leave. Your behaviour wasn't the only cause.'

'Forget Miss Petrie and reflect instead on the possibility of other, more serious, consequences of your conduct, Lisette,' said Julia. 'We want no more dealings with unsuitable men. I would have thought you'd have learned your lesson from what happened on Antigua with the Arandez fellow!'

'Aunt Julia! This is nothing like what happened on Antigua! If you want to know the truth, I talked to Miss Petrie about that, too, and she helped me more than you or anyone else! You just forbade me to see Ricardo again, or even to talk about him, and that left me feeling that I was somehow betraying Papa. Miss Petrie helped me to understand what Papa had *really* wanted.'

'Marriage to her brother, I suppose?' said Julia nastily.

'No! Oh, I can't talk to you!'

'Tell us, Lisette,' said Edward quietly. 'What did Miss Petrie say?'

'That I wasn't to worry any more about what Ricardo had said. Papa would want me to be happy. To know the world, before I made any big decisions. I still don't know what I feel about Ricardo, Edward, but I don't believe any more that we are betrothed. She at least did that for me. And now you've sent her away!' Lisette ran out of the room, and the door shut with a bang behind her.

'Was that really necessary, Julia?' asked Edward wearily. 'The child was already upset enough, without being reminded of Ricardo Arandez and what was probably the most distressing experience of her life.'

'Oh, I know where you stand, Edward!' snapped Julia. 'You're still so besotted with the Petrie woman, you'd see your niece marry her brother without doing a thing to prevent it. But I'll make sure she won't, if it's the last thing I do! In fact, I shall tell her so now!' Julia swept out and was halfway up the stairs before Edward could catch her.

'Julia!' he shouted.

She stopped and turned, her face contorted with spite. 'You won't stop me! That Petrie woman has turned Lisette against us all, and I'm not going to let her get away with it!'

She turned to carry on up the stairs, and screamed as one of the treads gave way with a large crack and she almost fell through the hole. She was still screaming as Edward leapt up the stairs and picked her up. He checked she hadn't seriously damaged herself, then carried her to her room. She was still kicking and screaming, swearing not to spend a moment longer in a house that showed every sign of wanting to finish her off.

Her maid arrived, but not all their efforts could calm her down, and in the end he slapped her, not too gently.

She stopped screaming and looked at him with loathing. 'I shall leave this house tomorrow, Edward! It isn't safe. It's tried three times to kill me and I won't wait for a fourth!'

'You've had a bad shock, Julia, but this is nonsense,' he said sharply.

'It isn't, it isn't! I refuse to live here! I want to go back to London tomorrow! I shall go mad if I don't.'

'In that case it might be wiser to go.' He thought for a moment. 'In fact, I think it would be better for all of us. You and the girls can leave tomorrow and I shall see that the house is properly shut down and follow you in a day or two. You'd better rest now. I'll leave you in the hands of your maid—she'll see to you. And I'll have a look at that stair. It will have to be put right straight away.'

He left the room and went to the head of the stairs. One of the estate handymen was examining the damage.

'I can't understand it,' he said, shaking his head. 'I've never known such a thing to happen before, Mr Barraclough. Never! Old Mrs Carstairs kept it all in such good repair!'

When Pip heard they were leaving she begged Edward to let her stay behind with him.

'I'll be good, Edward! I don't want to go to London, especially not with Aunt Julia.'

'I'm afraid you'll soon have to go to London. We're all leaving Wychford. But I'll see if I can persuade your aunt to let you travel with me. It will only be a day or two longer, mind!'

Julia, who was quite broken down by the latest accident, shuddered and readily agreed. 'My nerves won't take any more. The thought of being cooped up in a carriage with Philippa all the way to London appals me. By all means, let her wait for you! But Lisette must come with me.'

'Of course. Try to make friends again with Lisette, Julia. She's feeling very low. We don't want her to fall back into the melancholy state she was in last year. When you're feeling better you might think about dresses for her come-out. That should cheer her up.'

'Oh, I have great plans for that. I shall see if Madame Rosa will make some of her wardrobe. Daisy Ledbury was not at all sure she would. It seems Madame is in great demand, and can more or less choose her own clientèle. Perhaps I can persuade Lady Ledbury to put in a word for us.'

Edward saw them off with relief. Lisette was quiet, but she seemed to have repented of her outburst of the night before. The girl had been right, of course. There had been real animosity behind Julia's witch-hunt. Quite why, he wasn't sure. He wasn't sure, either, what he felt about Octavia himself. He had been less than impartial when listening to the story of her meetings with her supposed lover, of course. For a moment he had been beside himself with jealousy and murderous rage, unable to think clearly at all. The unaccustomed violence of his feelings had so shocked him that he had been glad to let her go. She posed too many problems, and he had decided long ago that what he wanted was a life without them. No wife, no one to remind him of his duty, no responsibilities. Above all, no one to make him feel as uncivilised as he had for a few minutes the day before. Never!

Except…he had a suspicion that, along with the problems, something else, something immensely important, had gone too, something he might regret.

* * *

Edward had no time for self-questioning during the next two days. He had a thousand things to do, the most important of which was to set in motion proper repairs to the staircase. Why *had* that stair cracked? The handyman couldn't explain it at all. He swore that the rest of the staircase was in excellent condition, with no sign of woodworm or decay. But what else could it have been? The idea that the house was trying to get rid of Julia was nonsense, of course! Hysterical rubbish!

There were other things to do. Wychford was a large house, and though there were still almost four of their six months' tenancy left, he doubted any of them would come back. Still, he wanted to leave it suitably prepared. Pip accompanied him everywhere, chatting, commenting, asking questions. Her talk was full of Miss Petrie and all the wonderful things they had done together.

'Of course, she did promise that she would see me in London. And I think she will, don't you, Edward? I hope she does. I wonder what she's doing now? I don't think she'll be a governess to anyone else. In fact, I don't think she's really a governess at all! She wasn't looking for a post when she first arrived, you know.'

Edward stopped in his tracks. 'What was that?'

'Well, she seemed surprised to find us here. And if she was hoping to be our governess she'd have known, wouldn't she? But she knew our name. It's funny, isn't it? I wish she could come back!'

On the last night, once Pip was in bed, Edward walked round the house checking that everything was in order. He came back to Pip's room to see that she was asleep, and as he came out he stopped by the narrow staircase up to the room in the tower. He had not been up there since…since that day. He couldn't avoid it any longer. It, too, should be checked. He went up the stairs, unlocked the door and entered the room.

It looked dim and ghostly in the faint light of his lamp. Ashes from the fire lit by Octavia lay in the fireplace. They could stay there. He walked to the chair and looked down. What a storm of feeling had filled this little room! For a short while the world had been on fire for him here… He turned, and a flicker from his lamp was reflected in the gilt of a picture frame on the table. He went over and picked it up. Mrs Carstairs's little daughter, Theophania. The child had been younger than Pip when she died, and there had never been any others.

The table was crowded with other pictures—miniatures, paintings, drawings… Obviously friends and family, people she knew. His eye was caught by one particular picture, a drawing of a young woman. It looked familiar. Picking it up, he held it close to the lamp. He had not been mistaken—it was a drawing of Octavia Petrie.

Edward studied the picture in his hand and wondered what Octavia Petrie's picture was doing on Mrs Carstairs's table, next to that of her beloved little daughter. He stood there for some minutes without moving. The room was cold, but he didn't feel it. Pip's words were going round in his mind…

She wasn't looking for a post when she first arrived…she seemed surprised to find us here…if she was hoping to be our governess she'd have known, wouldn't she?…but she knew our name…

Was this why Octavia Petrie had been so evasive about her background? He wouldn't have known anything about her family if he hadn't eavesdropped when she was talking to Pip. The keenly analytical mind that had made Edward such a success in the banking world was beginning to work. Was it possible that Octavia Petrie was Mrs Carstairs's mysterious niece? If Pip was right, she could well have come to Wychford merely to look it over, and their early arrival had taken her by surprise. But in that case why hadn't she simply explained? He now concentrated hard on that first interview. The more of it he remembered, the clearer it became that she had *not* come with the intention of working for him. No, by God, she wasn't any sort of governess! She had never said she was. The mistake had been his. But why had she not corrected him? Why had she embarked on such a mad escapade?

He shook his head. He had no idea. But one thing was clear even to an idiot like himself. She had pulled the wool over his eyes pretty neatly. Octavia Petrie had made a fool of Edward Barraclough, and had probably enjoyed doing it! What a fine joke it must have seemed to her—the prospect of being employed by her own tenant! No wonder he had seen irony in her eyes, had sensed challenge in her attitude, though none was ever openly expressed. How she must have laughed!

It must have been a shock to her when she found she was human, after all, when she had found herself caught in the end by something she *couldn't* control—little Miss Governess in the grip of straightforward, red-blooded passion. Of course she had fled! She was a fraud! Perhaps she *had* even introduced her brother to Lisette for her own purposes! He slammed her picture angrily down on the table, kicked the ashes so that they were properly spread, and left the room, locking it firmly behind him. He was finished with the whole business of his late governess! Miss Octavia Petrie was as dead to him as those ashes up there in the room. He had been saved from making one of the biggest mistakes in his life!

The next day he and Pip left Wychford. Pip made him pause at the bend for a last look. It was a dull day and the house had lost its quirky smile.

'What are you staring at, Pip? Wychford is empty.'

'But it isn't dead, Edward. I think it looks as if…as if it is waiting.'

'Come!' he said brusquely. 'I don't know what it could be waiting for. We're most unlikely to come back again.'

'Oh, look!'

'What is it now?' asked Edward a little testily.

'Didn't you see? The house smiled again!'

'Philippa, if you talk very much like that you will be thought mad. And your aunt will blame *me* for it! There are some stray patches of sunshine about. It was probably one of those hitting the windows. Now, no more talk of the house—it's London for us, midget.'

Edward decided he had one last duty before he finally put Octavia Petrie and her brother out of his mind. Lisette had clearly been very interested in Harry Petrie, and he owed it to her to learn a little more about the fellow, just in case he ever surfaced again. If he was the fortune-hunter Julia thought him, then he would certainly try to meet Lisette in London. The landlord had said he had the look of a soldier. So Edward selected one of the biggest gossips at the Horse Guards, a man for whom he had done a favour or two in the past, and went along to see him. Sir Charles said he would be delighted to assist. 'Petrie? Petrie… Let me think…'

'His brother Stephen was killed at Waterloo. Does that help?'

'Not much. Have you any idea how many were killed at Waterloo? But, wait! Petrie is the family name of the Warnhams. It's just possible that he's related to one of them… Leave it with me a day or two, old fellow. I'll do what I can.'

When Edward went back Sir Charles was triumphant. 'I was right! Lieutenant Harry Petrie of the Guards. That's probably the one you want. It fits together. He did have a brother who was killed at Waterloo.'

'Related to the Warnhams, you say?'

Sir Charles brayed with laughter. 'Related to them? I should say so! Indeed, I should! Young Harry will inherit the Warnham title one day, unless his brother Arthur can produce a son—which doesn't seem very likely now.'

'You mean…Harry Petrie is the son of an *earl*?'

'Exactly! The family is quite a large one—'

'Eight of them,' murmured Edward.

'What's that? Seven, dear chap. One of 'em died at Waterloo, remember. Now there are only two sons, the rest are daughters.'

'Respectable?'

'Highly! They're related to half the aristocracy in England. Their mother was a Cavendish, their paternal grandmother a Ponsonby, and, of the five daughters, one is married to the Duke of Monteith, another is the Marchioness of Rochford, a third married abroad—a French Count, I think… I forget the other, but it's equally respectable. Warnham's youngest daughter is the only one not married. She was one of the toasts of the Season a few years back, but she didn't fancy any of us. Pity.

She was rich, pretty, well connected. She'd have been a prize for some lucky man. A cool customer, though. Hard to please.'

'Was she, indeed?' asked Edward.

'Oh, yes! Lady Octavia's heart would never rule her head! Her mother died just before the end of the Season, and she never came back to London, but I'd have heard if she had married. Of course, she's worth a good bit more now. Inherited a handsome estate from her god-mother, I hear.'

Edward decided he had heard enough about Octavia for the moment. He said, 'Do you know anything about Harry Petrie himself? Is he wild? Does he gamble? Drink?'

'No more than the rest of them. Less than most, I'd say. Why are you so interested in young Harry? If you had a daughter I'd say you were pinning your sights on him, but you haven't. What's the interest?'

'One of my relatives came across him. I just wanted to check.'

'I hear Petrie is sending in his papers. If he enters the marriage market, you'd better get the girl's mother to work fast. He's bound to be one of next Season's mat-rimonial prizes!'

'Quite!' said Edward somewhat sourly. 'I'm very obliged to you, Stainforth. Let me know when I can do something for you.'

He went back to North Audley Street relieved, at least, that his niece had not fallen into the hands of a common adventurer. A match with young Harry Petrie ought to be approved by the stickiest of guardians. All the same, he sincerely hoped that Lisette would find someone else. The less he had to do with the Lady Octavia Petrie and her family the better it would suit him! Not just the owner of Wychford, but a star, the daughter of an earl, related to half the best families in the kingdom! What a clever little actress she was! How she must have resented his own and Julia's treatment of her—but never, not by a word, had she ever given a hint of her elevated rank. Why the devil had she done it? A cheap adventure? My Lady joining the ranks of the common people? Perhaps she had even done it for a wager!

Whatever it had been, he resented it. He resented the way she had deceived him, the fool she had made of him. He resented his own blindness. But most of all he resented the manner in which she still walked about his mind, taunting him with the memory of the way it had felt to hold her in his arms, filling him with unfulfilled desire. Damn the rich, beautiful, well-connected Lady Octavia Petrie! Why couldn't he forget her?

Octavia, too, was forced to postpone consideration of what had happened at Wychford. After taking the precaution of telling Jem put her down at the gates to Ashcombe and waiting till he had driven off again, she had asked the lodgekeeper to take her up to the main house. Here she was greeted with astonishment by Lady Dorney, and borne off straight up to her room, where she started to change.

'I should think so, too! Wherever did you get that shabby dress, Octavia? And what have you been doing with yourself? You don't look at all the thing!'

'I…I've had a difficult time during the past few days. Mrs Barraclough arrived, and there was really no reason why I should stay. So I came home.'

'What are your plans?'

'There are one or two things I have to do, promises

I made, and then we shall see. Tell me what has been happening here. I know that Harry is back—he came to Wychford to find me.'

'So that's where he went! There was quite a scene here when he first arrived home. At the end of it Harry stormed out without telling anyone where he was going. Tell me, has Arthur always been as overbearing as this?'

'Yes,' said Octavia briefly. 'Harry and I could never stand him. I don't expect Papa said much.'

'Well, no. But it was obvious that he really agreed with Arthur. Poor Rupert! He got quite agitated, especially when Harry left in such a temper. I had to spend the whole of the next day calming him down.'

Octavia smiled. 'It was lucky you were at hand. You are so good for him.'

'I'm glad to hear you say that, Octavia. As a matter of fact, your father and I…'

Octavia took one look at her cousin's expression and laughed. 'Don't tell me!' she said. 'Let me guess—you and Papa have decided to get married!'

'Do you mind?'

'Not in the least—it's what I wanted!' Octavia put her arms round Lady Dorney and hugged her. 'I am so pleased for you both!'

'We decided that we enjoyed each other's company so much that I might as well stay here all the time. It isn't what you'd call a great romance, Octavia. But at my age, I don't look for one.'

'Well, I think it very romantic! Papa is a lucky man!'

'Please don't think this will change things. I hope you will continue to consider this your home, my dear!'

'Thank you. But we shall have to see.'

After Lady Dorney had gone Octavia sat on the window-seat and stared out. She was truly delighted at this piece of news, but, in spite of what her cousin had said, there would be changes. The new Countess would take her stepdaughter's place as Ashcombe's chatelaine, and Octavia herself would at last be free to do as she pleased. Two months ago she would have been over the moon at the idea. But now... She sat for a while, then roused herself to go down and offer her congratulations to her father. Quite a number of things had to be done urgently before she could take time to think about her own future.

In accordance with her plans, Octavia drove over the next day to see her sister Gussie. Augusta, Duchess of Monteith, was now in her late thirties, but still had remnants of the charm and beauty that had taken London by storm twenty years before, and had enabled her to capture the Season's most eligible bachelor, the Duke of Monteith. Although the Duke was a large, lazy man with few pretensions to intellect, and Gussie a woman of energy and spirit, the marriage had been reasonably successful. She had presented her lord with four healthy children, the youngest of whom was about to go to Eton, and they now shared an easygoing tolerance towards each other, which satisfied them both. Octavia suspected that neither was wholly faithful, but if they did indulge in any affairs, they were very discreet ones. She had never heard any scandal about them. It was not the sort of marriage that had ever tempted Octavia, however.

The Duke was out shooting for the day, and the Duchess was at home and feeling bored. She was delighted to see her sister. They gossiped for a while, deciding that their father's proposed marriage to Lady

Dorney was an excellent idea, deploring Arthur's manners, and exchanging news of other members of the family. Eventually Gussie sat back and said, 'I'm honoured by this visit of yours, Tavy, but why do I have the impression there's something behind it?'

Octavia's colour rose. She smiled and said, 'I never could hide things from you! Tell me, are you and Monteith planning to do the Season next year?'

'I expect we shall. We always do. Don't tell me you want to, too! I thought you'd given up on London? Or has the news about Papa's marriage changed your mind for you?'

'I—it's not that, exactly. But I should like to do the Season again, and I don't want to risk having an invitation from Arthur to stay in town with them.'

'Perfectly understandable. You will naturally stay with us. I should love your company, Tavy! Monteith spends most of his time in London at his clubs, and I hardly see him. This is excellent news!' Gussie sat back and beamed at Octavia. 'That's settled then.'

'Actually, there's something more. I…I want you to recommend a governess to someone.' Gussie looked puzzled and Octavia hurried on, 'I'm very fond of a particular little girl. Her guardians will be looking for a new governess for her, and I want to make sure she has someone suitable, someone kind as well as efficient. Pip is a very special little girl. I remembered that your youngest is about to finish with the schoolroom, and thought of your Miss Cherrifield. Has she already found something else?'

'Not yet. I've hung on to her as long as I could! You could tell your friends about Cherry, if you wish. She would be ideal.'

'Er…that's not possible. I mustn't appear in the affair. You see, the woman who is most likely to choose a governess for Pip dislikes me. But a recommendation from a Duchess would impress her no end.'

Gussie looked at her sternly. 'You're not up to your tricks, are you? We're all very fond of Cherry here. I want her to find a good place. She is not to be made part of a game.'

'No, no! When you meet Pip, you'll see why I want to help. And when you meet her guardian's wife, you'd know why I couldn't do it personally! Please do this, Gussie. It's important to me.'

The Duchess looked at her youngest sister. 'I suspect there's more to this than meets the eye, little sister. Who is Pip? And what is your connection with her?'

'I... Gussie, don't tell Papa, but for the past two months *I* was Pip's governess! We were all at Wychford together.'

Gussie had never been easy to shock. She sat back and regarded her sister with amusement. 'A governess! So that's what you were doing there all that time! I did wonder. But...how on earth did you become a governess? And who is Pip?'

'Philippa Barraclough. There were two Barraclough girls—Pip and her sister Lisette.'

'Are they related to Edward Barraclough, the banker?'

'His nieces.'

Gussie put on a frown and said, 'Octavia Petrie, I am beginning to suspect the worst. Explain, if you please!'

'Wh...what do you mean?'

'Edward Barraclough is one of London's most eligible bachelors. *And* one of its most hardened. Are you telling me that you've been living down at Wychford with such a handsome brute for the past two months, teaching his nieces, and that is *all*? Impossible!'

'Well, it's true!'

'What? He employed Lady Octavia Petrie as a *governess*? Try telling that to the *ton*!'

'Er...not exactly. He didn't know who I was. He thought I was a parson's daughter.'

Gussie sat up and said, 'And to think I was feeling bored! 'Fess up, Tavy! I shan't rest till I've heard the lot.'

Chapter Thirteen

Octavia gave up and told her sister most of what had happened at Wychford. Not all. When she came to the end Gussie gazed at her sister in astonishment and said, 'Amazing! I would never have believed it!'

Then she put her head on one side and said, 'However, I think there's a little more to it, isn't there? I don't believe you spent all that time in Edward Barraclough's company without feeling just a tiny bit attracted.'

Octavia shrugged. 'You're right, of course,' she said a touch bitterly. 'I did what every governess is said to do. I fell in love with the master.'

'So this is why you want to do the Season? To try to win him? I'm sorry to have to say this, Tavy. You wouldn't be the first to attempt it, but you'd be the first if you got anywhere near him!'

'I wouldn't begin to try! For reasons which I refuse to go into, Mr Barraclough despises me.'

'He made love to you and you let him,' said Gussie, going unerringly to the heart of the matter.

Octavia nodded. 'And when he finds out who I really am he'll add deception to the list of my crimes. No, I don't think Edward Barraclough will fall for my charms. That's not the reason I want to do the Season.'

'Then what is it?'

Octavia leaned forward. 'I grew to love those girls, Gussie, and you will love them, too. I've told you about Pip, but there's Lisette as well. She's coming out next spring, and I want to help her, too. Julia Barraclough can't do nearly as much for the girl as I could. Could you use your influence with Sally Jersey to get vouchers for Almack's for the Barracloughs?'

'I should imagine Edward Barraclough has more influence with Sally Jersey than I have, my dear,' said Gussie drily. 'She has an eye for a fascinating man.'

'But it isn't the sort to get the patronesses to agree to vouchers! Gussie, Lisette is not quite seventeen, and she's the loveliest girl I think I've ever seen. And just as sweet-natured.'

Gussie blinked. 'That's praise indeed!'

'Harry thinks so, too.'

'Aha! Do I scent a plot, after all? Is poor Harry to be seduced into settling down and producing a family? You're the last person I'd have expected to find playing Arthur's game!'

'It would be a perfect match for him, I assure you, but I wouldn't try to force it. Lisette needs time. There's a young man on Antigua and she has still to decide what she really thinks about him...'

Gussie surveyed her sister. 'I'm not sure I'm doing the right thing, helping you like this with the Barracloughs. You're too close to them, Tavy. You might do better to put them out of your mind. *All* of them.'

'Please, Gussie! The best I can now do for Lisette is to help her forget her problems and have a wonderful Season. Please help me!'

'Oh, very well, I'll do it. Sally Jersey will hand over the vouchers, she owes me a favour or two. But I warn you, little sister, I'm going to keep a careful eye on you when we're in London!'

Edward Barraclough was not mentioned again, and for the rest of the visit they discussed practical details. Octavia left her sister feeling that things were arranging themselves quite well.

Her next move was to London to pay a visit to Bruton Street. Madame Rosa was surprised, but very gracious. She had been dressing the Warnhams' daughters, all five of them, for many years, and Octavia was a firm favourite.

'Lady Octavia! Zis is indeed a pleasure,' she said, with one glance destroying any illusions Octavia might have about what she was wearing. 'I see you need my 'elp. Immediately. Are you planning to do ze Season next year?'

'I rather thought I might, *madame*.'

'You will need a new wardrobe, of course. 'ow many years since you were in London?'

'Too many,' said Octavia with a smile.

For a while they discussed trends, styles and materials. It was too early to make final decisions or arrange times for fittings, but Madame asked Octavia not to leave it too late. 'We are so busy, milady! You 'ave no idea! All ze world wants Madame Rosa to dress zare daughters. I do not, of course, accept most of zem. Indeed, I accept very few new clients now.'

'I wonder if you might make an exception?' said Octavia. 'I have a young friend who, I assure you, will make a sensation in Society when she comes out next year. She is very beautiful, Madame. She would be worth dressing. A Miss Lisette Barraclough.'

'It is not easy…I 'ave so many valued existing clients, Lady Octavia…'

'As a favour to me,' said Octavia, with a touch of firmness in her tone.

'Zen I will! Of course I will! If you would bring 'er to see me…?'

'I can't do that. In fact, I should be obliged to you if you do not mention my name at all, especially not to the person who will probably come with her—her aunt, Mrs Henry Barraclough.'

'*Alors*, am I to make dresses for zees Mrs Barraclough, too?' demanded Madame Rosa.

Octavia smiled again. 'Not if you are too busy, Madame,' she said sweetly. 'Just Miss Lisette.'

Satisfied that she had done everything she could to smooth the way for her girls, Octavia went back to Ashcombe. She was at last free to think about her own future.

In fact, the delay had given her turbulent emotions time to settle. After the scene in Mrs Carstairs's room, she had already decided she must leave Wychford, so Julia Barraclough's accusations had not made any difference to her plans. But Edward's readiness to believe them, his harshness, his cruel interpretation of her motives, had been a bitter blow. She had expected him to think less of her after her wanton behaviour in the tower room, but he had been even more contemptuous than she had imagined. Gussie need have no fear that she would throw herself at Edward Barraclough in London! She wouldn't risk any more of his contempt.

The events at Wychford were now in the past, and

she was ready to pick herself up and start to rebuild her self-respect, without any interference from Edward Barraclough. She had been a fool. But foolishness was not a crime. And though nothing could excuse her wanton behaviour, she could see now that there had been reasons for it. Intense physical attraction had played no part in her experience of life, and she had been perilously unaware of its power. For a while in that tower room she had almost drowned in a sudden onslaught of desire, the irresistible excitement of a man's caresses. But now she was at least a wiser, if sadder, woman, with some sense of self-preservation. She would never risk such temptation again.

And what about the man who had brought about such a devastating change in calm, level-headed Octavia Petrie? What about her feelings for Edward Barraclough? It was truly ironic that the man whose opinion of her was so low had turned out to be the one man whose good opinion she wanted more than anything in the world, the one man she could love. It was unlikely that she would ever marry him, but it would be impossible to marry anyone else.

Octavia put this thought firmly behind her. Edward Barraclough was lost to her. But she had grown to love his nieces, and Harry was on the way to falling in love with Lisette. Knowing them both as well as she did, she truly believed they could be happy together. She had already done something towards smoothing the girls' way in London. Now she must deliver on her promise to make sure Harry and Lisette met again. Next year's Season was only a few months away.

The ache in Octavia's heart never quite went away in spite of all her famous self-discipline. But she was

kept busy with her preparations for London, and time
went by with surprising speed. Her father and his cousin
were married in December. The occasion was a quiet
but happy one, only marginally marred by Arthur's pon-
derous speech of congratulation. Christmas came and
went, and soon it was the end of January and time to
think of moving to London. By the end of February
Octavia was comfortably settled in the Monteiths' man-
sion in St James's Square, and the two sisters were busy
with appointments with the mantua maker, the milliner
and all the other purveyors of the fashionable image.

They went about London, renewing old acquaintances, seeing the sights, and completing their ward-
robes. Octavia breathed a sigh of relief when she
learned that the Barracloughs were staying with friends
in Gloucestershire, and were not expected back before
the middle of March. Her own visits to Madame Rosa
were more or less over, so there was no risk of seeing
any of the Barracloughs there. Though she knew that
they would all have to meet sooner or later, she pre-
ferred to choose her own time and place. It must not
happen by accident, before they were all prepared.

The moment came. It was announced in the *Gazette*'s
daily list of arrivals in London that Mr and Mrs Henry
Barraclough of Antigua, together with their two nieces,
had taken up residence in South Audley Street. Miss
Lisette Barraclough would be introduced to Society during the forthcoming Season.

There was no mention of Mr Edward Barraclough,
and Octavia could only assume that he had not yet returned to the capital. It seemed a good time to reveal
her true identity to the rest of the Barracloughs. Though
she had no liking for Julia, she had no desire to cause

her a public loss of face. Their first meeting must take place in private. On the other hand, if she sent a note asking Julia to receive her, and signed it with her own name, it would certainly result in a refusal. So, two days later, she wrote a note to the house in South Audley Street, asking if she might call on Mrs Barraclough the following day, and signed it 'Mrs Carstairs's niece'. Julia ought to be sufficiently intrigued to agree to see her.

It went exactly as she had foreseen. Mrs Barraclough had expressed her pleasure to receive Mrs Carstairs's niece, but when Octavia walked into the room she stood up and exclaimed in a voice quivering with rage,

'Octavia Petrie! What are you doing here? Who let you in? How dare you present yourself in my house!' She went towards the bellrope to summon a servant, but before she could pull it Octavia said quickly,

'Mrs Barraclough, pray forgive me, but please don't do that! Give me a few moments, I beg you. I really am Mrs Carstairs's niece. I'm afraid I have been very unfair to you, and I've come to apologise. I'd like to make what amends I can.'

Julia looked at her suspiciously. 'You! Mrs Carstairs's niece? The owner of Wychford? What is this nonsense?'

'If you'll allow me to explain… Perhaps I ought to introduce myself properly.'

'I already know who you are! You're Octavia Petrie. Or is that a lie? Are you really Octavia *Smith*, perhaps?'

'No, my name is Petrie. I'm the youngest daughter of Lord Warnham.'

Julia sat down suddenly. 'But…but that's not possible! You were a governess!'

'That was a misunderstanding, a mistake made by your nieces and…and your brother-in-law. I should never have let it continue. I assure you, I am Lord Warnham's daughter.'

'The *Earl* of Warnham?' Octavia nodded. 'You're the Lady Octavia Petrie?'

Octavia nodded again and said, 'Please forgive me for deceiving you. It was very wrong of me. That's why I've come today. It was certain we should meet soon, and I wanted to explain it all beforehand.'

Julia sat for a moment, then said slowly, 'So your brother—Harry Smith—is the son of Lord Warnham?'

'Yes.' For the life of her Octavia could not prevent a touch of coolness in her voice at Julia's eye for essentials.

'I see…' After a brief pause Julia said more warmly, 'But what am I thinking of? Will you not sit down, Lady Octavia?'

'Thank you, but I hardly—'

'I'm sure Philippa would never forgive me if I let you go away without letting her have a word with you. Lisette is here, too.' Julia went to the bell rope again, and told the servant to find her nieces.

Octavia gave in and sat down. 'How are they?'

'They are both in excellent spirits. Pip has a new governess—' Julia grew red, and hesitated before going on rather hastily, 'Miss Froom was unfortunately not free, but Miss Cherrifield came with excellent recommendations. I believe she has worked with the Monteiths for the past ten years.'

'Does Pip like her?'

This was clearly of less interest to Pip's aunt. 'I believe so. The Monteiths were most enthusiastic about Miss Cherrifield. I think we were fortunate to get her.'

'That is quite a coincidence,' said Octavia innocently.

'The Duchess is my eldest sister. I am staying with her at present.'

'Really?'

The door opened before Julia could say any more, and Pip came sedately enough into the room, followed by Lisette. But when Pip saw Octavia she gave a kind of whoop and launched herself at her former governess. Ignoring Julia's scandalised objection, Octavia gathered the child up and hugged her. Lisette came over to join them. She was smiling, but Octavia saw with concern that the indefinable look of sadness was back in her eyes.

'Miss Petrie!' Lisette took Octavia's hand, then threw a puzzled glance at her aunt. 'We didn't expect to see you here. So soon, I mean.'

'Lisette, we have been…er…mistaken. Miss Petrie turns out not to have been a governess at all.'

'I knew! I knew! I said so to Edward!'

Ignoring Pip's outburst, Julia went on, 'This is Lady Octavia Petrie. She is the daughter of Lord Warnham, and the owner of Wychford.' Julia turned to Octavia with a smile. 'A charming house!'

'That's not what you said!' said Pip. 'You didn't like it. You said it was trying to kill you. That's why we all had to come away. But I liked it a lot. Do you really own Wychford, Miss Petrie? Really and truly? May I come and stay with you?'

'Don't listen to the child!' said Julia, looking slightly flustered. 'Philippa, behave yourself and stop interrupting! Lady Octavia is far too busy to entertain a little girl like you.'

'I shall be in London for some time, Pip. But, if it can be arranged, you shall pay me a visit at Wychford before long. Meanwhile, Mrs Barraclough, I wondered if you would permit me to take the girls out one afternoon?'

'Of course!' said Julia instantly. 'When are you free?'

'Tomorrow?'

'Certainly. How very kind!'

'But, Aunt Julia, you said we were to go with you tomorrow to see Mrs Allardyce—'

'The arrangement was by no means fixed,' said Julia firmly. 'I am sure Mrs Allardyce will understand perfectly. Is your brother in town, Lady Octavia?'

Lisette started and blushed, but sat back when Octavia said, 'Not yet. He is still sorting out his commitments to the Army, and is at present in France. But I believe he will be here in time for the Season.'

'We should be charmed to meet him,' said Julia.

'Charmed to meet whom?' asked a deep voice by the door. Edward Barraclough came in.

Octavia was profoundly grateful that Pip was still on her knee, that her face was half-hidden behind Pip's curls. This encounter had come somewhat sooner than she had planned—she had thought he was still out of London. She felt herself grow pale, then her cheeks were warm again as the colour surged back into them.

However, she had many times thought about their first meeting in London, and how she would deal with it. The feelings of humiliation and self-abasement following her flight from Wychford were now all behind her, and she was determined to be herself again—level-headed Lady Octavia Petrie, and no one's fool, least of all Edward Barraclough's!

So, by the time Mr Barraclough had come far enough into the room to see who their visitor was, she was quite composed—on the surface, at least.

'Edward, may I present Lady Octavia Petrie?' said Julia with a little laugh. 'What a distinguished governess you found for the girls! I hope it isn't too much of a shock for you.'

'It isn't a shock,' he said evenly. 'I discovered Lady Octavia's true identity not long after she left us.' He bowed to Octavia. 'I hope you are well?'

Octavia set Pip down, then got up and curtsied. 'Thank you, sir. But you could have saved yourself the trouble of finding out who I was. As you see, I've come to make my own apologies for deceiving you all.'

'It was no trouble, ma'am. It was incidental. I discovered your secret in the course of investigating your brother.' His tone was coolly businesslike.

'Really?' said Octavia, stiffly. 'May I ask why you found it necessary to investigate anyone at all?'

Edward's smile of apology was less than sincere. 'You must forgive me. I had to make sure that my ward had not fallen into the hands of some adventurer or other. At the time "Harry Smith" seemed a very dubious character.'

'Edward!' exclaimed Julia. 'Mr Petrie is the son of the Earl of Warnham!'

'That is what I found, along with the truth about Lady Octavia here. Has she told you she owns Wychford, as well? However, being the son of an Earl would not necessarily guarantee Mr Petrie's respectability,' said Edward drily. He turned to Octavia again. 'You will no doubt be relieved to hear that I heard nothing to his discredit.'

'Relieved?' asked Octavia coldly. 'What can you mean, sir? I know my brother. Whatever *you* may have heard about him is a matter of indifference to me.'

'Edward, does this mean I could meet Mr Petrie with your approval?' asked Lisette hesitantly.

'Once you are out, and have been suitably introduced, it would be difficult to object,' replied her uncle with a touch of impatience. 'But there are many other equally eligible young men who would be delighted to know you, Lisette. Don't set your mind too early on anyone in particular.'

'Of course not,' said Lisette in a subdued voice.

Julia decided to intervene. 'Lady Octavia has offered to take Lisette and Philippa out tomorrow, Edward. Isn't that kind? And what do you think? Her elder sister is Miss Cherrifield's former employer, the Duchess of Monteith!'

Edward shot a sharp glance at Octavia, but she met his eyes and said calmly, 'A surprising coincidence. I knew my sister had finished with Miss Cherrifield's services, but that she should end up with Pip... I believe she is an excellent governess.'

'No doubt,' he said drily. There was a short pause, then he asked, 'At what time do you intend to call for my nieces tomorrow? I might be here to accompany you.'

'Edward! That would be lovely! Just like our walks at Wychford!' cried Pip.

Octavia was not sure quite why Edward Barraclough wanted to join them in their walk and she was not at all sure she ought to spend any time at all in his company. But it was difficult to refuse in the face of Pip's enthusiasm.

'That would be delightful, sir,' she said woodenly. 'Though I am surprised you have the time.'

'Not at all, ma'am,' he said smoothly. 'I shall count it well spent.'

* * *

The next afternoon Gussie watched in amusement as Octavia tried on one walking dress after another.

'Those two young girls must be very difficult to please,' she said.

'Why do you say that?' asked Octavia, twisting round to see how the latest attempt looked from the back.

'I've seen you discard three of Madame Rosa's best efforts, any one of which suits you perfectly. Especially the one in zephyrine silk.'

'The blue one? You think that suits me best, do you? Then I'll wear that,' said Octavia, nodding to her maid to find it.

'Tavy, why don't you tell me what you're up to? I refuse to believe that all this anxiety is in order to impress the Misses Barraclough. Are you quite sure that Edward Barraclough isn't accompanying you? Or are you planning to meet some other young man on your outing?'

'Of course not!' said Octavia indignantly. 'As if I would! The girls' uncle did say he might accompany us, yes. But I assure you, I have no desire to impress Edward Barraclough. I've told you, I'm now indifferent to him! Why this catechism?'

'Because you are behaving so unlike yourself! Martha has arranged that collar perfectly well, little sister, so stop fiddling with it. I wish to talk to you seriously.'

'I can't. I haven't time. Thank you for your advice, I think this blue outfit looks quite well on me. Goodbye, Gussie!' Octavia made her escape before her sister could probe any further.

Gussie looked thoughtful, then sent for her husband's secretary, who looked after her social arrangements. 'My rout party, James. I should like to add to the list of people to be invited...'

* * *

When Octavia arrived at the Barracloughs', she found another carriage already waiting outside. Pip was standing by it, and as soon as she saw Octavia she cried,

'Miss Petrie! We're going in Edward's carriage. He says it's better. And he says I can sit up with the coachman!'

'How kind!' said Octavia with something of a snap.

'You don't mind, do you? I'm sure you and he and Lisette will be more comfortable in the back.'

It was a sunny day, and Pip would be disappointed not to accept her uncle's offer. Octavia gave in gracefully, and prepared to descend. Edward Barraclough came out and took over from the groom who was helping her. Her hand jumped convulsively when he took it, but she controlled herself, and allowed him to lead her to his carriage and help her into it.

'Where had you intended to go?' he asked.

'I had thought we would take the carriage into the park, then walk for a while by the Serpentine,' said Octavia 'It's a poor substitute for the grounds at Wychford, but the girls might like to see the water fowl, and there are usually one or two small boats, too. But of course, if you have other plans, sir, you need not feel obliged to fall in with any of mine!'

He regarded her in silence. Then he turned, lifted Pip up next to his coachman, and seated himself opposite Lisette and Octavia. He surveyed them. 'What a very pretty sight! Hyde Park, it is!'

The carriage moved off and Octavia turned to Lisette. 'I never saw you riding at Wychford. I assume you do ride?'

'Oh, yes! I love riding.'

'Then you will enjoy seeing Rotten Row. We could perhaps go riding tomorrow or the next day.'

'Rotten Row. That's a funny name! What's rotten about it?' asked Pip, twisting round to talk.

'Nothing at all, Pip! In earlier times it was known as the *route du roi*—the king's road between Kensington Palace and St James. I don't know how it came to be changed.'

Edward drawled, 'Instructive, as ever, I see. Old habits obviously die hard.'

'Some more quickly than others,' Octavia said coolly, and turned her attention back to Lisette. 'In the Season it is the thing to be seen riding or driving along Rotten Row between the hours of four and six. You will see most of the polite world there. But the best time to enjoy a ride is before the rest of the world is about—at eleven or twelve.'

They drew up just past the entrance to the park and looked at the scene along the Row. Though it was still early in the Season, it was already quite crowded.

'I don't call that riding!' said Edward. 'A tea party on horseback, more like! It's quite impossible to have a really good gallop.'

'Not only impossible, but frowned on, too! You mustn't do it, Lisette. Not if you wish to be approved of by the ladies of the *ton*.'

'Lady Jersey has been very kind already, Miss—Lady Octavia. Aunt Julia has received vouchers for Almack's.'

'That's good news!'

'I wonder what good fairy arranged for that,' murmured Edward. 'Sally Jersey isn't often so obliging to newcomers.'

'I believe it was Lady Octavia's sister, the Duchess of Monteith, Edward.'

'Was it, Lisette? Well, well, well! What a surprise!'

Edward Barraclough was at his most sardonic. 'Shall we go on? Or do you wish to walk?'

'Let's walk, Edward!' said Pip, never content to stay inactive for long.

'Lady Octavia? Is this permitted to would-be leaders of fashion?'

Octavia ignored the irony in his voice and said, 'Certainly. Shall we walk to the Serpentine?'

As they walked along, Octavia was conscious that the polite greetings of her many acquaintances could not quite hide their curiosity. She nodded and smiled calmly enough, introduced the Barracloughs when necessary, and made sure that either Pip or Lisette was always between herself and Edward Barraclough. But after a while Pip could bear such a sedate pace no longer.

'Come on, Lisette!' she cried. 'Let's see the ducks!'

Octavia tried to protest, but Edward said, 'Let them go—we can keep them in sight. You're surely not afraid of being alone with me in broad daylight in the park, are you, Octavia? What do you think I could do?'

'Why, nothing, Mr Barraclough! Except to use my given name, when I don't believe you have my permission!'

'Oh, come! We are surely beyond that stage. In private.'

Octavia stopped and faced him. She spoke so calmly, in such a measured manner, that no one watching could have guessed the emotional turbulence behind her words.

'Mr Barraclough, I am no longer a governess in your employ. I know what you think of me, but what happened at Wychford is in the past. In the eyes of the world I am a member of an honourable family, and a lady of unimpeached reputation, who could hope to be treated with respect by someone who is no more than a casual acquaintance.'

'Casual acquaintance?' The mockery in his voice was evident. 'Is that what you would call it? Forgive me, Octavia! My memory is not quite so accommodating as yours, apparently.'

Octavia walked on, trying to control her anger. She had not expected this. For some reason she had thought he would be relieved to put Wychford and all that had happened there behind him. They were now beyond the crowds, though she could still see Pip and Lisette laughing at the antics of the birds round the lake. She had wanted to do so much for them, but if this man chose he could put an end to it all. Finally she said quietly, 'If you can't master that memory of yours, then I shall be forced to leave London. Is that what you wish?'

'Of course not! Why would you have to leave London?'

'There would be no point in my staying! I have no particular liking for town life. I only came this year because of my affection for your nieces. I thought I could use what influence I have in Society on their behalf.'

'Ah! The Duchess of Monteith. I thought as much. How very affecting!'

Octavia ignored this and went on, 'I believe I could do much more for them, but only if you stop reminding me of an episode I would rather forget. The gossips would quickly become suspicious if they heard you call me Octavia. Indeed, if you really wished, you could very easily destroy my credit in the world with a few well-chosen words. I could do nothing for anyone then.' She stopped again and looked up at him with lifted chin. 'So, which is it to be, Mr Barraclough? Can you forget the governess and her shameful behaviour, or shall I leave London and go back to Ashcombe?'

Edward Barraclough looked at her with a glint of admiration in his eyes, which disturbed her.

'What makes you so sure you know what I think of you?'

'You told me. I have not forgotten what you said on the last occasion we met.'

Edward paused, then said, 'I was angry. More angry than I've ever been in my life. I agree, I was mistaken. But why didn't you tell us that "Harry Smith" was your brother? Why did you leave me to believe the worst?'

'You wouldn't have listened. You thought you *knew* the sort of woman I was, and after my behaviour that afternoon I wasn't surprised.' She waved her hand in a gesture of impatience. 'But the sooner that's forgotten the better. The important thing is whether I can help Lisette and Pip. Am I to pack my bags? Or am I to stay and do my best for them? The decision is yours.'

There was a pause. Then, 'Lady Octavia,' he said at last. 'I concede defeat. I'll try to treat you with all the respect such a highly born lady deserves.' The words were placatory, but the tone was ironic. He went on, 'But I'm not quite sure how to proceed. How well am I supposed to know you?'

'As a good friend of your nieces. You needn't pretend anything more.'

'I'm not sure—' He stopped, then went on, 'Very well. But before we embark on this particular invention, I'd like you to tell me one thing.'

'Well?'

'What do *you* think of *me*?'

Octavia had not expected this. For a wild moment she was tempted to say, 'I don't know what I think of you, whether you're good or bad, kind or unkind. I only know I love you!' What a weapon that would give him! Would he be sorry for her, embarrassed, even? Or would he laugh? Perhaps he might feel he could tempt her to forget her vaunted respectability and have an affair with him, a rival for his mistress?

Octavia drew a breath and said, 'I admire your devotion to Lisette and Pip. But other than your nieces, we have little else in common. I certainly don't intend to pursue our acquaintance further than ordinary politeness would demand. Shall we join the girls? I think Pip is ready to move on.'

Chapter Fourteen

Octavia returned to her sister's house feeling as if her emotions had had enough buffeting for a while. For the next week she took care to visit Lisette and Pip when she thought their uncle would be out elsewhere. Plans for her sister's forthcoming rout party took up quite an amount of her time, too. She was annoyed, however, when Gussie showed her the guest list.

'What is Edward Barraclough's name doing here? I didn't ask you to include him! The invitation was meant for Mr and Mrs Henry Barraclough and Lisette! I thought you didn't want me to have anything to do with the other Barraclough brother!'

Gussie raised her brows. 'I could hardly invite one without the other, Tavy! Besides, brother Edward is much better *ton*, and twice as amusing as Henry and that awful wife of his. And, in the light of what you've told me, I want to see him again for myself. Why are you angry with me for including him?'

'I'm not angry! Who said I was angry? It was a surprise, that's all. There was no need for this!'

'Of course there was, Tavy dear! But don't look so annoyed with me. I think I have another beau for you, and we owe it all to Monteith's efforts. Now, there's a surprise for both of us!'

Octavia laughed in spite of herself. Gussie so seldom had a good word to say for her large, lazy husband. She asked, 'How did it happen, Gussie?'

'Oh, don't worry! Monteith didn't have to exert himself at all! The young man is the great-nephew of one of Monteith's numerous connections in Scotland, and he introduced himself the other day at Boodle's. Monteith liked him enough to give him an invitation to the rout party. I was delighted. It means that my dear husband has at least remembered that we are giving one!'

'Poor young man! He won't know a soul.'

'I shall invite him to dinner before the party. Harry will be there, too, and he can take Mr Aransay under his wing. I think they're about the same age, and Harry has any number of friends. Now, when am I to meet these Barracloughs of yours? Shall I call on them tomorrow with you? I wish to see beautiful Miss Lisette for myself. And Cherry tells me that Philippa Barraclough is just as bright and attractive as you said, too.'

Octavia was quite wrong about Edward Barraclough. Though he was not sure himself what he thought of her, he was certainly a long way from despising her. He might still be angry at the way she had deceived him, he might wish his harsh accusations unsaid, he might even still feel a lingering enchantment. All these and more he felt. But not contempt.

More often than he liked he found himself thinking about her, smiling at the memory of that imperious little figure by the Serpentine, chin lifted in defiance as she threw down her ultimatum. Treat her properly, or she would leave. He had started out full of suspicion, mistrusting her motives in coming round to meet Julia and the girls. He had invited himself on the excursion to Hyde Park with the intention of showing her how little her newly discovered status meant to him, prepared to cut her down to size with a few well-chosen reminders of their closer encounters if she adopted any airs.

But before long he had found he was enjoying their verbal fencing, had been unable to resist teasing her into defiance, delighting in the result. She had never been subservient, but now that she was free to talk to him as an equal, her directness, her readiness to take up his challenges intrigued and charmed him. Miss Petrie, the governess, had been like no other, and the Lady Octavia, youngest daughter of the Earl of Warnham, was equally rare a creature. He found her every bit as attractive.

Edward warned himself in vain against getting too interested in her. He reminded himself how she had deceived him, had probably laughed at him, had enticed him into near madness, but he found that he still wanted to know Lady Octavia Petrie better. He guessed she had been avoiding him, but was prepared to bide his time. She could hardly avoid him at the ball being held for Lisette.

Later it was generally agreed that the Barraclough ball was one of the Season's successes. Julia had done her work well, and, in a reversal of her previous attitude, had gladly accepted Lady Octavia's offers of help. As a result, most of the cream of London society was there, including a Royal Duke, two of Almack's patronesses, the Duke and Duchess of Monteith—even, briefly, the Duke of Wellington.

With her usual genius, Madame Rosa had produced

a dress of masterly simplicity for Lisette's début. A touch of silver embroidery on the sleeves and hem of her floating white silk dress was all the decoration she had permitted. Lisette looked like the fairy princess Octavia had first thought her, her dark hair, violet eyes and delicate colouring enhanced by the silver and white dress and the posy of white roses tied with violet ribbons that she carried. She was a sensation. She was quickly surrounded by admirers, and the polite world was soon talking with enthusiasm of Lisette's beauty, her modesty, her charm. Some were so impressed that they even forgot to mention her considerable fortune.

Edward was proud of his niece, but regarded the crowd round her with a cynical eye. It wasn't often that wealth was combined with such beauty. No wonder she and Julia were under siege. He could see several well-known fortune hunters among her admirers, as well as quite a few sons of the impoverished aristocracy. Lisette was going to need all his help in the coming weeks to weed them out. He hadn't saved her from the clutches of Ricardo Arandez just to see her fall prey to an English counterpart!

After a while he relaxed and started to look round. Lisette was safe for the moment. His eye roved over the company, searching the crowd for one slight figure. When he finally saw Octavia he made his way through to her, and found her with her sister.

'Lady Octavia,' said Edward, bowing punctiliously.

The Duchess watched as Octavia said coolly, 'Mr Barraclough!' and curtsied to an exactly gauged depth. 'I believe you've met my sister, the Duchess of Monteith.'

'I've only once or twice had that privilege, but I've

met your husband many times, Duchess,' said Edward,
bowing again.

Eyes full of amused interest, Octavia's sister drawled,
'I must congratulate you on your niece, Mr Barraclough. She's the loveliest creature I've seen in years.'

Edward eyed Octavia's sister with appreciation. This
was the sort of well-born lady he knew and understood.
He could see traces of a family likeness, but, unlike
Octavia, the sophisticated woman before him was very
aware of her charm, and used it with a deliberation that
was completely foreign to her younger sister. In other
circumstances he would have spent an enjoyable hour
or two's flirtation with the Duchess of Monteith. But
not tonight! He said with a smile, 'Thank you. We are
all very proud of her.'

'She has obviously been taught by an expert,
wouldn't you say?' This time the amusement was even
more evident.

Edward gave Octavia a sharp look, then said, 'Now,
what *can* you mean by that, ma'am? I suspect your
sister has been confiding in you. Am I right?'

'Tavy and I are good friends, as well as sisters. She
has told me about Wychford.'

Edward raised an eyebrow, and Octavia said rather
quickly, 'I've told my sister a lot about Pip and…and
Lisette.'

'Ah! I see. Yes. Pip and Lisette. Duchess, the Barracloughs owe a lot to Lady Octavia, not least for her
efforts on Lisette's behalf tonight.' He gazed round. 'A
brilliant company. I doubt the Barracloughs could have
managed it by themselves. My sister-in-law is delighted
with its success.' He turned to Octavia. 'I wish you
could have been here earlier. We had a hard time with
Pip when she learned she was not allowed to come to

Lisette's ball. I had to promise to take her to see the deer and primroses at Richmond tomorrow before she was mollified. In fact, she wanted you to come, too, and I said I would ask you. Will you come? To please Pip?'

'I…er…I…'

'Of course you will, Tavy! A drive out to Richmond would be just the thing for you! You mustn't disappoint…' There was an infinitesimal pause before the Duchess went on, 'Mr Barraclough's niece.'

Octavia shot her sister a puzzled look, but said calmly, 'Thank you, sir. At what time?'

He grinned. 'May we discuss that during the next dance? Will you excuse us, Duchess?'

'Certainly.' He bowed and, before Octavia could object, took her hand and led her away.

Gussie watched them go. Edward Barraclough might have eyed her with appreciation, but she was far too experienced not to know when a man's serious attention was elsewhere. It seemed to her that, whatever Octavia thought, he was more attracted to her sister than he was willing to admit. If it were so, his intentions could hardly be anything but honorable, and she would do all she could to promote this interesting state of affairs. To see Edward Barraclough caught at last would be very satisfying, especially if he was caught by her own little sister! She smiled. Richmond Park to please Pip, indeed!

'I thought you promised to treat me with respect!' hissed Octavia as Edward escorted her on to the floor.

'What on earth can you object to now?' he asked in amazement. 'It's perfectly in order for me to ask one of my nieces' closest friends to dance, surely?'

'It was the way you did it! You didn't ask me, you

simply dragged me away from my poor sister, who is now left alone!'

'My dear girl, half the gentlemen in this room have been waiting eagerly for an opportunity to ask your sister to dance with them! She won't be alone for long. She's a very fascinating woman, Oct—Lady Octavia!'

'She was always counted the beauty of the family.'

The movement of the dance took them away from each other. When they next came together Edward said, 'I've heard that *you* were one of the toasts of London when you came out. It doesn't surprise me. You look like spring itself in that pale green dress.'

'You shouldn't listen to gossip, Mr Barraclough. Nor should you try to flatter me. Casual acquaintances, remember? In fact, I'm not at all sure I ought to come with you tomorrow, in spite of my sister's intervention. It is almost certain to cause remarks.'

'Oh, no, you can't change your mind now! And I've been thinking about this casual acquaintances business. It won't work. Sooner or later London is going to hear about your "visit" to Wychford, and will wonder why we have pretended not to know each other. Let us say rather that we are distantly connected. That makes it respectable, surely?'

'Connected?'

'Through Mrs Carstairs! Have you forgotten that your aunt was a great friend of the Barracloughs? That I am still renting the house she left you?'

He watched as she absorbed this idea. 'You may be right,' she said doubtfully. 'London is bound to hear something sooner or later... Very well! We were about to settle on a time to meet tomorrow.'

'Richmond is a fair distance, and we shan't want to hurry. We'll call for you at eleven. Or is that too early?'

'Not at all. I'll be ready!'

The music came to an end and Octavia made to go.

'Not so fast,' said Edward, keeping hold of her hand. 'I want to take you to talk to Lisette.'

'But my sister—'

'Your sister is at present enchanting Charlie Stainforth. Look at her! She wouldn't welcome you. Come!'

He led her to where Lisette was standing surrounded by a bevy of young men. But when she saw Edward and Octavia she abandoned them all.

'You found her!' she said. 'Lady Octavia, I'm so glad I can talk to you at last! At the opening of the ball I hardly saw anyone, I was so nervous! Such a long line of people waiting to meet me! I want to thank you for this.' She touched her hair, which was held up with a delicate silver clasp.

Edward watched as Octavia smiled fondly at Lisette. He had never before realised quite how sweet her smile could be. Octavia's green silk dress was a perfect foil for her colouring, and its low cut, so very different from her Wychford dresses, revealed the lovely lines of her throat and bosom… He stood, not really listening to what they were saying, but watching the two of them talking animatedly to one another, the one so dark and the other so fair… He had been quite right about 'Miss Petrie's hair'. Tonight, of course, the loose knot on top of her head, the tendrils framing her face, had been artfully arranged by an experienced maid, and diamonds sparkled among the honey-gold curls. They were not hanging halfway down her back in the rain, or tumbled in disarray, reflecting the light of leaping flames… He drew a sharp breath as his body responded to the sudden memory. It was just as vivid, just as exciting, as it had been all those weeks ago…and he had thought he had mastered it!

Lisette had been claimed by someone else, and, with a smile of apology, she let herself be carried off.

Octavia turned to him, and said with determination, 'And now we shall return to my sister!'

Edward pulled himself together and shook his head. 'Wrong, Lady Octavia!' he said. 'Even the most critical tabby allows a young woman to have two dances with the same partner in an evening. I intend to have my second now!'

'But I promised Sir Richard…'

'What a pity. The poor fellow will have to wait.' Relying on Octavia's sense of propriety not to make a fuss at his high-handed behaviour, Edward took her firmly by the arm and led her back to the floor. This time it was a waltz. He took one of her hands in his, his other arm went round her waist, and they set off.

After a moment he said, 'Do you not find the ball-room remarkably chilly, Lady Octavia?'

She frowned at him. 'No.'

'Strange. I could have sworn there was an icy draught blowing down my spine. A Lady Octavia sort of chill.' An involuntary chuckle escaped her and he said, 'That's better! I had begun to think my fingers would drop off with the cold.'

'What do you expect, sir? I have pleaded with you to treat me as a casual acquaintance—'

'Distantly connected.'

'Distantly connected! But here you are singling me out! You may have stopped calling me by my given name, but you still treat me with a lack of ceremony, which will soon set tongues wagging if it continues.'

'That is nonsense! It's all in your imagination, Oct—

Lady Octavia! What could be more unexceptionable than that Lisette's uncle should pay some polite attention to a friend who has done so much for his niece? His *nieces*! Pip would have been far easier to deal with if you had been there today. Julia has no idea how to handle her. Now, have you any more complaints, or are you ready to enjoy this waltz?'

They danced for a while in silence, and, whatever their differences might be, their steps were perfectly matched, their bodies moving as if by instinct in harmony with each other. Edward drew Octavia imperceptibly closer. She looked up and smiled. For a moment he forgot the music, forgot the other dancers, forgot everything but the enchantment of having her in his arms.

'Octavia,' he murmured, his eyes warm as he gazed down at her.

Octavia, too, had felt the magic, though she wanted none of it. Firmly suppressing her wayward feelings, she decided to open the subject of Lisette's secret worries. He might be receptive enough to listen sympathetically.

'Mr Barraclough,' she said, uncharacteristically nervous, 'I've been thinking about Lisette…'

Edward was disappointed. He had thought her smile was one of pleasure, shared pleasure. Apparently not. Suppressing a sigh, he said, 'What is it?'

'Before I left Wychford I had intended to talk to you about her, but…but there was no time. Has she told you that, after she had met my brother, she and I had a long talk?'

This time the disappointment was sharp. Had he been wrong about her after all? The English aristocracy spent half their lives looking for suitable matches, by which they meant rich matches, for their sons. Or in this case, brothers. Why had he believed that Octavia was different from the rest of her kind? He said with resignation, 'I suppose I ought to have expected this. Have you any idea how many other young men would like to marry into the Barraclough wealth, Lady Octavia? You might say your brother has a head start on all the others, but that doesn't mean I shall look with any greater degree of approval on him. I'd like Lisette to be happy, but I'm not at all sure she should throw herself away on a good-looking young soldier who has already persuaded her to meet him in secret!'

Octavia gasped and began, 'I didn't—'

He brushed this aside. His eyes were no longer warm as he continued, 'I'm disappointed in you. However beautiful you look tonight, you surely can't have thought you could charm me into changing my mind on such a serious matter as this!'

Angry colour flooded Octavia's cheeks, and she pulled away from him. 'I doubt I could charm you into doing anything at all!' she said, and started to walk off the floor. He pursued her to the end of the ballroom, where they had left her sister. She was not there. Here Octavia stopped and turned. She said in a low voice, 'For your information, sir, I wanted to talk to you about something quite different! I am as anxious as you that Lisette should be happy, whatever her choice. But she would not be ''throwing herself away'', if she married my brother!'

Irritated at the turn the conversation had taken, he said coolly, 'Unlike the rest of the world, ma'am, I do not believe a title immediately bestows virtue on its possessor, so please don't quote your brother's prospects of an earldom at me!'

'I was not about to! You are impossible, sir!' Eyes sparkling, twin flags of colour in her cheeks, Octavia faced him angrily.

Edward felt his own anger drain away. 'Octavia—' he began ruefully.

'And *don't* call me by my given name!'

'Ah! There you are!' They both looked round. Gussie was making her way towards them. She looked from one to the other, and raised an eyebrow.

'Have you arranged a time?' she asked. 'As far as I remember, Richmond is more than an hour's drive. You'll need to be up early, Octavia.'

Edward decided that discretion was the better part of valour. He had a feeling that Octavia was in such a temper that she would cry off their excursion if he gave her the slightest opportunity. He said briefly, 'Thank you for the dances, Lady Octavia. I shall call for you at eleven. Duchess, do you by some miracle have the next dance free? May I?'

He led Octavia's sister on to the floor, and afterwards stayed well clear of the Petrie family for the rest of the evening.

The next morning Edward collected Pip and drove to St James's Square. In spite of her anger the previous evening, he was reasonably sure that Octavia would accompany them to Richmond. Pip was a powerful draw. And he felt a spurt of pleased relief when he saw that she was dressed and ready for them. He wanted to talk to Octavia—their quarrel the previous evening had left unfinished business between them, and it needed to be cleared up.

Pip greeted Octavia with her usual enthusiasm, then settled down between her and Edward, eagerly watching

the sights as they drove out down the Bath Road towards Brentford and the bridge at Kew.

Once at Richmond they left the carriage in charge of
the grooms and walked. Pip was delighted. 'Miss Petrie!
Look! Do you see the deer?'

'Lady Octavia will get annoyed with you, Pip, if you
fail to call her by her correct name,' said Edward.

'No, I shan't, Pip! But I behaved very badly in pretending to be simply Miss Petrie. I shouldn't like the
world to know about it all sooner than it has to.'

Pip fired up in her defence. 'You didn't behave badly
at all! It was my fault. I told Edward you'd come to be
our governess, and that was when it started. But I shall
really try to remember to call you Lady Octavia now!'
She added mournfully, 'It's just that "Miss Petrie" was
friendlier, somehow.'

'I'm still your friend, Pip! I always shall be.'

Edward said wryly, 'You're a lucky girl, Pip. You
should have heard the dressing down *I* got from Lady
Octavia for forgetting her name. Now, why don't you
go and take a look at those deer? Go quietly, mind—
they'll run off if you startle them.'

'I'll go with her—' began Octavia.

'No! Wait! Off you go, Pip! I need to make my peace
with Lady Octavia and I'd rather do it in private, if you
don't mind. I don't want you to see my authority un-
dermined.'

He said this so lightly that Pip laughed at the idea
and went off quite happily, to begin stalking the deer.
He looked at Octavia.

'I'm glad you came,' he said quietly. 'I was afraid
you wouldn't.'

Octavia stared coldly back at him. 'I wouldn't have, if it hadn't been for Pip.'

'I guessed as much. I was sorry for last night. I was wrong to leap to conclusions—' Edward stopped and took a breath. 'Heavens above, I seem to do nothing but apologise! What is it about you? I would say I'm normally a very even-tempered man, but you bring out the worst in me!'

'That's easily explained. It's because you secretly despise me.'

'What?' For a moment Edward was so surprised he could hardly speak. Then he exclaimed, '*Despise* you? What for? Of course I don't despise you. What a damned stupid idea!'

'It's quite obvious you do! You must! After the shameless way I behaved that…that afternoon. And the lies I told. Of course you do!'

Edward was stunned. 'Octavia— No, I will call you Octavia for this, so don't scowl at me like a cockatrice.' He took her hands in his and said earnestly, 'Octavia, I swear, I have never, not for one moment, despised you. How could you think it? Scorn is perhaps the one emotion you have *not* roused in me! I seem to have suffered from most of the rest. Suspicion, annoyance, fury, delight. Disapproval, admiration, respect, and…and yes, desire. And, of course, jealousy.'

'*Jealousy?* When was there any cause for jealousy?'

'I was choking with jealousy when I spoke to you that last morning at Wychford. That's why the accusations I made were so bitter.'

Octavia tried to pull her hands away, but he wouldn't let them go. 'No, you must let me finish. You think I *despise* you for what happened between us? You couldn't be more wrong. Your vulnerability, your innocence were all that stopped me from taking you completely there and then in that tower room. Your instant response to me, the passion I had roused in you, went to my head. You can have no idea how hard it was to resist temptation. Yet I knew I had to—'

This time Octavia wrenched her hands out of his grasp and put them over her ears. 'No! Don't say another word! I don't want to hear! If you knew how ashamed I am every time I think of it...' She put her hands down again and faced him with proud desperation. 'I can't expect you to believe this, but I had never...*never* before given way to such a disgraceful display of emotion. I had never before experienced it. And I was sure you must despise me for it.'

'The shame would have been mine if I had betrayed you, Octavia. We were both in the grip of a very powerful force in that room. How could I condemn *you*?'

'But the next day—'

'The next day, after hearing Julia's accusations, and hearing what the maid at the inn had to say—' He shook his head in angry rejection of the memory, and went on, 'The thought that you might already have had a lover, that you were not the innocent I thought you, was driving me wild. I was furious with jealousy. And *that* is an emotion that *I* have never before experienced.'

He waited for a moment. When she stayed silent he said, 'I hope you can forgive me. I hope we can put it all behind us, and begin again, as if I had met you as Mrs Carstairs's niece, and the owner of the house I happen to be renting. But whether we can, or whether we can't, you must believe that I have never despised you.'

Octavia looked at him uncertainly. 'Begin again?' she said. 'Forget what happened? If I only could... Would

it not be better to forget that we ever knew each other
at all? Go our separate ways?'

Not in a thousand years, was the sudden thought that
came unbidden into his mind. But he said quietly, 'Is
that what you want?'

She hesitated, and he waited stiff with tension, watching her conflicting thoughts cross her face. When she
said, 'I think it would be very difficult, if not impossible. What would Pip and Lisette say?' he let out a sigh
of relief.

'Exactly. I don't think that's the solution at all. So,
we'll begin again? This time as friends? At least, as
something more than casual acquaintances?'

'I'll try. But not if you leap to false conclusions about
me again.'

'I don't always seem to be rational when you are
near, Octavia, so I won't make rash promises. But I'll
certainly try not to! Now, what was it that you wanted
to talk about last night? You sounded nervous.'

'I was afraid you'd tell me it wasn't my affair. I
talked to Lisette about the man she knew in Antigua.'

'Ah! Ricardo Arandez. She said something of the
kind. I gather you tried to help her.'

'The trouble was, I was working in the dark. You
said once that Lisette's father found out something he
didn't like about Arandez. That was why he withdrew
his consent. Was it serious?'

Edward's face clouded over. 'Very.'

'So it's unlikely that your brother would ever have
changed his mind again?'

'More than unlikely. Impossible!'

'Don't you think it would have been better to tell
Lisette what was wrong?'

'Certainly not! She was a child.'

'But she's not a child now, and though she knows she is not betrothed, she is still half-convinced that Arandez was telling the truth when he said it was her father's last wish that she should marry him.'

'I thought we had scotched that!'

'No, your sister-in-law merely told Lisette she was never to mention Arandez again. She didn't say why.'

Edward was silent. At last he said, 'I see no necessity for bothering Lisette with the details of the story. She isn't in love with Arandez, and she has plenty to occupy her mind at the moment. If she hasn't yet forgotten him she soon will. Besides, in spite of Julia's fears, there hasn't been the slightest sign of him. No, I won't tell Lisette! It really isn't necessary.'

'I think you're wrong.'

'Then I'm sorry. But I won't change my mind.'

'Would you tell me instead?'

'Certainly not!'

'It's to protect Lisette! How can I help her when I don't know *why* her father wouldn't let her marry Arandez? You must tell me!'

Edward's expression darkened. He said stiffly, 'There's no question of it! I'd like you to leave this subject alone, Lady Octavia. Lisette is protected by those whose business it is! If Arandez ever dares show his face I'll know what to do, believe me!'

He sounded so fierce that Octavia saw any further effort would be wasted. She tried a different argument. 'But if he does, wouldn't it be wiser to let Lisette herself see him again? Isn't it better for her to face him, to discover what it is she really feels about him? She won't be happy until she does, you know.'

'Lady Octavia,' he said forcefully, 'you don't know what you're talking about! I would not willingly let that man anywhere near my niece!' Some demon made him add, 'Believe me, this is a much more serious matter than keeping at bay all those sprigs of the English aristocracy who simply have their eye on Lisette's inheritance.'

Octavia was already annoyed at his refusal to trust her. Now she was angry. 'I suppose you include my brother among those sprigs?'

'Yes, if you must know, I suppose I do!'

Octavia turned on him. 'That's *enough*! When will you realise, sir, that the Petries don't *need* anyone else's wealth. You do justice to no one—neither yourself nor my brother, nor Lisette—with such suspicions! I think I shall go to find Pip. I prefer her uncomplicated honesty to your pig-headed cynicism.'

Edward watched her broodingly as she walked angrily over the grass to where Pip was standing. He had done it again! Why did he always have to spoil things? He couldn't possibly have told her what Arandez had done, but with anyone else he would have managed to refuse more gracefully. As for that brother of hers... The trouble was, he had never come across anyone quite like Octavia Petrie before, and he wasn't sure how to deal with her. A lady of the highest society, yet she was as honest and straightforward as Pip, as gentle and caring as Lisette, a woman of courage and humour, and with a passion that could set him on fire in a way that Louise would never even begin to match. What was he to *do* about her?

'Marry her,' a voice inside him said. 'That's the only answer. Marry her before someone else does.'

Edward had started across the grass to join Octavia and Pip, but he now stopped short. *Marry* her? Give up his bachelor life? Join the ranks of those married men

he had pitied in the past? Never! Look at the state she
had got him into now, and he wasn't even engaged to
her! Oh, no! Marriage was a trap he would never fall
into. What a damned foolish idea!

Chapter Fifteen

The conversation during the return trip from Richmond was purely for Pip's benefit. Left to herself, Octavia would not have said a word to Edward Barraclough. She was angry and disappointed. One minute he was lifting her spirits by swearing, apparently sincerely, that he did not despise her, and two minutes later he was refusing to trust her with information about Arandez, and furthermore accusing her of promoting Harry's claims to Lisette's fortune! What was wrong with him? It was almost as if he deliberately picked a quarrel whenever they seemed to be getting closer. Octavia had no idea whether this was instinctive or deliberate, but to her mind it demonstrated even more clearly his reluctance to become involved. When they reached St James's Square she kissed Pip affectionately, and bade Mr Barraclough a very cool farewell.

Once in her room, she put Edward Barraclough firmly out of her mind and turned her attention to his niece. From what she had heard of the past year in Lisette's life, it wasn't surprising that she was sad. Time would heal the pain of her parents' death, but it was obvious that Lisette would never be happy and at peace with herself until she knew what she really felt for Ricardo Arandez. Edward Barraclough had dismissed the idea that she had ever been in love with Arandez, and Octavia was now inclined to agree with him. Lisette had felt affection for a young man she had known since she was a child, and she had trusted him. Why else had she been so ready to believe his story about the letter? However, during the past six months away from Antigua Lisette had done some growing up. Her interest in Harry proved she was no longer in love with Arandez, if indeed she ever had been.

But, as long as Lisette still half-believed what Arandez had told her, she would never truly be free to think of anyone else. Octavia wished she knew what had caused John Barraclough's sudden refusal to let his daughter marry him. Did Lisette herself know why? John Barraclough must have given his daughter *some* reason for breaking off the relationship so abruptly.

So, when she called to congratulate Julia on the success of her ball, she took the opportunity to invite Lisette to come for a drive in the park. Miss Cherrifield had taken Pip with her to visit some of her former pupils, so the way was free for a confidential chat.

'I've been thinking about what you told me about Ricardo Arandez, Lisette,' she began as they drove along in the spring sunshine. 'What sort of person was he?'

'I'm not sure any more. When I was young I liked him a lot, though he was much older than I was. He always said he wanted to marry me, and I quite liked the idea, especially as it meant I would still be near my own home. His family lives on the next estate, you see.

Mama and Papa seemed pleased, too, so I was very surprised when they changed their mind.'

'Do you know why that was?'

'Not really. But later I thought it must be because of some disagreement about boundaries. Edward thought the Arandez family had taken some land that belonged to us. Papa wouldn't talk about it, but that was the only reason I could find.'

'Were you unhappy? Did you badly want to marry Ricardo?'

'I thought I did at first, but not afterwards.'

'Why was that?'

'When Mama and Papa were killed and he told me that Papa had wanted me to marry him straight away, I wasn't sure I wanted to. So I told him I needed time.'

'My poor girl, of course you needed time! Your parents' accident must have been a terrible shock! Surely he understood that?'

'No. He said that Papa's last wishes ought to be a ''sacred duty''. He got angry when I still wouldn't do as he wished, and called me a stupid little girl. But then Edward and Uncle Henry saw him and sent him away. When they said I wasn't to see him again, I was almost relieved. But then, after Edward had left for England, Ricardo came back again and wanted me to go away with him. He was more like he had been in the past. He said he was sorry he had frightened me, it was because he loved me so much, and had promised Papa he would always look after me.'

'But you had your uncles to look after you! They were your guardians.'

'That's what I told him. I said I was quite sure Papa wouldn't have wanted me to run away with anyone. Then he showed me Papa's letter. We were just leaving when Uncle Henry saw us and called his men. That was the last time I saw Ricardo. I can't seem to forget it. The men were dragging him away and he was shouting that I must wait for him, that he loved me and would come for me. I...I think sooner or later he will.'

They were silent for a moment. Then Octavia said, 'And what will you say if he does?'

'I don't know! I once thought I was in love with him, but I'm not sure any more that he was telling the truth about Papa. And...and I met your brother and I found that I liked him much better! *Much* better! Lady Octavia, I just don't know *what* I would say!'

'I suppose in the end it comes down to one simple question, Lisette. If you think you're still in love with him, then you must persuade him to be honourable and wait till you have your guardians' proper consent. No running away again. After all, if it was just a matter of a boundary dispute, they may well come round if they see you're serious. But, if you are *not* in love with Mr Arandez, then you will have to tell him so. It's as simple as that.'

Lisette sighed. 'It does sound simple when *you* say it. I'll try to do it. Thank you for talking to me, Lady Octavia!'

After chatting with Lisette on less fraught matters for a while, Octavia thought she could safely take her back to South Audley Street. She was surprised at Edward Barraclough. The quarrel over the boundary must have been very bitter indeed to cause so much trouble in the family. But when she thought more about it, she decided that the delay it had caused hadn't actually done Lisette any harm. Without that dispute, Lisette might well have married Arandez and only afterwards discovered that what she had felt was affection for a childhood hero, not love for the grown man. She could have been very unhappy. As it was, she had a chance now to find out what she really wanted of life.

On the evening of Gussie's rout party her husband came in late to the salon just as Gussie was about to give him up and start dinner without him. He was accompanied by a tall, very presentable young man with blond hair and clear blue eyes. Introductions were of necessity rather hasty, but the Duke smiled blithely at his wife and in his rumbling voice presented his protégé as 'Billie Farquhar's great-nephew, m'dear, Richard Aransay.'

'You're very welcome, sir,' said Gussie. 'You must forgive our lack of ceremony this evening. The house has been made ready for later, and we are dining in the morning room. Perhaps you would take my sister, Lady Octavia Petrie, in to dine? And this is my brother, Lieutenant Petrie. I expect you two young men about town will find a lot to say to each other! Shall we go?'

Octavia found Mr Aransay an entertaining dinner companion. She gathered that he had just spent several weeks with his great-uncle, and his irreverent account of the activities of that eccentric peer reminded her strongly of Tom Payne. For a while her anxieties about Lisette, her sense of injury at Edward Barraclough's lack of trust, were forgotten as she laughed at Mr Aransay's stories, supplemented by those of the Duke, who had his own tales to tell of Lord Farquhar. The time passed very agreeably, and it was a surprise when Gussie rose from the table and announced that their other guests would soon be arriving. It was time to get ready to receive them.

* * *

The reception rooms of Monteith House were impressive, and tonight they were beautifully laid out for Gussie's guests. A table of refreshments surrounding a large bowl of fruit punch had been put out in the ornate dining room, and liveried footmen circled the rooms with trays of champagne and wine. There was no dancing, but a group of musicians provided a pleasing background of music. The salon was gleaming in the light of several hundred candles in its huge chandeliers, reflected over and over in the mirrors that lined the walls. Soon the rooms were filled with the hum of conversation interspersed with laughter, a sure sign of the evening's success.

The Duke had taken Mr Aransay off after dinner, presumably to exchange some further reminiscences, so Harry, who had been told by Octavia that Lisette would be present, was free to go through the rooms busily greeting old friends and members of the family, and remaining constantly on the watch for the arrival of the Barracloughs. As was Octavia. This time there would be no informal, accidental meetings, such as the one at Wychford. This evening Harry would be properly introduced to Lisette's family as Lieutenant the Honourable Harry Petrie, son of the Earl of Warnham, and, with one notable exception, she was fairly certain they would regard him with complaisance.

The Henry Barracloughs arrived with Lisette, who was looking exquisite in jonquil yellow. When Octavia introduced her brother, Julia almost simpered at him.

'We've heard about you, of course, Lieutenant Petrie. Your sister has told us you've recently left the Army. The Guards, I believe?'

Harry tore his eyes off Lisette and turned with one of his most charming smiles. 'Yes, Mrs Barraclough.

My father wishes to see more of me. I hear you are from Antigua? I believe it's a beautiful island…'

Octavia waited till she saw that Harry had the situation well in hand, busily charming Lisette's guardians, then moved away. She wandered through the rooms, finally acknowledging to herself that she was waiting for Edward Barraclough to appear, though what she would say to him when he did she had no idea!

'Exquisite! Truly exquisite!' Octavia turned round. Richard Aransay was behind her, his eyes fixed on Lisette.

'Indeed she is. And one of the Season's greatest successes.'

'I see your brother is with her at the moment?'

'Lisette has many admirers, sir. Would you like me to introduce you?'

Richard Aransay smiled. Octavia wondered why it made her uneasy. 'I hardly think that is necessary, Lady Octavia. Lisetta and I know one another quite well. You might say very well.'

'I beg your pardon, Mr Aransay?'

'Forgive me, ma'am, my name is Arandez. Richard Arandez. I'm afraid my host's vagueness misled you when he introduced me tonight.'

Octavia was looking at him in shock. 'You are Richard Arandez? *Ricardo* Arandez?'

'I see you've heard of me. Has Lisetta been telling you about us? I hear she thinks a great deal of you.'

'Mr Arandez, I'm sorry, but I don't think you should be here! The Barracloughs—'

'Have for some reason best known to themselves warned me off Lisetta. Is that what you wanted to say? But I am here by invitation, Lady Octavia. Since when have the Barracloughs decided who should be invited, or not invited, to Monteith House? My great-uncle was a very old friend of the present Duke's father.'

Octavia gave him a straight look. 'Did you know Lisette would be here tonight, sir?'

'Let us say that I hoped so. I have to talk to her.' He glanced at Lisette, flanked on either side by Harry and her Aunt Julia. Henry Barraclough was close by. 'But not at the moment. Is there somewhere where you and I can have a talk?'

Octavia eyed him for a moment, then, without speaking, she led the way through the press of people to the winter garden, which opened out from the last of the suite of rooms. 'I think this is private enough, sir. But I warn you, I'm not exactly prejudiced in your favour.'

'Of course you aren't! The Barracloughs have almost certainly poisoned your mind against me. I hear you're quite close to them. But do you think you're being fair, Lady Octavia? I love Lisetta. For many years I watched her growing up and, encouraged by her parents I may say, I looked forward to the day when she would be old enough to marry me. Her parents' death was a tragedy for me as well as those poor children. I not only lost two of my dearest friends, but the promise of future happiness with the girl I loved.'

Octavia was impressed in spite of herself, but she asked bluntly, 'Why don't Lisette's uncles like you?'

'They see me as a threat to their control of the Barraclough fortune.'

'I believe there was more to it than that, sir.'

Arandez stiffened and he frowned. 'I…I'm sorry. I don't understand,' he said somewhat warily.

Octavia went on, 'Wasn't there a quarrel? A dispute about some boundary?'

The frown lifted. He shrugged his shoulders and with

a rueful smile said, 'Ah, yes! That boundary. It caused a great deal of trouble. Much more than it was worth. Lisetta's father realised it was not a problem in the end.' He gave Octavia a direct look out of clear blue eyes. 'Now that you've met me, Lady Octavia, do you think I'm the villain the Barracloughs claim? Lisetta and I love each other. She will never be happy without me, and I…I want more than anything in the world to have the right to look after her, as her father wished. If only I could talk to her!'

Octavia was torn. She had some sympathy for Richard Arandez. He seemed sincere enough. Again she thought of how much he reminded her of Tom Payne, and Tom had been as open as the day. On the other hand, Edward Barraclough had made it more than clear that he wished Lisette to have no contact of any kind with Arandez. What should she do? Ricardo Arandez was an apparently perfectly respectable young man, sponsored in Society by her sister's husband. He would be accepted everywhere, and in the end he and Lisette were bound to meet *somewhere*—if not here, then certainly somewhere else. Surely it was better that they meet here tonight where she herself could keep a careful eye on them? She was risking Edward Barraclough's severe displeasure, but she was, after all, used to that!

'Very well, sir,' she said. 'I shall take you to Lisette. But I need hardly remind you she is one of my sister's guests tonight. She mustn't be upset, or put under any pressure. As far as London society is concerned, Lisette has *no obligation* to anyone other than her guardians. Do you understand what I mean?'

'Thank you! And, yes, I promise to be discreet. But I assure you, she will be delighted to see me! There will be no pressure, Lady Octavia, only relief.'

Octavia preceded him out of the winter garden full
of misgiving, not at all sure she was doing the right
thing. As they went through to the salon, she turned to
Arandez and said, 'I shall stay with you, Mr Arandez.
Lisette is very dear to me.'

'Of course, ma'am,' he said with a confident grin.
'But you will soon see how very dear she is to me, too!'

Henry and Julia Barraclough had left Lisette in
Harry's care and were being ushered towards the dining
room by the Duke, presumably for some refreshments.
Lisette looked happy enough, though she was rather
pale. The salon was quite warm, and several other admirers surrounded her, all pressing for her attention. Octavia quickened her pace to join her. Lisette was basically shy, and her success, far from going to her head,
was causing her some distress.

When she saw Richard Arandez with Octavia she
went even paler. She said uncertainly, 'Ricardo? What
a surprise! I…I didn't know you were in London!'

'Lisetta!' He bent towards her as if to kiss her cheek,
but she drew back nervously.

'Not…not here!' She gave him her hand, then turned
to Harry, who was standing behind her. 'Lieutenant Petrie! Let me introduce an old friend—Ricardo Arandez.'

Harry shook his head. 'Miss Barraclough obviously
knows you, Aransay, but why does she give you a Spanish name? I thought you were a Scotsman!'

'I come from Antigua,' said Arandez briefly. 'Lisetta
and I are very old friends, indeed, more than that—'
Lisette went even paler and drew in her breath.

Octavia stepped in before he could go any further.
'Mr Arandez!' she said with a smile. 'You'll find you
have quite a deal of explaining to do, I'm afraid. My

sister's husband is notoriously absentminded. You're probably known all over London as Richard Aransay from Scotland!' She paused, then added with a significance meant for him alone, 'I did warn you.'

He nodded and said easily, 'Lisetta and I were children together, Lieutenant, but we haven't seen each other for some time. May I take her away from you for a minute or two? I have news of her friends on Antigua.'

Harry gave Lisette a look of inquiry. She said hesitantly, 'I...I think I should like to talk to Mr Arandez, Lieutenant Petrie. For a short while. Will you excuse me?'

'Harry, you may take me to the dining room,' Octavia said before her brother could object. 'I'm so thirsty, and I know Gussie ordered some deliciously refreshing drinks. Let's go to find them. We won't be long, Lisette.'

Octavia led Harry away. 'What does all this mean, Tavy? Why are you encouraging that fellow? You know I like Lisette!'

'Don't worry, brother. There's no real competition there. My guess is that Lisette has grown up a little since she last saw Mr Arandez. Just give her time to find it out for herself. How did you get on with the Barracloughs?'

'I must say, I don't know what you have against Mrs Barraclough. She was very pleasant to me. A bit too gushy, perhaps, but quite easy to talk to.'

'Face it, Harry! You're quite a catch!' said Octavia, thinking she sounded every bit as cynical as Edward Barraclough.

'What about Lisette's Uncle Edward?' asked Harry echoing her thoughts. 'Has he forgiven you yet?'

'I'm not sure what the situation is at the moment. I suspect we shall fall out again quite badly as soon as he sees Ricardo Arandez with Lisette. He disapproves of Mr Arandez even more than he does of you!'

'Good! But why should he fall out with you? It's not your fault that Arandez is here.'

'Try telling that to Mr Barraclough! In fact, you can tell him now—he has just come into the room. I don't think he can have seen Arandez yet, though. He doesn't look angry enough.'

Harry looked towards the door. 'So that's Barraclough! He's a good-looking chap, Tavy. Powerful, too. I shouldn't like to fall foul of him!'

Edward Barraclough made his way over to them, hesitated fractionally while he eyed Harry, then bowed and said, 'Good evening, Lady Octavia.'

Octavia returned his bow and said in a neutral voice, 'Mr Barraclough. My brother, Lieutenant Harry Petrie.'

'Ah! Lieutenant!'

'Not for much longer, I'm afraid, sir. I've already sent in my papers.'

'Ah, yes.' There was a short silence during which the two men examined each other. Then Edward said, 'You know my niece, I believe.'

'I was introduced to her tonight, sir. In the company of your brother and his wife.'

Edward gave him a grim smile. 'Come, Lieutenant! You're surely not trying to tell me it was for the first time!'

'No, sir. I've met Lisette twice before at Wychford. And if you will permit me, I should like to meet her many more times still!'

Octavia drew in her breath, but Harry's audacity had done him no harm. Edward laughed and said more naturally, 'We'll have to see about that! You have a good advocate in your sister, at all events.'

'Tavy is the best of sisters, sir.'

'Tavy? What a pity to reduce a beautiful name like "Octavia" to "Tavy"!' He turned round and surveyed the room. 'But where is my niece at present?'

'Did…did you not see her as you came through? I…I think she is in the saloon, sir,' said Octavia swallowing hard. 'W…with an old friend.'

'Would you show me, ma'am? Excuse us, Lieutenant Petrie.'

Octavia cast a last despairing glance at Harry and took Edward's proffered arm. As she led him back towards the saloon she took a deep breath and began, 'I could have prevaricated, Mr Barraclough. But I choose not to. I hope you will give me credit for that at least. Your niece is with Mr Ricardo Arandez.'

Edward stopped. He said very quietly, 'What did you say?'

Octavia swallowed again and repeated, 'Your niece is with Ricardo Arandez.'

They had reached the wide doors to the saloon. Lisette was with Arandez in an alcove formed by one of the tall window embrasures. Arandez was leaning towards her, talking urgently. She was listening, but not particularly attentively, her eye wandering over the crowd, apparently in search of someone else.

Edward Barraclough drew in his breath with an audible hiss. 'Is this your doing?' he asked, his lips barely moving.

Octavia hesitated. 'Not exactly,' she said. 'My brother-in-law—'

As if the mention of his name had conjured him up, the Duke of Monteith clapped Edward on the shoulder.

'Barraclough!' he exclaimed. 'The very chap! I've got a young fella here from your part of the world. Jamaica, what? Come and meet him. You come too, Octavia!''

He steered Edward over to the alcove and gave a loud laugh. 'He doesn't waste time, I see! Already got the prettiest girl in the room with him! What a lad! Your niece, ain't she?'

'I thought my niece was with her aunt,' Edward said ominously.

The Duke brayed with laughter. 'Got to make allowances, Barraclough!' he roared. 'A pretty gel and a handsome fella—o'course they'll meet! She's perfectly safe, though. Good chap, Aransay. Know his uncle. Splendid fella!'

'You must excuse me, Duke! I need no introduction to Mr Arandez. But I should like to see my niece restored to her aunt and uncle.' They had reached the alcove. Ignoring Arandez, Edward simply said, 'Lisette?'

The Duke looked briefly surprised, then gave another laugh. 'Never knew you were such a stickler, Barraclough! Never mind, Aransay! I'll take y'to meet Puffy Rogers. Great chap, Puffy. Lost fifteen thousand last night. Didn't turn a hair. Come on!' He set off towards the card room.

Arandez looked uncertain, but Lisette said, 'Yes, do go, Ricardo! I want to find Lieutenant Petrie. I promised to introduce him to Edward. Edward, you stay here!' She disappeared in the direction of the dining room before anyone could stop her.

Edward said pleasantly, 'You'd better follow Monteith to the card room, Arandez. I have no desire to make a scene, but I'm not sure I can keep my hands off you for very much longer. Furthermore you'd better stay away from Lisette in future. As we both know, I could make London very uncomfortable for you if I chose.'

For a moment Arandez looked as if he might argue, but then he shrugged his shoulders and went. Edward turned to Octavia. 'You arranged this,' he said flatly.

'I didn't, but I would have, if I had known that Mr Arandez was going to be here tonight,' Octavia said defiantly.

'You don't fool me, Octavia! You arranged it with your brother-in-law, though you knew very well that I would stop it if I had known. How the devil did you get Lisette away from Julia and Henry?'

'I didn't have to. They had left her in Harry's hands.'

'I don't believe it! Julia wouldn't do such a thing! Especially not with Arandez in the house.'

'Mrs Barraclough didn't know Mr Arandez was here. But Harry is a very eligible *parti*, Mr Barraclough, and your sister-in-law sees no reason to discourage him! So she left them together. I was the one who brought Arandez over here to them. He wanted to talk to Lisette, so I...I let him.'

Edward's face darkened. 'If anything happens to Lisette because of what you've done,' he said harshly, 'I'll make you wish you had never been born!'

Octavia felt a pang of fear, but she faced him bravely. 'Don't be so blindly pig-headed! It is exactly as I said. Lisette has grown up a lot since she left Antigua. A few minutes in Arandez's company have been enough to convince her that she has outgrown him! Instead of berating me, look at her now! Does she look like a girl in danger of falling into his power again?'

Edward looked over to the other side of the room where Lisette was coming towards them, escorted by

Harry. They were both laughing as they approached. He hadn't seen his niece so carefree in a long time.

'Edward! Lieutenant Petrie tells me he's already met you! And I was so looking forward to introducing him myself.' Her voice faded. 'Why are you looking so angry? Aunt Julia likes him. She left us together…'

'What were you saying to Arandez?'

Lisette's face cleared and she came close and took his hand. 'You needn't worry any more about Ricardo, Edward. I shan't do anything foolish. I found out tonight that I'm quite cured. As soon as I can, I shall tell him so.'

Edward frowned even more heavily. 'You are not to talk to him at all, Lisette! Don't go near him!'

Octavia cleared her throat, and he turned to glare at her. Undeterred, she said quietly, 'Don't you think you're being a little draconian, sir? Since Mr Arandez is my brother-in-law's protégé, he is bound to be seen everywhere. It would be difficult for Lisette to ignore him completely.'

Edward set his jaw and turned to Harry. 'Lietenant Petrie, I must have a word with your sister. Do you think you could look after my niece for a few minutes?'

Harry looked doubtful. 'It depends on Tavy, sir. Does she wish to hear what you have to say? It doesn't sound as if it's about the weather.'

'The temptation might be considerable, but I promise not to strangle her, if that's what you're worried about.'

Octavia said, 'Take Lisette, Harry. And you needn't look so anxious, either of you! I'm not afraid of Mr Barraclough.'

Harry's face lit up. 'In that case, there's nothing I'd like better! Miss Barraclough, shall we go to find something to eat and drink?'

After they had gone Edward said, 'You should be.'

'Afraid? Of you? Never!'

A small smile flickered in his eyes, then disappeared. Then his expression changed and he said heavily, 'The fact that Arandez has appeared, and in such distinguished company, means that the situation is different. You seem so determined to refuse to do anything I ask that you force me to tell you more about him.'

'I would like you to.'

'Is there somewhere where we can talk?'

'My brother-in-law's library? We'll be undisturbed there.'

'You're not afraid of the gossips if we're seen? I seem to remember you were morbidly anxious about them a short while ago.'

'That is a trivial matter compared with this business of Lisette. Will you follow me?'

Chapter Sixteen

Once in the library—a room which was hardly ever used and certainly never by the Duke—Octavia turned and faced him, a challenge in her eye.

'Now, Mr Barraclough. I'm listening. But I warn you, I shall continue to do what I think best, whatever your prejudices about Mr Arandez. Indeed, I'm not sure why you are so worried. Lisette has told you she no longer thinks she is in love with him, just as I said she would. Once she has met him again to make that clear to him, I doubt you will be troubled any further by the man.'

'*Prejudices!*' He walked about the room, his every movement expressing anger and frustration. Finally he came to a stop in front of her and said abruptly, 'I simply don't know how to tell you this. Not even Julia knows the whole truth. But I can see that, unless I do, you will go your own headstrong way to disaster, and take Lisette with you.'

'Oh, come! Surely no dispute over boundaries can be as serious as this!'

'Is that what you think it is?'

'It's what Lisette thinks.'

'She must never know anything different. I want your word on that.'

Octavia hesitated, then said, 'Very well.'

He looked at her for a moment, as if he was still not sure. Then he made up his mind and said, 'Two years ago Ricardo Arandez abused and raped a girl of sixteen on the island of Jamaica. The girl died.'

Octavia stared at him, horrified, then sat down. 'I don't believe it!' she said.

'I assure you it's true. He has always been known for his harsh treatment of the slaves on the Arandez plantation, but on Antigua cruelty to slaves is not regarded as a crime. It's one reason why I left the place and became a banker. But this was different. This girl was not a slave. He ought to have been punished and disgraced, of course, but the girl's family was far from wealthy and Arandez's father was able to pay them off.' He watched her for a moment while she took it all in. Then he said, '*Now* do you see why I want Lisette to have nothing to do with him?'

'Yes, I…I… Are you *sure*?'

'Of course I'm sure,' he said impatiently. 'Do you think I'd make a statement such as that unless I was absolutely certain? I saw the girl's parents myself. I spoke to some of the authorities on the island.'

'But he looks so…so *decent*!'

'It's his chief asset.'

'Oh, God! And I encouraged Lisette to talk to him…' Octavia put her face in her hands.

'Quite!' He regarded her for a moment, then said, 'I would have spared you this, but—'

Octavia lifted her head and looked at him steadily. 'I wouldn't have listened to you otherwise. You are right to be so angry. I…I beg your pardon.'

His frown faded and a rueful smile appeared. Taking her hands in his, he drew her up from the chair and said, 'You've done it again, Octavia. It's very strange. I do get angry with you, you infuriate me. But I can never sustain it. Why the devil is it so?'

Octavia was finding it difficult to breathe. 'I...I don't know,' she croaked.

His eyes on her mouth, he said, 'I still fantasise about you, you know. I still have sudden memories of that tower room...'

'So do I,' she whispered.

He pulled her slowly towards him. 'Octavia!' he murmured, and bent his head to kiss her.

For a moment they were lost, locked in each other's arms, back in that room in the tower, passion mounting between them... But then they slowly came back to earth, unable this time to forget for long who and where they were. Octavia stared at him.

'What is it?' she asked, bewildered. 'It's still there, that magic. I've tried so hard to forget. You say you don't despise me, but—'

'Don't!' he said harshly. 'You mustn't say such things, not even think them. I don't despise you, Octavia. It's myself I despise for being so weak.'

'But it isn't *weakness* to love someone.'

His arms tightened round her. For a moment it looked as if he would kiss her again. Then almost violently he said, 'It is for me!' and turned away from her. 'No, Octavia! I've felt more for you than for any other woman. Some would call it love, perhaps. But it isn't *enough*. I have no wish to marry. I doubt I ever shall. I've no desire to tie myself down, to drown in a sea of domesticity, not even with you. And I respect you too much to offer anything else.'

He was as determined as ever. It was the end of hope. For a moment Octavia wanted to argue, to shout, to tell him what a fool he was to reject all that they could offer each other for so trivial a reason. But pride stopped her. She would beg for no man's love. Calling on all her training, all her pride, she managed to say coldly,

'It's as well you do. I would find any such offer very difficult to forgive.' She paused, then went on, 'As for marriage... You've been very frank, Mr Barraclough, so let me be equally frank. Since you don't intend to ask me, you'll never find out whether I would have accepted you or not. But, like you, I have always avoided marriage, and it would now take a great deal for me to give up my own independence, more perhaps than you have to offer. I am sure this feeling we have, however powerful, is transitory. It will die when we see less of each other—as we undoubtedly shall.'

'Octavia!'

She went on as if he had not spoken. 'It's time to go back to the salon and join Lisette and the others. Thank you for trusting me with the facts about Arandez. I shall do what I can to protect Lisette until something can be done about him. Do you wish me to say anything to my sister or brother-in-law?'

Her voice was polite, but still very cold. He frowned, and looked for a moment as if he wanted to say more, then gave up and followed her lead. 'I think not,' he replied. 'You can't tell them everything, so better not to say anything at all. I'll find a way of dealing with Arandez.'

Octavia nodded and they went out. She had to work hard to appear normal as they joined the crowds. She was still shattered at what she had heard about Arandez,

at how easily she could have encouraged Lisette into
danger. And a cold weight lay on her heart. However
strongly Edward Barraclough might be attracted to her,
it was now more than clear that Gussie had been right.
He would never commit himself to marriage. Her only
recourse was to rid herself of her own absurd weakness.

Edward's face was grim as they searched the rooms
for Lisette and Harry, but could find neither. His frown
grew even heavier. 'I thought I could trust that brother
of yours to look after her properly,' he said impatiently.
'Where the devil are they?'

Octavia caught a glimpse of jonquil yellow among
the leaves of the winter garden. She closed her eyes. A
scene between her brother and Edward Barraclough on
top of everything else would be too much to bear. She
said wearily, 'I think they're down this way.'

Edward looked and swore. 'That damned puppy! I
should never have left Lisette with him! Come!' He set
off at such a pace that Octavia almost had to run as he
shouldered his way through the crowd.

But Harry and Lisette were not enjoying a quiet tête-
à-tête in the winter garden. Arandez was with them, and
they were just in time to hear Harry say in a voice which
was quiet but full of warning, 'I've told you, Arandez!
Let Miss Barraclough go!'

'Damn you, she's betrothed to me!' snarled Arandez.

'I'm not, Ricardo! I told you! Why won't you listen
to me? I'm sorry, but I don't want to marry you. Leave
me alone!' Lisette sounded distraught.

Arandez jerked her to him. 'Never!'

There was a sudden howl of pain as Harry chopped
Arandez on the arm with the side of his hand, then
pushed him aside. He moved Lisette out of the way,

then told her gently to go back to her aunt while he dealt with her tormentor.

'I'll take care of him, Petrie,' said Edward as he moved forward. 'Oblige me by looking after Lisette and your sister. Take them out of here.'

'Come this way, Lisette,' said Octavia. 'We needn't go back through the crowds. You can recover in my room. Are you coming with us, Harry?'

Harry's face was flushed with anger. 'I think I'll stay, if you don't mind,' he said abruptly. 'Just in case the fellow tries any more tricks. But take Lisette to safety.'

Octavia didn't stop to question. She simply nodded and took Lisette away.

Some time later she heard a tap at her door. Harry was there.

'I've come to see how Miss Barraclough is,' he said.

'She's having a rest. I was just going to come down to look for her aunt. I think she should go home. Where is Arandez?'

'Gone,' said Harry briefly. 'You won't see him again tonight. Barraclough made it more than clear that he wasn't wanted. In fact, I doubt we'll ever hear any more of the fellow. It would take a braver man then Arandez to ignore Barraclough, I can tell you.'

'Good. Could you find Mrs Barraclough for me, while I stay here with Lisette?'

But Lisette joined them at the door. 'I'd rather you didn't. Aunt Julia will only make a fuss. If Ricardo has gone I should like to come down again, if I may.' She smiled at Harry. 'I'd like to thank Lieutenant Petrie for looking after me. And... I still haven't had any of those lovely looking refreshments.'

Octavia looked on in amazement as Lisette, who had

seemed on the point of collapse just a few minutes before, smiled even more widely at Harry and said, 'Will you wait for me? I need to tidy myself a little first.'

Harry nodded, and she disappeared.

Octavia raised both her eyebrows at her brother, then shut the door and went to help Lisette.

'Are you sure you're well enough?'

'Oh, yes. I'm not nervous when Harry—Lieutenant Petrie is with me.'

'You can call him Harry to me, my dear,' said Octavia with amusement. 'But don't let your uncle hear you! I have to say you're looking a lot better than you did.'

'It's as you said, Lady Octavia. Now I've told Ricardo, I feel happier than I've been for a long time. I'm free of him at last!' She paused, then said shyly, 'And Harry is even nicer than I remembered.'

'I'm glad you think so—I'm quite fond of him myself. But you must still go carefully with your uncle. There's no reason why Harry shouldn't have his approval, but there does seem to be a certain reluctance about him!'

'He'll come round. As you say, there's no reason why he shouldn't, and Aunt Julia approves. Shall we go down?'

Lisette opened the door, took Harry's arm and started off down the stairs. The difference in Lisette, her composure, her air of serene confidence was almost unbelievable! Was this all it had taken? To confess to Ricardo Arandez that she no longer loved him? Octavia's expression was wistful as she watched the two go down to join the company. It looked as if for them at least there would be a happy ending.

She went back into her own room, shut the door and

leaned against it. Solitude at last! The pain in her heart was getting worse. Edward Barraclough had admitted that he loved her, and in the same breath had taken away all hope that he could ever think of marrying her. What a stupid, stupid man he was! A sob escaped her, though her eyes were dry. What was she to do? Certainly not join the crowds downstairs again—Gussie's guests must do without her. This feeling of hurt was like a physical injury, which no balm could reach, nothing could alleviate. And to disguise the pain, to pretend that she felt nothing, was beyond her just for the moment. She needed time to overcome it....

Some one else was filled with pain and anger, and was less willing to suffer without taking revenge. Arandez was no longer able to convince himself that Lisette loved him, but he had by no means given her up. The prize was too rich and too lovely to be given up without a struggle. For the moment she was too well protected for him to get near her, but while she remained unmarried there was hope. His chance would come, he was sure.

But as time went on he found that the word had gone round. Fewer and fewer drawing rooms were open to him, and he was tempted more and more to seek his amusements in the sub-world of London society, a world that catered for the more depraved appetites. But the deeper he sank, the more he craved revenge. He began to promise himself that Lisette would be sorry for what she had done to him, sorrier than she realised. He had tried to deal honourably with her, but she had thrown his honour back in his face. The more gentle approach—persuasion, reproaches, his affecting stories about her father—had proved useless. Force was the only answer—as it was with all women in the end. His chance would come, and then she would pay… He went back to his underworld and bided his time, and urged his servants meanwhile to keep a vigilant watch on her movements.

After that evening Octavia had little or no contact with Edward Barraclough—no more confidences, no more arguments, not even about Harry. It was not difficult to avoid him. There were plenty of gentlemen only too willing to escort Lady Octavia, dance with Lady Octavia, talk to Lady Octavia, and in her own way she was having almost as great a success as Lisette. She showed the world a brave face, and no one suspected that Lady Octavia's heart was slowly breaking.

But as the Season wore on, and London got warmer and dustier, she began to think of Wychford, its greenery, its lake, the cool shadows among its trees and longed to go back there. The Barracloughs' six-month tenure was over and the house was now available to her. Her task in London was finished. Pip had her governess, Lisette had been launched as successfully as anyone could have wished, and it was now generally acknowledged that she and Harry Petrie would probably make a match of it.

Everyone, it seemed, was happy except herself. Life in London was just as stale, her admirers just as predictable, as they had been five years before, and this time the effort of keeping up appearances was proving harder with every day that passed. In the end she could bear it no longer; when the excuse to leave London came her way, she seized it eagerly.

It came during a visit to the Barracloughs in South Audley Street. Harry was as usual deep in conversation with Lisette, and Octavia was left talking to Julia. Her fortitude was sorely tested as Julia went into a long diatribe about Edward Barraclough's behaviour.

'He has never taken his responsibilities as seriously as I should have liked, but I have never known him as bad as this! He is the talk of London! I cannot imagine what has happened to him. Anyone would think he was deliberately trying to let the family down. He drinks and gambles to excess, and from what Henry tells me he is spending a fortune on that…that harpy of his!' Then, probably realising that she had been indiscreet, Julia said hastily, 'Not that I know about that sort of thing, of course. No decent woman would!'

At last, to Octavia's profound relief, Julia left the subject of Edward Barraclough's misdemeanours and turned to the rest of the family. But what she had to say was not much more comforting. She was worried about Pip.

'What's wrong?' asked Octavia. 'I thought she looked a little pale the last time I saw her! Is she ill?'

'Not exactly, but I'm afraid London doesn't suit her at all. She is forever talking of Wychford. Her governess has been very good—she has taken the child to all the sights she can think of, but you know Philippa. She has so much energy, and yet the heat and dust are sometimes too much even for her. London is not the best place for a child of her age and inclination. I don't know how we shall deal with her when Miss Cherrifield goes away.'

'Goes away? I thought she would stay as long as you needed her?'

'Oh, she will return. But it was arranged before she came to us that we would release her for three weeks

at the beginning of May. What Philippa will do without
her I cannot imagine! I have no time to spend on her.
My time is taken up with looking after Lisette. That
scoundrel Arandez is still in London, and Edward and
Henry insist that she must be chaperoned wherever she
goes. Your brother is very good, of course. He spends
a great deal of time with her.' She threw a fond glance
at Lisette and Harry, sitting on the other side of the
room. 'I think there'll be a match there, don't you? But
I can't even leave them unchaperoned for too long.
Which means I have very little time for Philippa.'

Octavia thought for a moment, then said, 'May *I* look
after Pip while Miss Cherrifield is away? I am thinking
of going down to Wychford and would be delighted if
she could come with me.'

Julia regarded her with surprise. 'You want to leave
London? Before the end of the Season?'

Octavia nodded her head. 'Shocking, isn't it? But I
would love to leave London, in fact. Pip's company
would be an additional attraction. Would she come to
Wychford?'

'I am very sure she would—she never stops talking
of the place.' Julia's tone conveyed her own opinion of
Wychford.

'Well, then, shall we consider it settled? In a week's
time, you said? Perfect! And…Pip can stay as long as
you can spare her. Miss Cherrifield could even join us
down there when she comes back. I doubt I shall return
to London once I leave.'

'Lady Octavia, it would be a godsend! I cannot say
how grateful we should be! Are you sure?'

'Quite!'

'Let me send for Philippa so that you can tell her
yourself.'

Octavia was concerned when she saw Pip. The air of crackling energy that had so attracted her was considerably diminished, and Pip's welcome, though enthusiastic, was less exuberant than it usually was. But when she heard of Octavia's invitation she went pale with excitement.

'You mean it? You really mean it? Oh, Miss Petrie, I mean, Lady Octavia, how good you are! Lisette, did you hear? I'm to go back to Wychford!'

Many were considerably surprised, of course, at Lady Octavia Petrie's decision. Gussie was extremely put out, and Octavia had a hard time reconciling her to the idea, but she remained firm. She was tired of London, and had no desire to hear any more gossip about Edward Barraclough. She suspected that he was doing his best to forget her, and she had no desire to be there when he succeeded and the secret, silken bond that had held him to her was finally broken.

So, after a busy week, Octavia, Pip and a small retinue of servants travelled down to Wychford. As they drove up the drive Pip could hardly restrain her excitement.

'Look, Miss Petrie, look! It's laughing!' She turned round. 'I'm sorry, I mean, Lady Octavia.'

Octavia laughed and put her arm round Pip. 'Call me what you wish, Pip. I shan't mind.' She looked out. 'I do believe you're right!'

It was sunny, but there was a slight breeze and the leafy branches along the way were swaying and dancing in the air. Their shadows, reflected in the windows of Wychford, gave the house an air of merriment, and Octavia felt a lift of heart. There would always be Wychford.

Mrs Dutton was waiting, and took the news that the owner of Wychford was 'Miss Petrie' with a comfortable smile and the comment, 'I always suspected there was something about you, my lady! We all hope you'll be happy with what we've done to the house. The repairs to the staircase went very well, though the men still don't understand what happened. It seems to be quite safe now, though. I've put Miss Philippa in the tower room, but I wasn't sure which room you would prefer. I've prepared both the main bedroom and your old one, as well.'

Octavia looked at Pip's pleading eyes and said, 'I'll sleep in my old room, Mrs Dutton, thank you.'

Soon they had both settled in and busied themselves exploring their domain, and if Octavia was less deliriously happy than her little guest, she found a measure of peace. But she never suggested that they should go up the stairs to the room at the top of the tower. When Pip asked about it, she said vaguely that she thought the key had been lost.

In London, meanwhile, Edward Barraclough was fighting a losing battle. He had seen very little of Octavia after the scene in the Monteiths' library, and whenever they did meet her manner was so different that she hardly seemed the same person. It was as if an invisible wall of ice separated them. She had clearly drawn a line under their long and curiously close relationship, and he was now seeing the Lady Octavia Petrie the world knew. Charming, well-mannered, and indifferent. A cool customer, as Stainforth had said. He ought to have been happy it was so, but in fact he could hardly bear it.

When he heard that Octavia was intending to leave

London it took considerable strength of will not to hurry round to the Monteiths' house to see her, but he had resisted the temptation. What could he say to her? Beg her to stay, to smile at him, to talk to him in her old way, to be his Octavia once more? Not while he was as determined as ever to avoid the trap of marriage. No, she had the right idea. Better that she should go, better that he should no longer be reminded of how it had been between them, better that he shouldn't catch sight of the proud lift of her head, her honey-gold curls on the other side of a room, and be seduced all over again. Better by far to let her go. Once she was out of sight he would forget her, he was sure. That was all it needed—her absence, and a little time.

But time proved him wrong. London was a desert without her, and life hardly worth living. Louise was no comfort, and after something of a scene he parted company with her. It wasn't long before she found someone else. Gambling lost its fascination, too, and even the cut and thrust of banking seemed a joyless affair. He lost patience with the Foreign Office, and after offending several important gentlemen there he left them to their own devices.

He viewed Lisette's evident happiness with Harry with a jaundiced eye, but could find nothing to object to in it, and decided after an uncomfortable search of his conscience that he was chiefly envious. When Harry asked for permission to pay his addresses to Lisette, Edward was just able to pull himself together and give his consent with reasonably good grace.

That same evening he went back to his house in North Audley Street and, as the fire died down and the house grew silent, he sat steadily drinking brandy and contemplating the wreck of his well-planned, well-organised life. What had happened? Just last September he had walked through Berkeley Square, pitying poor Trenton for having to marry, and congratulating himself on his own untrammelled, carefree existence. What had gone wrong? Why did it no longer seem sufficient?

After a while his mind turned to another problem that was occupying him, namely the behaviour of Ricardo Arandez. The fellow was being seen less and less in Society's drawing rooms, though he was still in London. After the warning he had been given in the Monteiths' winter garden, this was hardly surprising. But where was he spending his time? And why was he still in England, now that it was clear he had lost Lisette for good? Ricardo Arandez was not a man to give up lightly, nor would he forget anything he saw as an insult. Until it was absolutely certain that Arandez had gone back to the West Indies, Lisette must be guarded all the time.

This decided, Edward found it impossible not to go back to the other, all-important question. What could he do about his own, deep dissatisfaction? He eventually fell asleep, still reluctant to accept the answer. But just a day or two later, he found that his mind was suddenly made up.

Lisette missed Pip. And she missed Octavia. The thought that neither of them knew of her engagement, however unofficial, worried her, too. But her request to visit them at Wychford did not find favour with her aunt.

'Really, Lisette, that is most inconsiderate! You know I would have to accompany you, and the thought of that house makes me shudder. Besides, the Season will end quite soon, and I don't want to miss any part of it, especially not the Marchants' ball! You can surely wait till then.'

But when Harry saw Lisette's disappointment he hit on the happy idea of escorting Lisette to Wychford himself. But though Julia was tempted she vetoed it. 'It can't be done! Not before you are officially engaged, and even then I should be reluctant. No, Lieutenant Petrie, it's kind of you to offer, but it won't do.'

Julia had been made to feel guilty, and she was so annoyed that the next time she met Edward she expressed her feelings to him.

'I have devoted myself to that girl, got her engaged to one of the town's most eligible bachelors, and what is her response? She wants to drag me back to a house she knows I can't stand, merely to see her little sister! It's not as if they are missing anything, Edward. There's nothing official. The proper engagement celebration will come later when Lord Warnham has given his consent. Really, I wish you would speak to the girl! Instead of being grateful, she walks around looking as if I have committed a crime! But I can't allow her to go with only Lieutenant Petrie to accompany her. Apart from the proprieties, it isn't safe. Not with Arandez about.'

'I'll escort them.'

Edward's offer came quite spontaneously, and it astonished both of them. After a moment's pause Julia accepted with delight, and called Lisette to tell her so. Edward found himself making the necessary arrangements with them in a sort of daze, still not sure what had caused him to make the offer and wondering if he had gone quite mad.

Only later, when he was alone, did he finally acknowledge that to take Lisette and Harry to Wychford meant that he would see Octavia again, and that this was what he wanted most in the world. He had no idea how she would receive him, nor what he would do about it, but for better or for worse he had to know once and for all what it was that made life so impossible without her.

The decision made, life suddenly acquired a brighter hue, and the world seemed a better place.

Chapter Seventeen

The morning they left London was sunny and the countryside looked especially lovely as they bowled along. As they turned into the familiar drive Harry made them laugh with his account of how he had hidden among the trees the first time he had come, and they were still laughing as they turned the corner and the house came into view. Edward felt a surge of happiness. Wychford with its crooked gables, its sparkling windows and its odd little tower, looked welcoming and… expectant. That was the only word. Expectant.

Lisette had sent a message ahead, and Pip was waiting for them. When she saw the carriage she dropped out of her tree and raced up to the house, shouting, 'They're here, they're here, Octavia!'

Octavia stood framed in the massive oak doorway. She looked thinner, paler, than she had, but as the three visitors got out of the carriage her cheeks flooded with colour. For a few moments all was confusion and excitement as the younger Barracloughs greeted one another.

'I didn't expect you,' said Octavia distantly, looking at Edward. 'Lisette only mentioned herself and Harry.'

'I suppose you'd call me a kind of chaperon,' he said. He would have been astonished at how cool he sounded to her. At the sight of Octavia his heart had melted within him. He had forgotten everything but how much she meant to him, had wanted to snatch her into his arms and kiss away the look of unhappiness in her eyes... And he hadn't dared. For the first time in his life he was uncertain about his reception. He was paralysed by the sudden thought that Octavia might have found the cure that had eluded him, that she might no longer welcome his touch. But to restrain himself from taking her into his arms, to make himself sound anything like normal, had taken every ounce of his self-control.

He had been right. Octavia gave a little laugh, but the wall of ice was still firmly in place as she said, 'Of course. Julia wouldn't willingly come near Wychford again! She regards the house as dangerous.' There was a slight pause, then she went on, 'You must forgive me. I don't quite know what to say. The situation seems so odd. The last time we met here you were the master and I the governess, and now...' She shook her head, then began again. 'Will you come in, sir?' she said formally. 'I've arranged for some refreshments. They're in the little parlour—I wasn't expecting you, you see.'

'Don't treat me as a stranger, Octavia! Please!'

She gave a painful smile. 'I really don't know how to treat you at all. There were no classes for this sort of situation in my Ladies' Seminary. But come in. The others are waiting.'

As Edward stepped into the hall he looked around him. The hall looked the same as ever with no sign of damage to the staircase. The massive brass chandeliers gleamed in the sunlight shining through the long windows.

'Pip looks a great deal better,' said Edward, striving for normality.

'She loves Wychford,' said Octavia. 'We've had such fun together.'

'You spoil her.'

'Oh, no! I truly believe that Pip could not be spoiled. I shall miss her a lot when she finally has to go back to her aunt.' She bit her lip, then said brightly, 'Lisette has surprised me. I always thought that she and Harry would suit, but never that she would bloom as she has. Can I take it that Harry now has your approval?'

'Wait a minute or two longer and they will tell you themselves.'

Octavia led the way into the small parlour. On the table was a tray with glasses and an array of Mrs Dutton's delicacies. Beside it stood a wine cooler with a bottle in it. She hesitated, then turned to Edward. 'Would you…?'

Edward opened the bottle and poured its sparkling contents into the glasses. Octavia handed them out one by one, even passing a small one to Pip. She raised her glass.

'First of all, welcome back to Wychford,' she said. And waited, a small smile on her lips as she looked at her brother and Lisette.

Harry cleared his throat. 'Tavy, we've come today to ask you to wish us happy. Lisette and I… That's to say…Lisette has agreed to marry me,' he said. 'And her guardians have given their consent.'

Pip gave a cheer, and Octavia's smile widened. 'My darlings! This is wonderful news!' She put her glass down and embraced Lisette. 'Harry, you always did have all the luck in the family, but this is the best of the lot! I can't think of anyone I'd like more as a sister.'

Edward said, 'With your permission, Lady Octavia… To Harry and Lisette! Long life and happiness!'

They all drank. Pip was so excited she hardly tasted her wine before she begged them all to excuse her. She had something in her room for Lisette. She disappeared, having made them promise not to talk about their plans till she was back.

There was a silence. Harry drew Lisette aside. Edward looked at Octavia. For a moment they were both lost in each other, lost in memory… Then Octavia shook her head and turned away.

'This…this won't do! I won't…I can't…' She stopped and took a breath. 'I wonder what Pip is up to,' she said with determined cheerfulness. 'I think we ought to go to see.'

They went into the hall and came to an abrupt halt. Mrs Dutton was there, looking terrified; surrounding her was a gang of men armed with pistols.

'I'm…I'm sorry, my lady. They burst in when I opened the door. I couldn't stop—' She gave a little scream as one of the men bundled her out of the door to the servants' quarters and locked it. He turned round and looked at his leader, still holding his pistol at the ready.

Harry took an impulsive step forward and the pistol was instantly turned in his direction.

'Don't move, any one of you!' said Ricardo Arandez. 'My…friends are all ready to shoot. Stop where you are!' The men spread out and faced the end of the hall where Octavia and the rest were standing. It could be seen that there were four of them, not counting their leader, though to Edward's experienced eye they looked a poor lot. Still, men with guns were always dangerous.

His eyes fixed on Arandez, Edward said abruptly, 'Better do as he says, Petrie. There's no place for a dead hero here.'

Arandez circled round and stood at the other end of the hall, behind his men. Octavia was horrified at the change she saw in him. Any resemblance to Tom Payne had vanished from this emaciated creature. The fresh complexion was blotched and pale, the blue eyes bloodshot. He looked on the verge of a collapse—and all the more dangerous because of it.

Arandez noticed how Edward and Harry were measuring their chances as his men approached, and he said quickly, 'Don't get too close to them, you fools! Can't you see they'll leap on you if you get too near. Keep the guns pointed at the beautiful young lady in the yellow dress. My future wife. If anyone moves, fire. But no one would dare, would they, Barraclough? Not if it meant Lisetta would die. She's my safeguard.'

'What do you think you can do here?' asked Edward harshly. 'You're mad, Arandez!'

'Perhaps I am. But I'll have Lisetta, even if I have to kill the lot of you first. I might even begin with you, Edward Barraclough. You're the one who has caused all my troubles! Your damned brother was happy enough for me to marry Lisetta till you told him about my activities in Jamaica! Yes! I might just begin with you!' He lifted his gun and pointed it at Edward. 'Beg for your life, Barraclough, or you'll die here and now!'

In this moment of tension when the eyes of everyone else were fixed on Arandez and Edward, Octavia saw a slight movement on the gallery immediately above Arandez. Pip was quietly climbing on to the balustrade.

Arandez and his men, who were all facing away from her, were unaware of it.

Octavia caught her breath and looked fleetingly at Edward. It was clear that he too had seen Pip. He cast a quick glance at Harry, then raised his voice and asked loudly,

'What do you wish me to say, Arandez? That I'm sorry? I might say something of the kind—but only if you tell your men to take their guns off Lisette first. They don't look very reliable to me. Do you really want *her* killed, too?'

Pip was now on top of the balustrade. Arandez said, 'Very well. I would really enjoy hearing you crawl, Barraclough. Do as he says!'

His men lowered their pistols, and at the same time there was a bloodcurdling yell and Pip landed with a thump on Arandez's shoulders. He staggered, and his pistol went off somewhere into the ceiling. With a roar of rage he threw the useless weapon away and dragged Pip down, fighting to release himself. The moment of distraction had given Edward and Harry their chance. Kicking and punching, they soon had all four of Arandez's accomplices on the floor, and were relieving them of their weapons.

Arandez was still fighting Pip. To her horror, Octavia saw him take out a knife, with the clear intention of using it to free himself from the child's leech-like grasp, and she hurled herself at him, screaming, 'NO! No, you mustn't!'

She took hold of the hand with the knife and hung on to it, dragging it down and away from Pip with all her strength. He pulled his hand free with a curse and flung Octavia from him so violently that she hit the ground several feet away, and lay in an inert heap, her head against the edge of the fireplace.

Edward had finished with his man. He looked up just in time to see Octavia fall, and leapt over to her. Pip was already there, kneeling beside her and desperately calling her name.

'She's dead!' wailed Pip. 'Octavia's dead!'

Edward cradled Octavia in his arms. 'Don't be a little fool,' he said roughly. 'She isn't dead! She can't be! She mustn't be!' He put his fingers against the side of Octavia's neck...

A sudden howling gust of wind swept through the hall and set the huge chandeliers swinging wildly. Arandez took a couple of paces towards Lisette.

'Lisetta—' he began uncertainly, stretching out a hand in appeal.

The fixings of the chandelier over his head suddenly gave way with a groan, and it crashed down on top of him, followed by a mass of plaster and dust. The noise was deafening. Arandez crumpled and fell. The silence that followed was uncanny.

It was broken by Edward. 'Thank God! Oh, thank God! There's a pulse there. She's alive.' For the first time he looked round and saw the chaos in the centre of the hall. 'My God!' he said in an appalled voice. He looked round at the servants who had broken their way in, and were standing at the end of the hall wide-eyed. 'See if you can help that poor devil under the chandelier. Come on! Step to it! And fetch a doctor. Immediately!'

Harry had been comforting Lisette, but now they came over. 'Octavia ought to be in bed. Let me take her,' said Harry, bending over his sister.

'Leave her alone!' said Edward fiercely, pushing him

away. 'She's mine! I love her and she's mine! I'll take
her!' Harry looked at him in astonishment, but didn't
argue. Edward picked Octavia up in his arms, and, as
he walked to the stairs, he said over his shoulder, 'Get
Lisette to look after Pip. Her knee is bleeding. And
Harry—see what's has happened to Arandez. I doubt
we can do much for him, but you'd better take a look.
Don't let the girls anywhere near! Bring the doctor to
Octavia's room as soon as he arrives.'

Edward carried Octavia slowly up the stairs. He laid
her on the bed, covered her, and knelt down beside her.
For a moment he buried his head in the covers, then he
said in a broken voice, 'Dear God, Octavia, don't leave
me now! Not when I've only just found out how much
you mean to me!'

Octavia's eyelids fluttered. But then she was once
again still. He looked at her white face, the blue bruise
on her temple, and said even more desperately,

'Dammit, you mustn't die, Octavia! Without you
there's no happiness, no joy. You've *got* to live! You've
got to give me time to tell you what you mean to me!
I want to marry you, take care of you, live with you
forever! I love you so much! I don't think I could face
life without you! Please wake up!'

Octavia opened her eyes. 'Edward!' she said con-
tentedly. 'Was that you I heard? Saying you wanted to
marry me?'

He started to tell her how much, but stopped and
looked more carefully at her. After a short silence he
said slowly, 'You devil, Octavia! You heard it all!'

'Most of it,' she said.

'You mean, you let me carry on believing you were
badly hurt, perhaps dying, when all the time…'

'I think you owed me that much. I *was* badly hurt.

But by you, not Arandez.' She sat up. 'Where is he? What happened to Pip?'

He pushed her back against the pillows. 'Pip is perfectly sound apart from a few grazes. Lisette is with Harry. And Arandez is dead.'

'Dead! Did you…?'

'No, I didn't, though given the chance I might well have killed him. I'll tell you about it later. I expect you'll say that the house did it. But now you must rest till the surgeon comes.'

She would have protested, but Mrs Dutton came in at that point with the surgeon, and Edward was dismissed.

Octavia's questions had reminded him that he had some clearing up to do and he went downstairs. The servants told him that the men Arandez had brought with him had recovered and vanished while no one was looking, presumably back to their haunts in London. The surgeon had seen Arandez's body and it had been taken away. The chandelier, too, had been lifted away, though most of the dust and plaster was still there. Edward looked at it, then up at the ceiling.

'I don't know how it could have happened, sir,' said Mrs Dutton tearfully. 'After what happened to Mrs Barraclough the men went over everything, including that chandelier. It should never have fallen the way it did. They're saying in the kitchen that it was all a judgement. He was a wicked man, sir. He could have killed Lady Octavia. Do you think it was old Mrs Carstairs…?'

Edward shook his head. 'No, Mrs Dutton,' he said firmly. 'There's nothing supernatural about it. Look at this.' In the rubble on the floor was a broken piece of the chandelier's supports. Something had cut a neat hole right in its centre. 'That's a bullet hole,' said Edward. 'When Arandez fired his pistol into the ceiling that's where it went. Chance, perhaps. But nothing supernatural.'

He went towards the stairs, but heard Mrs Dutton say, 'Well, you may call it chance, if you wish, Mr Barraclough, but it was a very funny chance, and I know what *I* think it was!'

Edward smiled and went upstairs. Lisette and Pip, with Harry in close attendance, were already with Octavia, who was sitting up looking pale but fully conscious. The surgeon was on the point of coming to look for him. Octavia, he said, had had a narrow escape. She was shaken, but he had not found any serious damage. Rest and quiet for a few days ought to cure her. He departed after promising to call in two days' time to see how she did.

Edward came to the bedside, and said calmly, 'Now that everyone has seen you're not dead, Octavia, I expect you would like Lisette and Pip to show Harry the house. I want to talk to you.'

She sat up even straighter. 'No!' she said in some agitation. 'I don't want... Pip could stay...'

'No, she can't,' Edward said firmly. 'I promised to tell you what happened, and I intend to do so. Without an audience.'

Harry grinned at Lisette. 'I think your uncle means it,' he said. 'And after having seen him in action this afternoon I would hate to fall out with him.'

'Good man,' said Edward. 'You're not too bad in a fight yourself. You can call me Edward if you wish. Goodbye.'

Pip cast a knowledgeable glance at her uncle. 'I know

why you want to get rid of us,' she said. 'I heard what you said when we thought she was dead. And I don't mind going if it means you're going to marry her. I always said you ought to.' Lisette laughed and dragged her away.

When they were gone Edward sat on the bed and said softly, 'Now, my love, we shall have a little chat.'

'Rest and quiet. That's what I'm to have,' said Octavia.

'You shall have all the rest and quiet you could wish for,' said Edward.

Octavia's face fell. 'Oh!'

'But not before you've told me two things. The first is why you pretended you were unconscious.'

'I was unconscious for a while. And then when I came to you were saying such wonderful things…I wanted to hear you say more.'

'Such as?'

'That you loved me. That you wanted to marry me. In fact, I'd quite like to hear it again…?'

Edward said firmly, 'Not before you tell me the second thing I want to know.'

'What is it?'

He put his hand on her cheek and said very seriously, 'That you forgive me for being such a fool. That you love me in spite of it.'

'You *are* a fool, Edward!' she said softly. 'Of course I love you! I couldn't have behaved so…so shamelessly with anyone else.'

He laughed triumphantly and took her into his arms. 'My dearest, sweetest Octavia! I can't possibly tell you what your shameless behaviour did to me! But now I want so much more. I want you to share your life with me, let me look after you, grow old with you, have children, *your* children.'

'But Edward! You said—'

'I know what I said, all the things I swore I would never even consider. And there's only one woman in the world who could have changed my mind for me. You. Only you. I adore you.' He took her hand and kissed it. 'Marry me, Octavia, and I'll swear I'll do everything I can to make you happy.'

Octavia's pale cheeks were suffused with colour. 'Of course I will, dearest Edward! With all my heart.' She leant forward and kissed him, then drew back and smiled. 'Indeed, I hardly dare say no! Aunt Carstairs brought you here. Think what Wychford might do to me if I refused you!'

Gently, carefully, Edward leaned forward and gave her a long, lingering kiss. A sigh, a faint breath, soft as a summer zephyr, and perfumed with the dry scent of herbs, passed through the house and out into the summer air. Wychford was content.

*　　*　　*　　*　　*

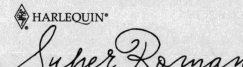

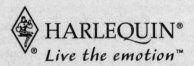

If you enjoyed what you just read,
then we've got an offer you can't resist!

Take 2 bestselling
love stories FREE!
Plus get a FREE surprise gift!

THE
ELLIOTTS

Mixing business with pleasure

The series continues with

Cause for
Scandal

by

ANNA DePALO

(Silhouette Desire #1711)

She posed as her identical twin to meet a sexy rock star—but Summer Elliott certainly didn't expect to end up in bed with him. Now the scandal is about to hit the news and she has some explaining to do…to her prominent family and her lover.

On sale March 2006!

OPEN SECRET

by Janice Kay Johnson

HSR #1332

Three siblings, separated after their parents'
death, grow up in very different homes,
lacking the sense of belonging that family
brings. The oldest, Suzanne, makes up her
mind to search for her brother and sister,
never guessing how dramatically her
decision will change their lives.

Also available:
LOST CAUSE (June 2006)

On sale March 2006

Available wherever Harlequin books are sold!

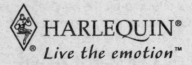

HARLEQUIN®
Live the emotion™